Strong at the Broken Places

Clayton Lindemuth

Hardgrave Enterprises
SAINT CHARLES, MISSOURI

STRONG AT THE BROKEN PLACES/ Clayton Lindemuth — 1st ed.
ISBN: 9781976836985

DEDICATED TO LOREN FAIRMAN

(details at back of book...)

IN THE DESERT

I SAW A CREATURE, NAKED, BESTIAL,

WHO, SQUATTING UPON THE GROUND,

HELD HIS HEART IN HIS HANDS

AND ATE OF IT.

I SAID, "IS IT GOOD, FRIEND?"

"IT IS BITTER—BITTER," HE ANSWERED;

"BUT I LIKE IT

"BECAUSE IT IS BITTER,

"AND BECAUSE IT IS MY HEART."

—STEPHEN CRANE

THE WORLD BREAKS EVERYONE AND AFTERWARD MANY

ARE STRONG AT THE BROKEN PLACES.

BUT THOSE THAT WILL NOT BREAK IT KILLS.

—ERNEST HEMINGWAY

..

Prologue

Tuesday wanted a dog. She was six and we went through the regular conversation—she promised to feed it and fill the water dish, and when it messed on the carpet, she'd be responsible for cleanup. No child makes this promise intending to fail it.

As I looked at my daughter's bright eyes, I couldn't help but love her so much I didn't care if the dog shat everywhere and she left it for my wife to clean. That was eight years ago, after I signed with my first big sponsor.

But the other side of the dog equation is the dog.

Life forces us to make decisions that affect the fates of others, sometimes that determine the fates of others. Every morning we wake wearing blindfolds fashioned of our fears and pick up suitcases filled with yesterday's bad choices, and careen about our day from one impact to the next.

With my new, big sponsor, I sensed a crossroad. The world was becoming serious about ultra-distance running. The world, with its money, was inviting me to the table. As I launched my athletic career I struggled to teach Tuesday how to care when another life depends on you. Really care.

Sometimes caring requires distance.

I studied my daughter's eyes. As a boy her age I had been desperate to own a puppy—a mix of German shepherd and

••

malamute. It watched with intelligent eyes that seemed never to frolic, almost as if he stood transfixed by a vision of his future.

He was an upstate New York outside dog. We brought him into the garage when the temperature dropped under ten degrees but otherwise he lived in a wood slat dog house, tethered by a chain of rusted links. In the winter his water bowl froze and often the chain would flip over the food dish. My father had assigned that I'd right the bowl daily and fill it with food, and knock out the giant ice cube from the water dish and refill it with hot water so it would remain liquid a few minutes longer.

When the dog was young I loved him and took him exploring in the woods. I'd share my peanut butter and jelly.

But after the age of ten, other people's decisions pressed in on my world. Mother left. Father drank. At an absurd age I ran absurd distances and discovered the more exhausted I became, the less the world mattered. The stronger my will grew, the less I had to surrender to externalities I didn't understand.

I charged into myself and the dog became a burden.

I was in bed. Outside the dog howled. It was the night of my first half marathon: earlier I had run up and down the driveway while my father stood in front of the garage with a rifle trained on me.

Sprawled on the mattress after it was over, with teenage rages flashing against the inside of my skull like primal bonfires on a cave wall... I heard the dog howl and for the moment I allowed him to enjoy his torments while I enjoyed mine. I was in a broken place, yet with a new understanding

••

of that place and the power of my will. I thought about how cold my wet boots were. Maybe my father would sober up enough to feed and water the dog.

The dog howled.

My father burst through my bedroom door. "Supper scraps still in the dish? So I checked on the animal! Water froze. Fifteen degrees, no food or water all day."

He seized the back of my neck and dragged me from bed, dropped me to the floor. A half hour before, he was so drunk he couldn't stand. Now he was ready to brawl. He rolled me with his foot. Cigarette ash fell to my face but it was cold and I didn't move.

He sputtered, searched for words as toxic as he.

Finally he pointed.

On legs that almost couldn't move I got up and fed and watered the dog. When I was back inside and had removed my boots and coat, my father yelled to put the dog in the garage because it was going to get cold overnight. I put my boots and coat back on, struggled outside again, leashed the dog and took him to the garage. I arranged an old army blanket against the back corner that shared a wall with the house. I took off the dog's collar and pet him.

His growl said he found love intolerable.

When he grew so old he would no longer run off in search of bitches in heat, we removed his chains. One winter night he left. My dog eventually died somewhere cold and alone, the sorry conclusion of a life chained to a boy growing up without illusions.

Tuesday wanted a dog and I wondered how I would die. If it would be brutal or triumphant. Sudden or slow. Every ultra-

••

runner dreams of having the courage to run right up to the line that, if crossed, would shatter his heart and drop him drooling to the dirt. In all my victories, I've never found the line. I've found pain. I've found unconsciousness. But never the line. The more I train the farther out it hides.

Life is a mad race to accomplish something before the clock unwinds—while embracing the absurdity of the exercise. Knowing that the best part of exertion is the trance that washes through us and convinces us it will never end. And all the people we've ignored and the pain we've converted into miles underfoot will someday be justified by the magnificence of our achievements.

We dream.

My six-year-old daughter Tuesday wanted a dog and I stood at a crossroad. I felt compelled to help her understand the gravity of the responsibility she coveted, and the pain that would accrue to an innocent creature if she proved unworthy of the task.

At the hardware store I purchased a chain—not heavy, but capable of securing a child. At the pet store I bought a pink collar.

••

Eve of Badwater 135

TOMMY: You know, Nick, a lot of people question how you prepare so you always peak on the day you need to. I mean, let's face it. You've been doing it a while, and every time you run, it seems like your best yet.

NICK: An athlete trains to get the body capable of victory. But in any race, there are always a handful of people who are physically able to win. The one who does is the one who has put an equal effort into conditioning the mind. Your attitude is either working for you or against you. When your body breaks, only the will can compel it to burn past the limits it chooses. That's the most important thing you'll ever hear me say. Limits are choices. If we want to excel, we must condition the will beyond the body.

MADDY: What are your predictions? Overall winner?

NICK: I want it more. I always want it more.

--DistanceHippy Podcast Pre-Race Interview

I sat with my left leg on the floor and my right across the mattress, pressing hard on the lumpy area where the surgeon removed the meat, and where I spent the last year seeking to restore it through training, diet, and lifting weights.

"You want me to do that?" Lisa said.

"That would be helpful."

She went to the refrigerator and pulled out a bottle of beer.

"When did you get that?"

"The Indian shop where Mary bought the blanket."

"Oh."

Instead of working on my leg, Lisa sat on the second bed, arranged the pillows. Grabbed the television remote from the night table and turned it on.

I kneaded the knot in my calf and then slipped under the covers. After a half hour I rolled. "You want to turn off the television so I can run the biggest race of my life in seven hours?"

I opened my eyes. Her face was red and shiny. Tiny shudders rippled from her chest.

••

Mile 26: 4 Hours, 13 Minutes

Floyd Siciliano first slept with my wife three years ago. Correction: First my sister, then my wife.

Floyd Siciliano died a few hours ago.

I'm twenty-six miles into the last race of my career—Badwater 135. I will win and set a new course record, and afterward, disappear from racing and most of the elements of my life. Lisa joins me fifty yards before I reach the support van, exchanges my empty bottle for one full of electrolytes and water. The temperature is already one hundred and ten. She can't hold my pace.

"Floyd's dead," she says, again. "We heard it on the radio."

"They said his name this time?"

"No, but who else could it be in the Furnace Creek Hotel, and involved in the race?"

"When he didn't show at the start, I figured it was something."

Floyd Siciliano was my crew chief, responsible for the support vehicle and everything in it. Back home about three years ago, Floyd became my sponsor. And my wife Lisa started preferring his bed to mine.

I think of the police—how long until they attempt to pull me out of the race?

I arrive at the van and stop. My sister Mary parses my face with hydrocodone eyes. She takes the drug for non-pain issues and it keeps the pilot light of her sentience trimmed to a tiny blue nub.

I run in a suit of white, UV-blocking fabric. Mary waves a sprayer wand and soaks me with a gallon of ice water. I can almost hear it evaporate.

Death Valley receives less than two inches of rain per year and measures some of the hottest temperatures on the planet. Furnace Creek, ten miles behind me, has recorded one hundred and thirty-four degrees—only two shy of the hottest temperature on the planet, reached in the Sahara.

Death Valley's heat reduces you to nothing, if that's what you are.

As Mary sprays, Lisa, my damp-eyed wife, swaps the bottle I just drained for a full one and gives me half a peanut butter and jelly sandwich. The first bite is moist; the last, like half-done toast. I wash the bread down with water.

Mary and Lisa struggle to coordinate themselves without Floyd. Mary has taken over driving his van, a white Chevy sniper special with a cardboard nameplate NICK FISTER #100 taped over the gym name and logo: The Bench Press and Pound, replete with my face atop a running stick figure.

Lisa stuffs three Gu foils—110-calorie packets of syrup flavored like chocolate or berries and given angst names like Chocolate Outrage—into my belt. Mary places the sprayer in the back of the van and drops to her knees before me, then kneads the back of my right leg. "That good?"

I grunt.

A small band of runners passes, many in white outfits like mine, several in tanks and shorts, slathered in pasty sunblock. One of them is square chested and soldierly, barking

••

comments and motivations. We're a single marathon into a race consisting of five, plus another ten miles straight up the side of Mount Whitney, and this man has energy for words.

Lisa stands blank faced beside the van. Her lover is dead and she must now take his place to support the husband she's cuckolded.

Does she wonder if she's gotten away with a three-year affair?

Floyd's death will introduce new challenges into the race, but also new pains. I use pain like a quality complex starch.

I'm somewhere close to sea level, looking ahead to the first of three battleship gray mountain ranges I will ascend. The sun hammers near a ninety-degree angle. The locals say Charles Manson came to Death Valley to find a doorway to hell.

I open my right arm all the way, stretch an elbow that remains tight years after injury. The pain of extending my elbow steals my thoughts for a moment, before returning them to the desert at the bottom of the world.

What am I thankful for, today?

Pain.

Death Valley looks like any other valley baked in an oven for a million years. The floor shimmers into the hazy forever ahead. The land is hazy yellow brown. The sky is hazy blue, and the distant valley walls are scorched-hazy ugly.

Although I trained by running summer afternoons wearing black trash bags duct taped tight, and by running in place in the sauna, and by putting the treadmill in the laundry room and routing the dryer vent into my rain poncho, I was unprepared for Death Valley. The sun attacks like a fighter swinging two fists at once. The first comes face level and burns skin and eyes, steals breath. The other punches the liver

••

and kidneys, extracting minerals and fluids the body needs to sustain life.

Death Valley sunlight is not the happy sunlight John Denver wanted on his shoulder.

As I take off from the van Lisa steps forward, mouth open. She trots beside me, her face splotched in red. Her t-shirt clings to her skin showing the contours of a body men—Floyd—noticed. Her arms are pink as her cheeks and her eyes are wet.

"You're going to keep running?"

I concentrate on my stride and follow as close to the white line as I can, though it is hours until the road will peak at one hundred seventy degrees.

I sustain a nine-minute and forty-second pace because it will bring me in at twenty-one hours, besting the existing record by an hour. Every minute I stop to rest will decrease my margin. I've trained at nine forty for six months and my legs are like a pair of upside down metronomes.

Learning efficient form took years of my youth. After tens of thousands of miles, I still must be present with every stride, conscious of landing with my forefoot under my center of gravity, rolling off my foot, slightly leaning and falling perpetually forward.

Form is almost insignificant during a short run, but Badwater?

This run will last three hundred and fifty thousand strides—opportunities for ripple effects to mingle, procreate, build new agonies. Prolonged heel striking tears muscle, flattens cartilage, crushes red blood cells and fractures bone. Extra wear begins a vicious cycle: premature tiredness, poor posture, poor respiration, and the machine is even less efficient. Less oxygen absorption, poorer digestion, all

..

systems spiral downward. Bad form is most costly in the most critical race, the internal, where resources deplete faster than the body replenishes. In a hundred and thirty-five-mile race, every mistake matters.

Complicated reasons for ignoring Lisa.

She jabs my arm. She wears salty tear streaks on an exasperated red face.

"You're not going to finish this race," she says. "Floyd was your crew chief! We can't go on without him. I can't run this crew with just Mary! She's taken so much dope she can hardly talk. And I don't know what I'm doing. Everyone else has a bunch of people in their crews."

"It's medicine. Not dope."

Her calling Floyd my crew chief makes me think of the old television commercial that called a hamburger chopped steak. Floyd was a gym hound who built muscle for show as if self-esteem resulted from a look instead of an action. He drove a red Corvette. He sponsored my running so he could lay my wife.

"You have to drop the race," Lisa says. "I'm not doing this! I can't think. I can't make it."

Mindful of my stride, and keeping the correct form with my footfalls, I turn my head until I see her dead on. I remove my shades and force my eyes to remain open despite the searing dryness and sting.

"What?" she says.

I muster three-years' rage and project it without words.

"Okay," she croaks. "Okay."

Lisa stops running and I glance at my Garmin. I've drifted ten seconds fast. I throttle back to nine minutes and forty seconds per mile, and empty my mind of Lisa and Floyd Siciliano.

● ●

The hotel cable weather channel indicated temperatures will max out at a hundred and twenty-three today. It feels like we're only a few digits shy, but it's probably more like a dozen. After a couple of minutes the van passes me, Lisa and Mary on their way to our next rendezvous, two miles ahead.

I'm striking on the heel. My shoulders have rounded.

I shake my body loose. The heat is working on me faster than I anticipated. My mind is working on me.

I look down the road and see where I want to be. It's always that way.

••

Mile 28: 4 Hours, 21 Minutes

MADDY: "Last time we talked was a few years ago—"

NICK: "Before Western States, right?"

MADDY: "Yeah, that was before States. Last time you said you got your start running ultras early in life. I know a lot of runners don't get into it until they have a track and field career in college, and then they find distance is their thing. But you did distance early."

NICK: "That's true. I told the story last time—are old podcasts still up on your site?"

TOMMY: "Yeah, sure."

NICK: "So anyone can listen. I was introduced to distance when I was twelve, and for me it's everything. I'm not a fast guy. I don't train the hardest. You look in history and some guys have put up some amazing training numbers. Marshall Ulrich averaged four hundred miles a week running across the country. Guano calling batshit crazy, right? But you know for me it's always been the feeling that I could go forever. I don't want to go as fast as possible, and then break down. I want to know I don't ever have to stop. Ever. Someday when I die whatever's left will keep on running.

--DistanceHippy Podcast Pre-Race Interview

Running.... Thoughts string together disjointed and clumsily bound. Random but connected by invisible threads. What would it be like to decipher dolphin squeaks? What would I tell the dolphins? Take me to your leader? What would I ask him? Or her? What makes a dolphin sexy? Do dolphins get horny? Do they cheat?

I regret the summer when I was thirteen and every afternoon raided my grandmother's garden for carrots to fuel my long runs. How did they find Floyd Siciliano? What did Floyd think as the light faded from his eyes?

Dead, did he loiter before crossing over?

Do the dead ever truly leave?

I allow my feet to guide me while my eyeballs slip dreamily behind my eyelids' welcome moisture. Eyes closed, I am the cartoon Roadrunner, levitating on a spinning obloid of legs. The road is straight and my gait is perfect; I'm in a moment, an unthinking execution of perfection. Each stride lands on the ball of my foot, directly below my center of gravity, rolling forward, leaning forward, one hundred and ninety footfalls per minute. Effortless. The atoms of my body and the air are indistinct and the glucose that fuels me wriggles through eternity and arrives in my blood stream by osmosis. I could run forever.

To my right an animal grunts, startling me. I blink open my eyes.

"Weak," she says. Her accent sounds as hard as her body looks.

Is this the Swede who promised to humiliate all American men by kicking my ass?

She runs beside me, redness showing through the deep tan on her legs. Above she wears a white solar-block top, billowy and light, but her legs, where she generates heat, she leaves exposed to the baking sun and radiating road. Her left shoe cricket farts as she accelerates to pass.

••

I tell myself I'll let her open some distance and ride her down later, but she slows and maintains her lead a mere step or two ahead.

My advantage: I maintain even splits over immense distances—I run my last mile at the same pace as my first. Many runners begin fast, burn excessive calories and build more lactic acid than they can clear, not to mention the thousand other bio cycles they warp for the exhilaration of early speed... They sweat more fluids and minerals than they can replace—to claw ahead time they will be forced to yield when their self-inflicted damage catches them.

In the end, their average time is the middle of the inefficient extremes. My average time is the locus of efficient moderations.

One might think perfect efficiency arises from inflicting the discipline of even splits, running each mile the same speed. Neither wasting energy doing donuts in the parking lot at the beginning of the race, nor crawling on all fours the last hundred yards. While this is generally true, I've found the optimal pace is a state, not a speed, and I maintain the optimal state by adapting speed and a host of other run elements, from hydration to salt to music, and that in the end I run even splits because I have mastered my body, not because I have mastered the clock.

The fast athletes are miles ahead. This blonde takes her time passing—not like those who pass hard to inflict emotional damage on a competitor, or on knoll so they can disappear quickly.

This barelegged blonde struts within grabbing distance for a quarter mile. Her left cheek, then her right, then her left, then her right. Hypnotic.

••

The taunt makes me dwell on her and that's what she desires.

I slow and she drifts a dozen paces ahead. She tilts her head sideways, noticing my changed cadence, and turns on the speed. Her glutes appear to pop. Her elbows swing hard and a breeze wafts a mild stink of ambition.

Last night I saw Maddy and Tommy, of DistanceHippy Podcast outside the Furnace Creek Hotel in a 1985 Toyota motor home. They caught me in a moment of introspection, handed me a bottle of Dogfish Ninety Minute IPA, which I waved off, and invited me to talk. They sat side-by-side on a bench built into the wall and I stood in the entrance with the door closed behind me to keep some of the cool air inside, though the air conditioner struggled and the interior smelled like the bodies that occupied it, sweat, beer, and coconut sun block. Maddy moved a microphone to the partition between us, pointed it at me. "We're recording now, but we can edit the dull stuff."

I sniffed the coconut air and Tommy said, "Smokin', huh?"

I must have looked blank.

"The woman who just left was Nova Bjorkman."

Maddy nodded and the interview was on. They did a quick intro, rapping on the scene, passersby, and the unbearable Satanic heat of Furnace Creek, seventeen miles from the lowest point in North America, Death Valley. I readied the routine: I was feeling fine, looking forward to the run, optimistic about the morrow, while nonetheless respectful of the competition.

"What time you thinking?"

"Twenty-one hours, less disasters. But you never know. Weird things happen."

••

"Well, your humility is becoming," Maddy said.

"Becoming boring." Tommy said. "A lot of people are looking for someone—all due respect Mister Fister—to kick your ass. So what's your take on Nova Bjorkman? Is she the one to end your eight-year streak?"

"Jork who?"

"Nova Bjorkman. She's a Swede."

"Never heard of her."

Maddy and Tommy traded exaggerated looks. Maddy drank from a sweaty bottle of Sierra Nevada and Tommy laughed. "She's heard of you, brother."

I shrugged.

"For the listeners, Nick Fister just shrugged loudly."

"I guess she's somebody?"

It's difficult to get into the game sometimes. You find your roadie sleeping with your wife. You deal with it because the sport is more important, but you miss things like one more ultra-runner pinning your photo to the bathroom mirror to focus her ambition. Nova Bjorkman.

"Nick, I know you're aware of this, but for our audience, let me mention that women have been placing well in ultra-running events for a long time. Researchers treat it as proven science that women endure pain well, and their bodies are better at converting fat to fuel."

"That's right," Tommy said. "Women have been overall winners of many of the best-known courses, and Badwater is no exception. Pam Reed won in what? 2002—overall winner, beating the entire field."

"And 2003."

"So you haven't heard of Nova Bjorkman?"

"No," I said. "What's her story?"

••

"We interviewed her right before you. That's why the place smells nice. Over the last two years, she's been the overall winner of every event she's run, mostly stuff you wouldn't recognize and we can't pronounce. Races in Europe—completely unknown in the US, but here's the skinny: every single hundred kilometer or longer race, she's beaten the course record by at least thirty minutes."

"No kidding?"

"And she mentioned you, Nick," Maddy jumped in. "She wants to take you out."

"She wants your crown."

"Funny. I've never run Badwater before. Last year's winner—Stu Flanagan's here. Why doesn't she gun for him?"

"I guess she's heard this is the last run of your career, her last chance to take you face-to-face."

I've won enough races that I'm a target for anyone with a mouth and an ass to carry it.

Turns out the Swede—Barelegged Nova Bjorkman—has legs like a locomotive, but she started too fast.

Fear is a perennial challenge. It pushes runners into a war of attrition against their bodies. The average person can only absorb thirty-four ounces of water per hour, yet the skin can sweat three times that. The liver can process about three hundred calories per hour, but the running body will burn a thousand. In each dimension, the body fights a losing battle. The lines intersect.

Worse, all the variables change with degrees of effort and difficulty of conditions. A perfect strategy of calorie, mineral, and fluid replacement will leave a runner utterly depleted, given too fast a start, or a large change in environment.

••

The faster Nova begins, the greater my advantage. Badwater forces fast runners to pay for their extravagance. The hotter the temperature, the greater my advantage. The attrition against the body accumulates faster, inflicts deeper damage, and takes longer to recover from.

I am confident because I will keep an optimal pace while the rabbits pull off the road to puke and massage their cramps.

But I am also aware my confidence and my ability diverge. I am not the runner I was a year ago.

For now, the Barelegged Nova is aggressive, young and used to setting records. She has a big mouth and I'm betting she runs a foolish race. Hunger is good when it leads to discipline and courage. But if it makes a runner witless, she's better served by humility.

I glance at my watch and estimate Nova's pace at seven minutes per mile.

I'll pass her this afternoon once she wanders into the desert in search of magic.

*

I built a tree house to escape being beaten with a telephone cord, tied up, and locked in the potato cellar. Instinct told me the more time I spent away from the house, the less opportunity my father would have to scare up reasons to pound me.

My mother left when I was ten. My father got worse. He made his living working in stores like Sears and Montgomery Ward selling stereos and televisions in the eighties, appliances in the nineties. The more he drank and beat my sister Mary and me, the farther his career devolved into a job and then a part time gig at a Radio Shack.

••

He drove one Chevy pickup or another. In flush times it was a Silverado. When he lost the Sears job he switched to an S10, but boasted it had the same motor—he called it a motor, not an engine—as a Corvette. He took the rifle rack out of the Silverado and had a friend who junked cars in his back yard modify the rack to fit the smaller truck.

He wore a short sleeve shirt, a black clip on tie that always sparkled with dandruff, and a bowler hat.

After work he'd throw cigarettes and hat to the end table, his keys into a dish on the kitchen counter. A few minutes later, every day, he'd emerge from his bedroom in a t-shirt carrying a strapless guitar by the neck. At the kitchen he'd pour a glass of rye and then carry guitar and whiskey to the living room, reunited with his cigarettes and bowler.

Sometimes he'd put the guitar down, stand up, and practice flipping the hat to his head and a cigarette to his mouth in one elegant sweep. It would have looked good on stage, if he could have fingered the chords to follow.

I watched him slink out of the truck seat one time, flip the hat to his head, and it seemed the salesman personality kind of vibrated out of him and his walk got easy and smooth, his eyes sharp, at the thought of rye whiskey and rotten blues.

Before I discovered running I spent afterschool time in the woods beside the house. Skinny black cherry trees poked through here and there, bare of limbs for twenty feet until they reached the canopy and battled for light. I liked the rare white pine. They smelled cleaner.

Kneeling at the base of a hemlock, I unpocketed a book of Holiday Inn matches that my father left by the ash tray. Somewhere I'd learned the intoxicating work of matches, how a flame could turn a piece of wood, or a feather, or an ant, into something that would float away.

••

I raked the ground bare of needles with my fingers and grabbed every pine cone within reach. They were dry and perfect tinder, constructed by nature to allow maximum airflow. I piled them in the center of the black earth and struck a match.

A feeble flame grew until it consumed the cones and wavered a foot taller, grasping after something in the air to let it keep climbing. I swiped more dried needles away from the circle, expanding it, then sat with legs crossed, elbows on knees, and rested my chin on my palms. The heat on my face made me drowsy and the dancing orange was hypnotic.

I didn't see my father arrive home. I didn't hear him approach or see him with his balled fists or bowler askance until the rustle of leaves jarred me alert and I looked up as he stripped off his belt and taught me right from wrong about twenty times.

My behind was so sore I couldn't sit. Then he went to the house and drank rye clean. Later he busted open the door to my room. I was belly-down on the bed to keep blood from the sheets. He leaned on the jamb and pointed down the hall.

"Solitary," he said.

Solitary was his word for the potato cellar, where he sent me to ensure a lesson took.

I slipped on my shoes and grabbed another shirt in case he left me there all night.

He followed me downstairs and when I'd climbed inside the potato cellar, a six by six-foot cube of cement blocks, filled half full with potatoes, and with a single light bulb hanging from the ceiling, he closed and latched the door behind me.

I hated the spiders most.

When he released me hours later, Mary had already gone to bed, and by the time I scrounged supper and brushed my

••

teeth, my father sat on the sofa, passed out, with the guitar on his lap and his head cocked back so far I could have hacked it off.

His bowler had fallen to the floor.

Next day before I did any of my after-school chores I got the ladder my father left on the back porch and climbed to the roof, where the previous evening I'd weighted his upside-down bowler hat with a rock.

I ran to the rear of the house and circled to the woods. In the mound of ashes I'd left the afternoon before, I filled the bowler with pinecones and pine needles. Lit them and they flamed high and orange.

I turned my back to the fire and watched to ensure my father didn't arrive home from work early. The heat warmed my back. The burning wool smelled like poison.

When my father came home, the fire was gone, and all that remained of the bowler was a circle of gray ashes.

*

I have not run the Badwater 135 before. In my thirteen-year ultra-running career I have won on two dozen courses and set sixteen course records. I have run a hundred thousand training miles. I have beaten head-to-head, at least once, every elite ultra-distance athlete in the world.

Badwater 135, often hailed the most difficult course on the planet, will be my capstone.

I am not the best runner ever; thinking so is silliness. I'm only the best today because in the pain of achieving it, reality fades. Winning affirms the will, and gives evidence the

••

identity I choose is more real than the one I don't. My achievements are no more permanent than I am, but we are bound together and cannot exist without each other.

I run downhill at the end of a career, aware that the same sort of calculus that determines how long a runner will last in a race—the attrition between consuming and replenishing, calories and water and salts and calcium—that same battle inexorably ages my muscles and bones so tomorrow I will be less than today.

Everything comes down to this one last race.

*

One harsh, ten-degree February day I was bundled up on the school bus. I sat close to a heater and opened my coat and removed my hat. Arriving at our stop, I tucked books under arm and exited with Mary.

If my father would have seen me it would have been a beating with the telephone cord because we couldn't afford cough medicine, but he never came home before the bus dropped me off, or even while I walked the quarter mile driveway.

By the time I was twelve my father had been drinking hard for a year. He'd become a mediocre guitarist, able to strum most of a song before cussing himself and starting over. Mary and I would spend every night after our chores staring out different windows, empathic, in tune with one another in a way our father could never muster with strings.

Before he arrived home, we tore through our chores. The first of the evening for me began when I exited the bus. My job was to fetch the mail. I huffed a cloud of moist breath into the frozen air and followed Mary off the landing.

··

The bus door slammed. The engine revved. As the bus passed behind, I heard laughter and felt the insulting heavy sting of a balloon snapping open against my skull, and after a pregnant moment of terror, the splash of luke-warm water against my neck.

Before I turned and saw his leering face I knew it was Frank Licona. His father Vince drove the bus.

I grunted a scream—full volume but throttled back, painfully enclosed in my throat, rasping chords and shaking teeth. The water steamed about my head and neck and I smelled it. Saw the color dripping from my skin and hair to the snow.

It was piss.

I hurled my books, slipped and scavenged for a rock in the snow, and finding none made a ball in a sweeping move, packed and threw it in one motion. The snowball fell short of Frank's moronic face, which he held sideways, tauntingly out the open upper window.

The bus ground away over packed snow and ice. My ears burned and Mary watched.

I slipped about the icy surface, picked up my books, dusted them off and found the only wetness came from the snow I threw them into. My homework papers scattered.

My ears were numb.

Mary walked homeward.

I gathered loose papers and still on the run, now getting cold, trotted past Mary and continued toward our house, which sat far off like a dead bug on a white windowsill.

After fifty yards, lungs burning like my ears, I walked fast instead. Fresh snow had fallen on the driveway since my father cut tire tracks through it that morning, and the

••

driveway would remain unplowed until he returned from work and let the tires pack the fresh snow again.

I walked in the tracks, but on a rough driveway, invariably I'd slip and wet my ankles.

At the house I changed out of my wet coat and dunked my head in a sink of soapy water. Toweled my hair. Standing beside the wood burner, waiting for the faded embers to return to life, I shivered into a sweater and hat, and then my damp piss-smelling coat again, and headed back out to face the half-mile round trip to the mailbox.

At the mailbox, for the first time in my life I opened the lid and discovered a box addressed to me. I wouldn't have noticed my name except the box was on top. It was small but oddly heavy on one end.

Its contents rattled inside.

Someone had been mistaken in sending the box to me and if I opened it knowing it didn't belong to me, I could look forward to a few hours in potato cellar solitary. Although I'd grown wise to the misery and stowed a blanket inside, during winter the tiny prison barely lingered above freezing.

I guessed the contents of the box at each step to the house. I had no one to send me a gift. My mother?

Impossible.

Who?

My father—as a trick?

The mystery wore on me. I stopped. Held the box aloft and peered in the waning light. It still read my name.

The right thing to do was turn the box over to my father. Though I'd probably never see it again, I would avoid his wrath.

I stuffed the box in my pocket.

••

At the house I dropped the rest of the mail on the kitchen table and set about my chores. When I was done I went to my room.

I lay the box on my study desk and placed my Buck pocket knife beside it. Stepped backward to the window and looked out, and then at the box. Dug at my ear with my pinky.

The box was addressed to Nicholas Fister and I only knew one: that's what my mother had called me when she was angry.

I listened to the silence. Looked out the window. Opened my pocket knife blade and cut the tape, pulled apart the cardboard flaps. From inside I withdrew a heavy wad of newspaper, spread it open and read *New York Times*.

A lump of gold fell to the desktop and marred it.

I stared at the metal and slowly realized the flash of gold was reflected sunlight. The gold coin was a burnished medal affixed to a ribbon. I ran my fingers across raised letters and an image of runners and buildings. It read: *1985 New York City Marathon*.

I studied each side of the paperback-sized box as if to manifest a clue. It had no return address, but in the center someone had printed *Nicholas Fister, 1421 Old Spark Road, Greenville, NY 14411*.

Maybe one of my father's relatives had sent it?

Although not solid gold, the medal was magnificent, from another planet where anything was possible. I didn't know how long a marathon was, only that most people said the word with confused contempt, such as they might employ to discuss the sport of sawing off one's arm or bathing nude in diesel and applesauce.

I kept the medal, studied it. At school showed it off.

••

From the library Encyclopedia Britannica I learned history I've never forgotten. During 490 B.C. the Athenians beat back the Persians at a place called Marathon. A guy named Pheidippides ran about twenty-five miles to Athens with news of the victory. For the 1908 Olympics, the third Olympic running of the marathon, the distance was lengthened by another mile and two tenths so the course would include a lap inside the White City Stadium, and finish in front of the Royal Box.

The history... the pomp... the insanity of it was grand. People actually ran twenty-five miles, then another one point two so the royalty could watch them finish.

I carried the medal with a sense of stewardship confused with stolen valor. I carried it but couldn't display it. I held it but didn't own it. I showed it off the way a man might show off a piece of amber with a bug inside. There it is. Look at it. I don't know what the hell made it but there it is on my land. Mine.

One morning I studied it before leaving for school. My father yelled, "It'll be your ass if you miss the bus."

I dropped the medal on my dresser, grabbed my books. Ran.

••

Mile 30: 4 Hours, 51 Minutes

MADDY: So what I was saying a minute ago is that you started early, right?

NICK: That's right.

MADDY: Have you read any of the studies about the muscular damage you might have caused? Because with your accident and comeback, it seems like something you would have come across.

NICK: I'm not sure I know what you mean.

MADDY: Well, for instance, Bruce Fordyce wrote that after fifteen years of seriously heavy training, the muscles don't work the same. It becomes impossible to train enough, and it isn't just a function of age. It's a matter of how many years of pounding the muscles have taken.

NICK: Yeah, okay. I'm familiar. I've read about biopsies of muscle tissue in a guy who ran thirty some miles a day for seven weeks. Instead of helping, his leg muscle fiber was messed up. Especially the fast twitch fibers.

MADDY: What about after a career of it?

NICK: Yeah. There's damage. This isn't yoga.

--DistanceHippy Podcast Pre-Race Interview

The heat is beyond what I manufactured in the dryer room. Beyond what I thought possible only an hour ago. I sweat and my skin remains hot and dry. The air scorches and I feel my veins turn viscid, as if the heat renders my blood into sludge.

The woman with the bare legs who passed me less than a mile ago is ahead, maybe a hundred yards. She shimmers like a belly dancer in the heat. I cut away my stare, blink hard until the sting goes away, and next I look she folds on the side of the road.

Nova vomits.

Her van will find her soon. Crews worry about everything the runner doesn't have the capacity to worry about, or is forcing herself not to worry about. No crew enjoys seeing their runner suffer.

Except mine.

I've known about Floyd and Lisa's affair—I hate how that word makes animal betrayal sound intrepid and passionate. No middle-aged lay is worth the lie.

Was it a perpetual casual thing, each of them barnacled to me so long as I gathered sponsorships? Did they think I'd die on the trail? –As I could have in New York?

Or someday their lust would fade and they'd part, no one the wiser?

Happily, Floyd Siciliano is dead.

I smack my face. Blink myself into a new consciousness.

No need to indulge those thoughts now. I'll require them later.

My mind is no sooner clear than I think of my daughter Tuesday, five days dead.

I see her smirking behind a cell phone, rolling her eyes, or bringing her knees to her face as she watches television and pretends she doesn't hear her mother and father cursing each other. Hollowness takes over my chest and presses out, crushing my heart and filling me with palpitating anxiety.

No need to indulge those thoughts either...

••

I run my way. My time; my stride. For a moment Barelegged Nova doesn't seem to get any closer, though she remains doubled over. Maybe her van is ahead of her, waiting at their next rendezvous. Between now and then she must steel herself. I suspect Badwater is more difficult than any of us virgins suspected.

The sun is at an early afternoon angle; it's been a happy nuclear blast all day and the accumulated heat smolders. Finally I near the Barelegged Nova.

She retches.

Her water bottle rests sideways on the road. She gags and hacks and mumbles as I pass. She voices delirium. I slow.

This is the kind of heat that makes delirious people wander off in search of moondust.

I return to her. "Hey? Your people up ahead?"

"Uhharrrggh."

I stoop to her water bottle—empty. I unscrew the cap, dump the water from mine to hers. All I have.

The sun stares down, evil and angry.

"You been eating? What's the last calories you had?"

She convulses with dry heaves. I reach to her back but stop short and instead present her bottle. "Drink. I gave you my water. What color is your crew vehicle?"

"Yellaghh." Her voice turns to dry heaves. I study her, the pavement, heat waves. Is that hiss the sound of her flesh searing?

"I'll tell them to come back for you. Drink the water and let your body catch up to you, and the next time you feel strong, you'll be twice as strong as before. Today hasn't seen your best. Let your body catch up."

••

I push off knowing the compulsion in her is strong. I will see Nova again.

I look down the road to where I want to be.

*

I'm home before my father. It's March, two months after I left the marathon finisher's medal on my dresser. Almost a year since my father's bowler disappeared and I spent a weekend in the potato cellar. He removed the light bulb before putting me inside, so I ate potatoes not knowing what I ate with them.

In those months I discovered the periodic table of elements, and decided regardless of my future the entire table would be good to know. I committed to memorizing the symbols and the small numbers beside them, so someday when I knew what the numbers meant, I would be ahead.

I sat at my little wood desk hunched over the chart when my father's truck door slammed outside with more force than usual. Part of me shrank inside. I ran through my chores in my mind and I'd already completed them, so it was fifty-fifty whether my father would punish me. Sometimes he made up rules just to punish me for breaking them. Sometimes he didn't bother making up new rules.

He made his normal noise in the kitchen, then in a few minutes the guitar rang out, accompanied with my father's grunted vocals. I caught the first whiff of cigarette smoke and opened my window a crack, even though a late season snowstorm had hit midday.

The music stopped. I read the same symbol over and over, FE26, iron. Footsteps, creaking house. Creaking door. I felt

••

my father's eyes on the back of my head but was afraid to turn. I ducked as if his hand was near.

"Who'd you steal this from?"

I turned. My father wore the marathon finisher's medal on his neck. Cigarette in his teeth, he squinted.

"It came in the mail. I still got the box."

"And you opened it."

"The box had my name."

"Bullshit. It wasn't yours."

I shook my head. No. It wasn't mine.

"You know how many miles is in a marathon, boy?"

I didn't say.

"Twenty fuckin miles. Twenty fuckin miles. Twenty fuckin miles. Now, how far can you run?"

I started to shrug, and caught myself because he'd beat me for shrugging him. He lurched at me. "I don't know!"

"Well that didn't keep you from wearing it, did it? Like you was somebody. Time to teach my son a lesson, wants to be a somebody. Put on your sneaks. I'm going to show you something. In case you haven't seen it yet. You live in New York. You live where nobody gets to do what they want. PUT ON YOUR SNEAKERS."

I darted to the sneakers tucked under my bed with the toes sticking out, dress right dress, and hooked them by the laces. They were split where the fake leather upper met the rubber sole on the outside of my right foot. I dragged them over my heels and stood.

My father inhaled from the cigarette and the cherry glowed. He removed the cig from his lips, drank the last of his whiskey, and dropped the butt in the glass. It sizzled.

"Outside, thief."

●●

I shrank, anticipating his cupped hand on the back of my head. I didn't think to grab any more clothes than I wore—corduroy pants and a flannel shirt over a long underwear top. He pushed me into the door jamb as I passed him.

"Outside."

His feet clomped behind me until he stopped to grab his deck of smokes and light one.

Mary peeled potatoes at the kitchen sink with a paring knife. She paused, the blade frozen, her shoulders curved as he passed behind her. I held her stare through the kitchen window reflection. She seemed to nod and instead of not being friends and not being enemies, we knew each other.

I stood a moment like I'd forgotten my directions.

"Wait for me by the truck."

One of my chores was to shovel snow from the dirt path we used like a sidewalk. The falling snow had dusted it since I'd cleaned it after school. I grabbed the shovel thinking I'd stay warm while I waited and maybe take some of the steam out of my father's temper, but I'd no more cleared three feet when the front door slammed.

I worked until he said to stop and then leaned the shovel against the house. He'd taken a moment to don a fluorescent orange hunting coat, a furry balaclava over his ears, and trigger mittens on his hands. He rested the butt of a 30-06 with a scope on the top of his boot.

"Twenty fuckin miles, you want to wear this." He threw the medal in the snow next to the truck tire. "Driveway's a quarter mile here to the road. Out and back is how far, genius?"

"Half mile, sir."

"Out and back twice is what?"

"Mile."

••

"So you got forty trips for your medal."

Snow fell, tiny, stinging pellets more like ice missiles than flakes. From the dial thermometer on a porch post I read nineteen degrees. My hands and head were bare but with anger I was warm.

"Run out to the mailbox." My father thrust the rifle. "Get moving."

I stood with my hands balled into fists thinking I should run somewhere he'd never find me again. He swung the rifle barrel at me and the crazy in his eyes made me backpedal.

I turned. One foot in front of the other. Snow worked into the gaps around my ankles and into my heel, and in moments the right side of my right foot stung with wet cold. I jumped to the most recent track cut by the S10 tires.

"I'm gonna train this scope on you," he called when I was fifty yards away. "I'll see if you turn before the mailbox, ya cheat."

Snow sheathed ice. My legs were unaccustomed to running on lopsided terrain. Ice pellets blew into my face and I cupped a numb hand over my eyes and tilted my head—and kept putting one foot in front of the other. I stopped to tuck in my shirt so it didn't flap in the back, then slipped my other hand inside my sleeve and swapped them frequently.

At the mailbox, fear refined to rage. My hands were fists and I aimed my face to the wind so the ice would cut my cheeks. The pain flowed to my legs, and fueled them.

I stood a long moment, shook a numb fist toward the house. I grunted profane words so hard I hiccoughed. A moment later a bullet zinged nearby and I heard the report from my father's rifle. The shot didn't pass so close that I feared his intent as much as his ability to miss.

..

The cold air burned my lungs. I wiped a snot string from my nose with my flannel sleeve only to feel it turn to ice against the side of my face. Then slipped and landed on my knee.

I neared the house. My father strutted in a small landing of tamped snow, held the rifle in one hand and pointed at me as if to punctuate a thought he'd share when I was closer.

"That's a half mile. You got nineteen more 'til you deserve a medal. Turn around, thief." He hoisted the rifle to his shoulder, swung like to sight a deer on the run. He held his whiskey in the other gloved hand and I figured if he ever set down the whiskey, and I was close, I'd worry.

At the turn my chest and abdomen were warm but my snow-soaked thighs, ankles, and feet were stiff. I balled both hands and turtled them into my sleeves. My hair was too long for a boy, as my father said, but it kept my head mostly warm.

I returned to the mailbox, and then my father, and the mailbox, and my father. Fear turned to anger and then hatred. My thigh muscles burned from lifting and dropping sodden feet. It felt like running in ice cold glue. The pain in my knee grew worse. I couldn't tell if it was a muscle injury or a tear in my skin.

I longed for the warmth of the house.

"That's two mile." My father pointed the rifle at me. "You got eighteen more. Turn around."

Now he smoked a cigarette and his glass was empty. I stopped before him and opened my mouth, an exhausted apology stuck in my throat.

My thighs burned. Each step stretched fire from deep in my hips down through my knees, into my shins, my ankles, even to my numb feet. As I thought about the pain, it spoke

••

to me, suggested inside the house was warmth. My bed. Shame is a little thing. Shame goes away. Comfort—safety— is more important. I smelled pork and beans, potatoes, and onions. Calories and sizzling taste. I could almost smell the heat inside the house. I could almost feel warm bathwater.

I held my father's eyes.

He tilted his head toward the mailbox.

In a half-step I opened my mouth.

He lifted his head. Eye to eye.

I stopped.

He studied.

I stared. Inside his eyes and smirk I saw darkness. Like finding myself staring into a beast, a satan—and yet—I recognized my thin lines in his haggard ones. Saw my features in the contours of his addled face.

He needed me to quit because he was a quitter. And I could never give in because to do so meant becoming him.

I turned away and left the house at my back. Veered from the Sio tracks and cut my own path through the snow, and perceived in my exhaustion a growing sense of fortitude. Physical exertion and rage coexist. Tie them together, the knot is confidence. The knot is energy pulled from a vacuum.

My pace slowed but I owned the run.

I owned it.

My next lap I ran within two paces of my father. He jerked backward, eyes rounded. I swiveled and headed back to the mailbox, thinking, if I ever stop it will be because my father quits or my body quits. I—the part of me that is not body, the part of me that commands—will never quit. I will not quit. I will run until I pack this driveway to ice. Until my legs fall off.

••

Until my father sleeps and wakes sober and asks himself why his dead son is covered in snow.

When I next arrived at the house my father's seat was empty and his rifle leaned against the wall. Mary stood where my tracks rounded and when I turned she pressed a black bundle into my hands.

"He's inside getting more whiskey. Open it a little ways out," she said. She stood with shoulders bent against the cold and I stood with shoulders squared against my little universe. Our first moment as allies.

Fifty paces out I opened the bundle, a black knit cap stuffed with gloves, a can of Coke, an apple, and chunks of black pepper deer jerky. I wore the hat and one glove, held the apple and Coke while chewing on the jerky.

I left the Coke inside the mailbox and ate the apple on the return to the house. My legs were numb. Each step felt like it had to be the last, but another always followed.

I imagined humbling my father, completing forty laps and saying different things. "Give me back my medal," or, "Someday when you think I'm cool I'll still think you're a dick."

I walked a few steps and the rhythm was awkward. Running was easier.

Returning to the house I followed my prior tracks and approached within a few feet of my father. He glanced at my hat and his eyes narrowed. His face was blank. The longer I ran the less he seemed to know why I was doing it.

And the more I did.

I turned from him again without word. At the mailbox I opened the Coke, drank a few swallows, and left the can inside. I turned at my father, and next lap, completed the soda. The sugars from the food replenished my blood glucose.

••

Now wearing hat and gloves, my overall body temperature was good, except my feet stung with numbness.

Frostbite...

During an act of rebellion an injury becomes a badge of honor. All my running has been rebellion.

I would willingly suffer frostbite because running back and forth to the mailbox wasn't a demonstration of physical strength. I was young and had little. It was instead the benediction of my will. The first inkling of self-respect, rooted in the dawn of understanding that if I could withstand every extreme and pain and punishment—if I could take all of that and not quit, then no matter the outcome I would prove my father's view of me didn't matter. If my will triumphed over my body, then it—and I—was supreme over everything else. My father. School. The world.

The elements of will—self-control, self-direction, self-worth—crystallized with all the reality of the snow under foot.

It didn't matter if I completed the distance my father demanded. His number didn't matter. My number was whatever it took for my willpower to outlast his. Even if I collapsed of exhaustion, I would win if I fell forward and my last conscious thought was resolute. I found power in this knowledge.

Later when I read Camus and Sartre I recognized the same strain, that the universe is stark, there is no one responsible but I, because I either bear the burdens foisted upon me or I choose that they are intolerable. Either way I choose—but being conscious of the choice I become an agent capable of exerting himself against the world, rather than being merely subject to it. In choosing life over nihil, I affirm the only worth is will, the only power is will, and of the two possible

••

choices to evil, only one affirms my right to live another moment—and that, only if I fight for it. In that driveway run I formulated a twelve-year-old's existentialism. My identity, my worth, my protection were all faces of my will, and I would stoke whatever rage was required to keep it white hot.

After sixteen laps my father snored in a lawn chair with his rifle across the blanket spread on his lap.

Mary greeted me with a paper bag with a roast beef sandwich, a raw, peeled potato, and another can of coke. "Socks and boots," I said, and next time, she had my work boots and wool socks. My father snored through me changing them.

"You should come inside. When he wakes he won't even know."

"I run until I can't or he says I'm done."

"He might sleep for hours."

"Then I'll run for hours. I'm better than him."

"What if he comes in the house and forgets?"

"Then I'll die running."

"You're being stupid."

I looked to the crater in the snow where the medal had fallen. "He doesn't win tonight."

Mary helped me no more.

My legs moved as if by their own ambition and my feet stung as warm blood started retaking numb flesh.

At the next turn my father woke, rose shivering from the lawn chair and said, "You want to come inside?"

"No."

My boots were much heavier and I no longer ran, just shuffled, and sometimes walked quickly. But each time I came to the house I forced myself through the pain in my

••

knee to accelerate and hold my head high. I locked my gaze on the house so a chance outburst wouldn't throw me.

Or offer tempt me.

After what seemed like half the night had passed, but was really four hours, my father stood as I approached. He looked into the bottom of an empty whiskey glass, then stumbled into the turnaround path I'd cut. "That's ten laps," he said.

I stopped, staggered forward, unable to carry myself now that I wasn't moving. He was right in front of me and I could have reached to him for support. Instead I braced my hands against my knees. My back was on fire with stiffness and my legs trembled below my hands. "That's twenty-six," I said.

"Well, that's no closer to a marathon. Get your ass inside before you get pneumonia."

He left. I pitched into the snow near the medal he'd tossed and laid there until I realized if I didn't move I would be in trouble. I removed my glove and clutched the medal. Crawled to the truck, climbed the front tire, and standing, wobbled inside the house.

"That proves that," he said, unaware of the medal in my hand, or much at all. He slouched down into the sofa and tipped his baseball cap over his face like a cowboy needing shuteye.

I dangled the medal in the air in front of him. "That proves that," I said, daring him to open his eyes.

I made him back down. Through brute, total, absolute self-control, I made my father back down. Nothing in this world can hold a man prepared to trade his existence for going farther.

Even those who enjoy a great imbalance of power—such as a father holds over a son—find their power useless unless they stand ready to use it in the extreme.

••

To overcome my tyrant, I displaced him.

In my room I found a thumb tack. I pressed it into the center of the wall at the foot of my bed and hung the medal where it would be the first and last thing I saw every day.

It was there when the house burned.

••

Mile 32: 4 Hours 58 Minutes

TOMMY: You come across as a student of the sport.
NICK: To me, it's impossible to think of pushing the boundaries without knowing the lessons learned by the people who got them pushed out to where they are now. I study the sport.
MADDY: So with all the training and study, how do you find time for the rest of your life? For balance?
NICK: Balance is mediocrity.
TOMMY: Then by your achievements you must be one of the most out-of-whack people on the planet...
NICK: That's fair.

--DistanceHippy Podcast Pre-Race Interview

At a curve in the road I glance backward and glimpse a pulsing glob of light that distills into two pale headlights—a car five-hundred yards back. Though every crew vehicle is required to have its headlights on always, day and night, this vehicle belongs to no crew. The roof carries a low-profile deck of red and blues and it speeds toward me with alternating headlights.

I beef up my obstinacy. I will not slow, I will not stop. The only way they stay my progress is by tackling me. The only way I don't get up and keep running is if they shackle my feet and drag me across the back seat of the cruiser. I will not slow.

I will not stop.

Glancing at my Garmin I see I've increased my pace. I ease up.

The car pulls beside me. Hot pavement makes the tires sound like they're rolling through wet oatmeal. I run face forward. The car noses into my peripheral view, white with an angled blue streak on the side.

"Sir, are you Nick Fister?"

A woman's voice, hard at the edges, burnt like everything else in the heat.

"Sir?"

"I got a stride going. What's up?"

"I'm Deputy Edgerton. This is Deputy Bly. We need to ask you a few questions. You mind stopping for a few minutes?"

"I'm running a footrace."

"We're stopping several runners for questions, so you don't have to worry about your place."

I look. In the driver's seat sits a young woman with butch hair and a wrinkled brow. Everything about her is vertical, nose, neck, brow. She exudes virtue. Clarity and discipline. In the passenger seat is a slouched, shadowy profile, a man perhaps pulled from wandering Death Valley, slipped into a uniform.

"I'm not running against runners; I'm running against time. So any time I give you costs me. Can't this wait until the finish line?"

"Mister Fister?"

"Yes."

"Sir, this is a homicide investigation."

I take off my glasses and when my eyes adjust to the glare, "I'm seventeen hours from a course record. I've trained a year

••

for this run. It's the last race of my career. I'm not going anywhere except the finish line and Floyd Siciliano is going to be just as dead in seventeen hours as he is now."

The female deputy talks with the other.

"Besides. You really want to get out of your air conditioning now? Talk to me at the top of Mount Whitney."

I turn my attention to the white line and keep sending purpose to my feet. Shimmering desert heat can hide things in plain sight. Ahead is a yellow van, probably the crew of the Barelegged Nova, parked on the opposite berm. I slow but the patrol car matches me. I speed and the car responds. The driver looks at me through sunglasses she wasn't wearing a moment ago.

"What's your name?" I call.

"I am Deputy Edgerton of the Inyo County Sheriff—"

I spin on my heel, shoot behind the vehicle and across the road. In a moment I'm at the side of the yellow van. The driver is a man with frizzy hair and a razor burned neck.

"You crewing for the lady in a white top and yellow shorts?"

"What do the police want?" His voice is European.

"Dunno. Is that your runner?"

He nods. Glances at the sky. Back to the police car.

"I gave her my water. Passed her a mile back puking on the road. She's in bad shape but she'll get through. You mind replacing the water I gave your runner?"

His nose twitches. "She will defeat you."

"Sure."

Another crewmember in the back of the van speaks in gobbledygook. Another laughs.

Lisa and Mary will soon spray me with ice water and replenish my drink. This is a mere blip, a discourtesy, a cheap

••

mind game, and as I cross the road I realize the rudeness is not personal. Young Barelegged Nova has decided this is the race of her life and she's prepared to be relentless, to get personal and be offensive. Her crew has fallen in line.

I return to my pace.

Deputy Edgerton stands beside her car door. I'm already swinging my left leg forward, leaning into proper form, midway through the launch of a controlled fall that will last a half mile to my next rendezvous point.

I point across the hood of the police car and veer onto the road, kicking off fast. The twenty seconds of rest dealing with Barelegged Nova's crew chief has rejuvenated my legs. Deputy Edgerton allows me to cross and then gasses the engine and tools beside me—breaking the rules. She remains in the far lane and I on the left, facing traffic. With the added distance I see the bottom half of the other deputy's face.

"What's your name again, deputy?"

"Edgerton. What did you communicate to the person in the van?"

"Their runner is down a half mile back. Leggy blonde in a white top. You must have passed her."

"We offered her assistance. She said she's coming for you."

"A lot of people gunning for me."

"Why do you suppose that is?"

"You know anything about this sport?"

"I'm familiar."

"What have you run?"

"Couple marathons."

The other deputy scowls, turns his head away.

"So you know why I'm not stopping to have a conversation."

••

"We understand each other. For now. What can you tell me about Floyd Siciliano?"

"He's my crew chief. He didn't show this morning at the start."

"Did you go into his room?"

"I knocked for about five minutes and said to hell with him."

"You said to hell with your crew chief? At Badwater? Did you and he have poor relations?"

"You could say that."

"And you chose to run without him? Seems like an odd thing to be prepared for."

I look at my watch. Heart rate up. All this talking while I'm running is wasteful.

"My wife, sister, and Floyd have crewed before. They know what to do. Every run, shit happens. You don't prepare for details. You prepare resilience. There's always a way to deal with contingencies."

She tilts her head. "Your crew chief's murder is a contingency? What can you tell me about Mister Siciliano's death?"

"My wife told me a few miles back that he's dead. She guessed from hearing radio reports. He didn't show up at the start line. He's chiefed my crew for the last three years. He gets a little publicity out of it."

"And what about the manner of death? Ever imagine Floyd dying like that?"

"Like what?"

"The manner of death. Someone would have to hate a guy to do that."

"My wife said he's dead. That's what I know."

"Where were you at the time of his death?"

••

"How the hell do I know?"

Edgerton's mouth twitches. Something attractive lurks beneath her surface. Her face is stark with a button nose that makes her starkness girly.

I bet that nose pisses her off.

A muscle in my right thigh twitches. Not pain, but a sharp sensation. The strain of the heat and miles. I'm baked and I can already tell I have sweated out half of the chemicals my body keeps on hand for day-to-day operations. I muse about Edgerton in the nude and realize I'm sliding into that unclear state runners achieve when the body diverts glycogen to the muscles instead of the liver, preventing the brain from participating in the refueling.

If Edgerton keeps asking questions I doubt I'll be wily enough to engage her very long. I don't run races to think.

"So this morning... tell me about your whereabouts this morning."

"I started at the eight-a.m. start. I was in bed until six."

"What then?"

"I got up, used the bathroom, showered, ate breakfast, weighed in, and went to the line."

"What were you doing at four a.m.?"

"Sleeping. My throat's getting raw from talking in the dry air. I didn't kill Floyd Siciliano. I don't know who did. If you've got any worthwhile questions, we can try this again later."

I do my best to ignore the car. Edgerton keeps pace and talks with the other officer. Her window is down and I hear snippets, nothing that allows me to cobweb a meaning.

I try to coax a swallow from my bottle but the last drop has long turned to steam. My mouth feels full of sand. Even my eyes feel parched and I notice tightness in my right calf

••

that will soon become a cramp. I need water, electrolytes. I'm afraid to consume the Gu on my belt without being able to drink water. It will pull liquid from my body wherever it can, until competing systems—heat transference from my core, and sweating—assert priority over scarce body water and shut down the process. Then the lump of sugar will lay in the bottom of my stomach and ferment until enough water arrives to bring it to the right osmolality to be absorbed.

Trusting I'll see Mary and Lisa soon enough to prevent catastrophe, I pull a Gu, tear the top, and squeeze the Chocolate Outrage into my mouth. It comes out liquid, syrupy and slimy, but I swallow until the slick mass is gone. I cut the side of my mouth on the foil.

"We're going to return later with more questions," Deputy Edgerton says. "For now I've only got one more. Who would have wanted Floyd dead? Enough to do that to him?"

"Do what to him?"

"Floyd Siciliano was stabbed multiple times."

"Where?"

"He was found in his hotel room. Who would have wanted him dead?"

I can't help but snort. "Floyd? Sweetest guy in the world. I'm shocked."

Edgerton observes me without expression. The other deputy nods as if registering some grave insight. He speaks and Edgerton powers up the window. She nods and the car slows, swings wide, and cuts a U-turn behind me.

I twist to watch the sudden movement and glance my right foot on the side of the pavement. My ankle pops and pain knifes through me. My right leg, rehabilitated for a year, amplifies the shock and for a moment the ground rushes toward my face. I roll, lifting my leg and twisting to my back.

••

The pavement sears and I twist through, arrive seated on the edge, both ankle and ass in searing pain.

I've twisted ankles dozens of times and though the injury can be debilitating, it isn't a death sentence. My first concern is my leg. While my behind yet burns on blacktop, I rub along the tibia, feeling the notches where it healed. I remember the flash of blinding light that New York night that sent me sprawling into a bed of sharp rocks. I remember the face of the stalker who broke my bones.

Fearing, I place my fingers on my tibia, rub along the bone and feel the old scars and hollows. But the bone is fine.

From the back of my leg I press into a cavity, a muscle sinkhole, along the fibula. Neither pressure produces pain. Satisfied it is only my ankle, I twist to rise and see a scorpion, tail raised, in the shadow of a roadside rock.

Though my leg bones are not broken, as I put weight on my ankle I sense the damage is deep. Pain rarely matters—but I suspect this pain does.

*

When I was ten years old an old man lived in a trailer a couple hundred yards from the end of our driveway on the other side of the road. James Bliss—never Jim or Jimmy. James was frail, eighty some years old, with a left hand curved like a claw. When I visited he told me stories, sometimes the same stories. As a young boy he slipped in a barn, caught his left wrist on a nail, and ripped out a couple of tendons. He'd spent most of his life with an almost useless hand. He was gentle but so old he was terrifying.

James had a son when he was in his fifties. Denny drove a tractor trailer and kept a hotrod parked under a couple of trees by the road. It had yellow paint, a fastback design, and a roadrunner decal on the driver side rear window. The windshield was spider webbed by a rock—long before I had the teenage balls required for vandalism. The car was the second coolest thing about Denny.

The first was Raggedy Ann—his daughter.

Denny—in his thirties in 1991—could keep neither a job nor a woman. I leaned in when James talked about Denny because son rarely visited father but when he did, I wanted to know about it.

I saw Raggedy Ann for short clips that only expanded into significance in my imagination. She had a round face and was squatly built—a twelve-year-old girl who could kick a fifteen-year-old boy's ass—and then turn into the prettiest creature ever sprung by the time she was eighteen.

One summer we played Frisbee and I got stung by a half dozen hornets fetching the plastic disc from a spruce where they had a nest.

No one was in the house.

I ran inside. Raggedy Ann followed. I stood at the kitchen sink running cold water on my hand and she shifted to her knees, nestled between me and the sink, dropped my shorts and put my mess in her mouth.

"I ain't stung there!"

I jumped away before she could bite it off, or whatever she had in mind. I stood confused and thrilled, shorts at my knees while she ran out of the kitchen. I watched her race half down the driveway before pulling up my shorts.

James Bliss died that summer and Raggedy Ann never returned.

••

Looking back I can only remember Raggedy Ann's face for a moment before it morphs into Tuesday's, they look so alike.

Tuesday was the kind of pretty that made you look twice—to guess if she was legal. Red hair and freckles, a face carved from oil soap, soft and pretty but no baby fat, as if whatever youth in her departed quickly, leaving a young woman with a perceptive eye for reality but a precocious habit of assuming herself in control of it.

When she brought a boy home to study I knew his mind—and I remembered Raggedy Ann well enough to guess what might have been in Tuesday's.

"How you doing." I was heading out for my second run of the day, a ten-mile evening jaunt. Total for the day would be twenty. I was tapering miles before heading to a hundred miler at Greenville New York, a nothing race that would become the most important of my career. This evening run was my last before flying out the next day.

Tuesday's study friend didn't slow as he walked past me. "Fine." They headed down the hallway toward Tuesday's bedroom.

"Tuesday, stop. What are you doing?"

"Studying for a history test tomorrow."

"Study in the living room."

She exhaled. Cast aside her hip like to throw it from her body.

They looked at each other, then turned around, planted their stares on the floor and filed past me. The boy's face was red. Probably already had the evening's details worked out.

While he avoided looking at me I studied him. Jeans slung low like a gun belt across his groin. Boxers, white with gay blue ribbons. Long frolicking hair. Doors t-shirt, as if he read Jung and Nietzsche, grasped the complexities of their

••

arguments, and had something to add. Young Thornton—
Thorny as he liked to be called—was making a statement.

They opened their books in the living room. I filled a
water bottle, took a last look at them on the sofa, and went
out to run.

I was gone an hour and twenty minutes.

••

Mile 34: 5 Hours, 17 Minutes

MADDY: If you were giving advice to a young athlete who wanted
to achieve some of the things you've achieved, what
advice would you give?

NICK: Good question. I don't know anyone in this sport who has
really raised the bar who isn't a perfect balance between
two well-developed and competing forces. One is an
outsized sense of destiny, and the other is an outsized
sense of personal responsibility. Put the two together, you
have someone willing to pay the price, and the body falls
in line.

MADDY: So is there advice in that?

NICK: Yeah. You gotta be warped.

--DistanceHippy Podcast Pre-Race Interview

The night my father held a rifle on me to teach me I wasn't
worth a damn, I realized the cost of liberation wasn't so high.
I didn't hurt so bad. Exhaustion felt good, even better because
it proved my willpower and reminded me I had pushed back
the limits of the possible.

Shaky-weak legs felt better than a back laced with a
telephone cord, or the misery of shivering in a locked potato
cellar. We all get to choose our torments, even if it is only to
die sooner, or another way. We are all pregnant with
rebellion.

That night when I went to bed my father told me to put
the dog into the garage. Afterward, I realized the thirteen

miles hadn't consumed all my strength. I had something left, and I wanted to regain the feeling I'd attained cutting a trail through the snow, looking up at the stars and discovering reserves of strength within me. Feeling ice pelting my cheeks, knowing that I too could become a force of nature.

I climbed out of bed, locked my feet under the edge of the frame and did sit-ups until stomach cramps stopped me. I rested and did more. When I was done I had to roll to my side and push up with my arm. My stomach, back, and legs had reached muscle failure, and the feeling was like discovering a footlocker of gold under a rotted cotton blanket.

When I woke the next morning my legs were sore like I'd never experienced. The pain of moving them was worse than the pain that caused them to be in that condition. I couldn't adjust my legs without cramping my back, thighs, calves, and feet, sending wild bleats of pain through my brain. I pushed myself upright. The pressure of the sheets against my toenails felt like needles. I threw back my covers and slid my legs to the left. I counted five blisters, one filled with blood under the nail of my middle toe.

I knew nothing about recovery techniques that would have lessened the effects of the workout.

Just as a wolf pup has no inkling to complain about falling snow, a child has no perspective outside the house he knows. Fairness doesn't exist. Snow does. Hunger does. My environment sometimes included violence against me—like snow falling in the woods, covering the scent of game, bringing an impersonal, unobligated starvation. My father taught the same lesson: Violence doesn't result from reason: it just results. Like snow falls.

The lesson carried a personal corollary. I was useless, growing up in a land where opportunity existed for no one.

••

The folks around us were poor; no one in my family was anybody, my mother found her rural existence so intolerable she vanished like a dying Elijah. It wasn't just my father creating inevitable failure. Disappointment was in the air. Even after I set myself against my father, I exerted not against his worldview, but the world.

"Nick!" The door jarred with my father's fist. "Where the hell are you? Time to get up."

It was time for breakfast. I heard Mary in the adjacent room close her closet door. It was my turn in the bathroom. Flexing at my knees I drew my feet toward me, pushed a blister, felt fluid move under the skin.

The cold wood floor brought quick relief to my feet. I waddled to the closet and removed a safety pin from one of my shirts. At my desk I sat and pricked each blister, then pressed out the slippery fluid with my thumb. The pain increased when they drained. After showering, I slipped them uncovered into socks and shoes.

At school I walked stiffly. Mary told someone in her grade—one ahead of mine—that I'd run thirteen miles in the snow. Word spread and my classmates had varying responses. I had no close friends but the boys I spoke with most often thought the feat otherworldly... possibly a lie.

Frank Licona approached me in algebra before Mr. Grant entered to start the class.

Boys horse around whether they like each other or not. We took turns punching one other in the shoulder until someone turned aside in pain, earning the chorused epithet *Chickenshit!*

It wasn't good enough to weather the torment. You had to appear to enjoy it.

We learned that creating fear in our opponents was worthy gamesmanship in its own right. When a boy approached another with fist raised shoulder high, middle knuckle out, or with his hand wrapped around a sawed-off stub of broomstick, the challenge was thrown.

If the other turned his shoulder toward the challenger's fist, the match was on.

Licona hovered over me at the open side of my desk, his fist in front of my face. He had his middle knuckle raised and locked in place with his thumb wrapped tight to the side. Before I registered the challenge and could turn my shoulder, Licona drove his knuckle straight down into the tight muscles of my thigh. My leg instantly spasmed. I bounced my desk and books fell.

Licona threw back his head. "Chickenshit!"

"Asshole!" I twisted out of my seat and lunged but my leg locked with a charley horse. I shoved him back and his laugh turned into a snarl as he caught himself and charged.

The door slammed. Noise ceased. My neck shrank.

Licona froze. His eyes expanded. It could only be Mister Grant. Licona eased backward and by the time I realized Mister Grant had approached he pinched my ear between his age-hardened fingers. The pain was excruciating, worse than my thigh. Grant levitated me by my ear and led me out of the classroom. He paused at the door.

"Class, turn to page one hundred and sixteen and begin writing your homework problems on the board, starting with you, Jonell."

Mister Grant didn't release my ear until he steered me into a seat in the assistant principal's office.

Mister Smits sat ramrod straight. Shoulders square. Brow furrowed. Chest out and stomach in. He glowered at a document on his desk.

My ear radiated heat.

••

Mister Grant said, "Young Nick Fister was engaging in—"

"I'm sure he'll tell me."

Mister Smits scribbled on the form, buzzed his assistant to come remove it from his desk. We waited in silence, then:

"Mister Grant, I'm certain young Fister will tell me why he is here."

Mister Grant backed out of the office, somehow accumulating dignity while doing so.

"So? You are here because?"

"My leg was sore. Someone punched it. I shoved him and cussed him. That's when Mister Grant came in the room."

"I see. And your leg was sore because you ran thirteen miles last night?"

I squinted.

"Young Fister, in my view telling lies is more dishonorable than starting fights or cursing around young ladies. You understand?"

"Yes sir."

"So this rumor I heard in the cafeteria today?"

I nodded.

"It's true? You ran thirteen miles last night... in the snow?"

I tried to understand the shifting context—how I could be in trouble for running. I nodded.

"Why did you run?"

"I wanted to."

"And who did you have the altercation with in Mister Grant's classroom?"

"Licona."

I looked away, tricked. Feeling queasy like a rat ought to.

"Good. Turn sideways and place your hip against my desk."

••

I stepped closer, wondering if he would lunge.

"No, place your hip directly against the side of my desk. Good. Now lift your right leg and place your heel on the edge of the desk."

I studied him.

"Follow my instruction."

I lifted my leg no higher than my knee. It was torture. I wobbled—didn't want to place my hand on his desk for balance without permission.

"It's okay to steady yourself."

I did.

"Can't lift your leg. Excellent. Now bend slowly forward at the waist and let your arms hang. It'll be very tight in your back, but just let your body hang while you count to thirty."

I counted, every second expecting to hear him ready the paddle behind me, wondering how it would feel to be spanked bent over. But he remained seated behind his desk.

"Okay, slowly lift yourself upright. Good. Now lift your right leg and place your heel on the edge of my desk."

The stretch loosened my leg enough that I could lift it to the desk.

"Good. After a hard exercise your muscles stiffen. When you stretch them the pain goes away faster and the next time you run, you go farther and faster. You are not aware because we have not yet made an announcement. In fact, I have not accepted yet—but I have been asked to take over the high school track and field team, as well as the cross-country team this fall."

"Uhm."

"I'd like for you to join the cross-country team. I'll need you here at the school in June. Between now and then I want you to keep running like you did last night."

••

"I don't know that my father will allow me to join a school sport. He wouldn't be able to pick me up after practices."

"How far away do you live from the school?"

"Half hour on the bus."

"Then I will arrange for your transportation until you are able to run home after practice."

"But I don't have shoes."

"What did you run in last night?"

I nodded toward my boot, still on his desk.

Mister Smits glanced at my foot and then watched me a long moment. "Would your father object if the school provided adequate footwear?"

I shrugged. "No telling. Probably."

"Turn around and change legs. Stretch the other one. And the matter is settled. I need boys with integrity and diligence. Boys that don't back down from hurting legs. Boys with discipline. As to your fight with Frank Licona, I don't expect to hear of any more trouble. Your future is too bright to risk sinking with stupidity. Am I clear?"

"Yes sir."

"Good. Do these stretches after every run. Move out."

By late afternoon the soreness in my legs and back had receded. I'd taken everything my father could dish and kept him in the cold longer than he wanted when he started. Coach Smits had begun to distill the mash of thoughts I'd been cooking since the night before, and by evening all that remained was a few jewels I still carry today.

Late in my thirteen-mile run my father asked me if I wanted to quit and go inside the house where it was warm. I said no. The longer I suffered, the longer he suffered.

••

In learning to endure, I learned to inflict.

My context expanded from victim to victor. I wasn't a nobody from a hopeless nothing town. I could tolerate more suffering than my father could dish. Than anyone—even I—could dish. I could persist, and not quitting when everyone else was quitting meant I won. Coach Smits isolated the values for me, integrity, diligence, discipline—and if I could be true to the words I would be untouchable.

The lesson applied to everything. I didn't have to be skilled, fast, smart. If I lasted longer, I would win.

Riding the bus home that day I sat partly sideways so I could keep tabs on Licona in the back. The bus wasn't the right place to settle the score, but I had an idea of how I'd do it. When I got off the bus I got the mail, and walking back to the house, I tested my sore legs and found I could trot along. I wasn't fast, but I wasn't walking.

I carried the mail back to the house and instead of following the tire tracks from my father's Chevy S10, I tracked the path I'd stomped flat going back and forth twenty-six times the night before.

"Integrity, diligence, discipline."

I fed the dog and gave him hot water. I looked at the list on the refrigerator, written in my mother's hand three years before, and enforced by my father since she left. It was the only way anything got done around the house. It was Wednesday so I got a sponge and cleaned the top of every heater vent in the house, except in Mary's room, where I wasn't allowed to go. I went to the garage and straightened up the tools on the bench, and swept the basement with a push broom. My last chore was to clean the bathroom toilet, the mirror over the sink, the sink basin, and sweep the floor. I rushed through the routine but paid attention to every detail.

••

A half hour after arriving home, I put on a pair of sweat pants, wrapped my right foot in a plastic bag and put on my tennis shoes, crunchy from sitting next to the wood stove all day, and a hat and gloves. I ate an apple because my stomach felt like a pit, then ran to the mailbox and back until I'd run six miles. I thought about making Coach Smits proud and my father angry.

The run loosened my legs and on my second day of running I learned a lesson that would define my approach to training.

The best recovery is more running.

I dreaded seeing Frank Licona and felt a spike of angst every time I heard his raucous laugh. Aside from algebra with Mister Grant, I had another class with Licona, English with Miss DesForge, a wisp of woman prone to fits of Shakespeare-speak. *I wit not what ye speaketh of.* Her classroom was adjacent Mister Grant's. A few students migrated from one room to the next and waited the remainder of period change as other students trickled in from farther parts of the school.

Licona took his seat.

Miss DesForge stepped out.

I'd broken a pencil point during the prior class. Leaving my books on my desk I started for the sharpener mounted on the wall beside the chalk board.

"Chickenshit," Licona said. He turned to watch the reactions of the few other students in the room.

I swung back to my desk, grabbed my algebra textbook, and in the same swinging motion, smashed it against the back of Licona's skull.

••

The thud turned my stomach with fear.

Licona slumped forward, rolled sideways from his seat, and lay with his legs tangled above him. His eyes were open and blank, jaw slack sideways.

Six of us stood over him.

"You killed him," Regina whispered. "We have to get somebody."

But no one moved.

"Oh man that was sick," said Trunzo.

I nudged Licona's foot.

"Holy shit, he's really dead."

"Oh you are so screwed."

Licona's eyelids fluttered and opened. They grew wide and his face began to twitch with emotion. He straightened his jaw. Started to right himself with his elbow. Jerked his legs from the chair and rolled to his side and pushed himself from the floor.

"Oh dude!" Trunzo said, "You are SO CHICKENSHIT!"

Licona stumbled a few feet to the left then steadied, gathering his wits. His face splotched crimson and his eyes glazed with tears.

"Trunzo!" Miss DesForge shoved into the growing crowd. "Trunzo, stand in the corner. Steve, now! What's going on?"

"The corner? I'm thirteen."

"Fine. Go to the principal's office. Now what's going on here?"

"It's Licona," Regina said.

"What happened? Are you ill? Frank, dear, oh. What's wrong?"

Licona wrested his shoulder from her outstretched arm and stalked from the room. Miss DesForge watched as Licona left.

••

She twisted slowly, absorbing our looks through squinted eyes.

"Regina—what happened?"

"I—I don't know. Frankie, uhm, just fell out of his chair. Then I think he was embarrassed by the commotion."

By now most of the students had arrived and silence gave way to excited murmurs, "I just passed Licona in the hall. I think he got bad news or something. He's crying."

"Take your seats everybody. Everyone sit. We're about to begin."

Frank Licona never said anything to me again, never looked harshly, never spoke to or about me. When our eyes connected his face always seemed to masque the fear that I would do something horrific without him preventing or defending.

Show a bully you'll go farther, he's helpless.

*

I've often thought about the events that led to my success. It takes rage to subjugate your entire life—what you eat, when you take a dump, what you drink, how long you sleep, what you read and think—to a training regimen. An idyllic childhood would have allowed me to be mediocre. My latent talent is minimal. VO2 Max, lactic threshold, nothing special. I'm like the dumb kid who studies hard and gets the best grades. I win races not because of genes, but because of total submission to the sport—and that wouldn't have existed without my father's negative influence.

The last time I saw him was when our house burned.

I was eighteen, looking forward to starting college on a track and field scholarship.

••

Mary was nineteen and pursued dating with standards decreased by desperation.

Our father sat in a cross-eyed stupor. His guitar sat on the sofa beside him face-first on its strings like a fallen soldier, untouched in months. His half-empty tumbler rested on his knee, balanced between two fingers like a fat cigarette. He sat in the shadows, no television, no radio, just the static in his mind.

Five minutes before Mary's date arrived she trotted down to the basement to the dryer. She wore a robe and I wondered whether she could put herself together in time.

I worked in the kitchen. During long summer runs I wore a small backpack stuffed with peanut butter and jelly sandwiches and plastic soda bottles full of salty water and honey. I filled bottles and in a couple of minutes Mary came back upstairs, now clad in a crimson top, untucked, and blue denim skin from the waist down. She'd soaked the butt and threw the jeans in the dryer to make them tighter.

Our father reached out and grasped her thigh as she passed. She froze.

"Where you going?"

"I have a date."

"Not dressed like a whore."

Mary's eyes darted to me but before I could move she tore away.

Through the open screen door I heard a car. Her date, Pete, approached in a red Ford Tempo with a green hood taken from another car.

"Pete's outside."

Mary hurried to the door, slammed it, and then slammed Pete's car door as well.

••

I followed outside a moment later, not looking at my father or exchanging words.

I ran thirty miles and on my return smelled smoke from the blaze from five miles out. I saw the flames more than a mile away, and when I arrived the fire only then began to wane. My father lay on his back on the grass, so close to the house his clothes smoked.

He coughed. His breaths came choppy, raspy as if drawn through a reed in his throat. His red skin flickered with light from the fire and part of his hair was burned down to a bubbling red scalp.

I looked at the S10. "You got your keys? I can take you to the hospital."

He rolled his eyes toward the house.

I set off down the driveway for the nearest neighbor and before I'd progressed a hundred yards, headlights turned onto the driveway. I waited and in a couple minutes Mary arrived, Pete bringing her home early.

I flagged them down and told Mary our father was on the grass, catastrophically drunk and mostly dead from smoke inhalation and burns.

"You think he'll live?"

She and I looked at each other a long time.

A few minutes later we put our father in the back seat of Pete's Tempo and they drove forty-five minutes to the hospital in Albany, St. Peters.

Mary sat in the back seat with our father.

The hospital pronounced him dead.

*

I first met Floyd Siciliano when Mary brought him to meet Lisa and me over Thanksgiving dinner. Their relationship was short. Months later, I suggested to Lisa that I wanted a Bowflex or some free weights to add a dimension to my training. There was room in the basement.

Lisa gave me Floyd's card. She'd met him at a fundraiser for sexually abused girls who needed legal help. Small world, they knew a lawyer in common who was starting a nonprofit.

It turned out Floyd's gym was the closest gym to our house, only two miles away. I drove to check out the equipment. Floyd stood behind the desk and my first thought was that he'd bought the gym so he could work out all the time. He looked like a shaved buffalo, heavy on top, legs neglected. I couldn't help but grin at his lopsidedness and think how easy it would be to knock him on his ass and watch him struggle to make his skinny legs right all that chest.

Years earlier, upon going professional, my training and diet approach was to reduce my body to only the musculature essential to rapid, never ceasing self-propulsion. I thought the best way to accomplish that was to run at a slight caloric deficit until I'd lost enough weight that, even accounting for overtraining, I suffered a decrease in running capacity. I lost weight until it didn't help.

As I aged I began to think differently. I didn't want to be heavily muscled, but a running human is a machine, a symphony of coordinated actions, the legs, arms, chest, stomach, back, and head. Each moves in concert, each utterly necessary. The body is a finite system limited by its weakest component. The head stabilizes the body as a counterweight in a tower steadies the building during an earthquake. The arms add thrust to the legs merely by swinging harder. The stomach controls form and cant. Running requires all of

..

them, and running strengthens all of them. However, as I aged I began to wonder if I might forestall the decay of my speed by increasing the power of my other muscle groups.

My mind grew stronger, harder, and colder, about pain. Nothing occupied me more heavily than my goals. I ran knowing the laundry and dishes needed doing, groceries needed bought, and that I hadn't spoken in depth to my wife or daughter for months. I ran with everything else in a state of perpetual neglect, so I might accomplish the thing I chose to do well.

As I aged I grew not merely wiser and colder. I became more capable of drowning the voice telling me I was losing my humanity. I was more willing to listen to the violent part of me that wanted to quash every manifestation of increasing age.

When I was young I ran effortlessly. Collapsed and rebounded overnight. Legs of endless energy, every springy stride affirming my immortality. But as I aged the same fears possessed me as any older person. I attempted to slow time— and when I wanted to stop to enjoy the barest moment, urgency blared in my mind. I couldn't afford to rest. I couldn't afford to enjoy anything.

I had to push deeper into pain and beyond if I wanted to sustain what I was, and this understanding grew in a shadow: soon I would not struggle to remain, but to resurrect.

In the back of my mind floated the absurdity of it all. I couldn't stop time or be as good as I was before I broke every cell in my body. Before I abused my organs to the point of complete failure. But knowledge didn't prevent me from remaining fixated on my mantra. My belief compelled further belief. I drowned the opposition. I plugged my ears and chanted when reality knocked at the door, and I won. She went away, for a while.

But reality gathered herself together, unwilling to be put off. I knew she was coming and I ignored the pounding on the door because I needed one more perfect race before I could admit the truth. My best days were behind me.

Every man or woman chooses a yardstick. The one I chose prefers youth, not experience, and will measure me shorter and shorter every day until I die.

As I age the peripheries of life, my wife, daughter, sister, become less important. The body degenerates at speeds that surprise. One morning I run and the pain in the ball of my left foot is sharp and won't go away. It wasn't there yesterday, but it will be there tomorrow.

It didn't work that way when I was twenty.

Mile 35: 5 Hours, 26 Minutes

TOMMY: As you think about Badwater 135... it's billed as the toughest race on the planet. Any fear?

NICK: No, not in the way you might think. I've run enough miles to know bad things will happen. Tonight, tomorrow morning, and through the race. Nothing happens the way we plan. But I also know that in the past, I've dealt with it. So I respect the environment and the competition. I respect Death Valley. But I don't get twisted about the unknown.

--DistanceHippy Podcast Pre-Race Interview

Every second step launches pain rippling through my twisted right ankle, right calf—where I broke my leg last year—through my knee, to my back and brain. It cripples, figuratively and literally, my being, overtakes thought. It is the heat of Death Valley refracted to a focal point in the middle of my mind. My heart beats—and I am nearly unaware.

Floyd is dead, wonderfully dead, and I almost forget.

Sometime soon the local police will question me again.

*

Three years ago I gave my first interview to DistanceHippy Podcast's Maddy and Tommy. After I agreed to talk via email they called me on the telephone and, among other things, asked how I started running. I related how I'd received a 1985 marathon finisher's medal in the mail that didn't belong to me when I was twelve.

I'd thought about it a thousand times as a quirk of fate, but never as an unfulfilled obligation. I never questioned why the medal arrived with my name on it.

A week after the interview, I rounded a turn on a long run and noticed a pickup truck trawling behind me. I run against traffic. I thought the driver must have been looking for a turn or gotten confused. St. Louis roads are built for locals and the signage presumes as much.

When I glanced back again, the vehicle still followed at the same distance. The fellow inside the cab appeared to lean into the wheel, watching me with close attention. He removed a green Deere cap and wiped his brow, nodded, and his oddness made me cut onto a trail through the woods that I sometimes used to lengthen a run before arriving home.

I arrived at my house to find the truck parked on my driveway. The man sat on his open tailgate, legs dangling close to the ground. He sported a military haircut and wore tan cargo shorts with a light blue tank top. His skin was white with little red spots here and there, like blotches or pimples, and he backed up his half smile with a direct stare that left me uncertain if he was upset or insane.

"Been following you a long time," he said.

I hesitated. On the road just now, or my running career?

"Saw that documentary you did about the treadmill last summer. Watched it a few times because I thought I must have missed you saying the truth, but you never did. Been seeing you win these races here and there. I run, you know. I do distance like you, but I never really had a chance."

..

I resumed walking. "Something I can help you with? I'm on my way inside."

"I come from Greenville."

"You should have talked to my publicity people."

"You remember Greenville, New York, where all the Fisters come from? You grew up in Greenville, I bet. Your website doesn't say much. Make a fan wonder. Not the good wonder."

I stopped. Looked him over for some sign of his intent or evidence of a concealed weapon. Lisa was inside and Tuesday would be getting home from school any minute. "Why are you here?"

"Nick Fister, I'm you're biggest fan. And I heard what you said on the internet radio station last week and I thought I better give you the opportunity to set things right. You finally spoke the truth and so I drove down here so you could set things even righter."

"You caught me at the end of a run, and being an athlete yourself, you know that the ten minutes after a long run is the most important for recovery. If you want, send me a letter, or if you feel that's not sufficient, have your attorney send me a letter. I need to go. Please leave my property."

"Oh, no, Nick Fister. You know what I'm going to do?"

I stepped backward.

"You know the origin of the name Fister goes back to Germany, right? You should know that, being a famous Fister. It's an occupational name, like Smith makes horseshoes and Jones wants drugs. They used to spell Fister with a P in front, and Pfisters made bread. I suppose because they beat the dough with their p-fists—but that's just me speculating."

••

I glanced to the garage door. Closed. I always entered the house from the back after a run so I didn't have to carry a key. I'd run forty miles with the trail extension, and I'd pushed a little harder than usual in the middle of the run to help burn off a slight flu I'd been fighting for a few days. I could sprint for the back door, but if the man gave chase and caught me, he'd have me down in the back yard, hidden from all. And who knew what he had hidden in the small of his back, or his shorts' cargo pocket?

"What exactly can I help you with?"

"You never did say that you come from Greenville."

"I grew up in Greenville."

"That's right, see? That's why I came all the way down here to settle this face-to-face. You have property that belongs to me."

"Say again?"

"I'm asking the questions here. Unless you want the law involved."

"I wouldn't mind getting the law involved."

"So you're about thirty-five, right?"

I nodded.

"I'm thirty-nine." He grinned at me, the conclusion obvious.

"And?"

"I was in track and field in high school. You want to guess what high school?"

"Not particularly."

"You know I went to Port Jervis? You ever hear of the Port Jervis Raiders? That's what we were. But that sounds more like your M.O."

"This is all interesting. But I have to go."

..

"You know the students from Greenville New York, 12771 went to Port Jervis High School, and the kids from Greenville, New York, 12803, went to Greenville High School? You guys were the Spartans. That right? You see where I'm coming from?

The random pieces of information started falling together. The podcast interview about the marathon medal. Two New York towns with the same name. He ran track and field in high school. "So I guess your name is Nick Fister."

He put his finger on his nose and pointed at me with the other hand, grinning clownishly behind it. He giggled. "You got it, buddy! We're goddam doppelgangers."

My stomach grew tight. I twisted to my right, pressed my left nostril and blasted the right. His elation tamed.

"I even looked up your granddaddy on the internet. We're not exactly kin. In fact, you got to go back to the seventeen hundreds to find our common grandpa. I don't think folks are truly kin, you got to go back that far."

"I suppose not."

"So listen, grand champion ultra-runner Nick Fister, I'm Nicholas Fister, and the medal you got in 1985 belonged to my uncle Jeremiah Schwartz. He ran the New York Marathon and sent that medal to me. But since he didn't know the address, and called information to get it, they gave him your daddy's address because you was the only Fisters in Greenville. And they looked up your Greenville instead of mine because yours was bigger."

"That's interesting. I'm going inside."

"I want my medal."

"Good day."

"You can't steal everything from me. Not forever." He sat swinging his legs. He slammed his hand to the tailgate.

••

Removed his hat and finger-combed his hair, kept long on top. "You should have found me. Don't take a genius. You knew that medal wasn't yours and you built a career out of it. All that glory, you son of a bitch. I'm your biggest fan. So don't get me wrong. But that medal's mine and I come for it. I very damn well come for it."

I back stepped like I was facing a bear. Talk to it slow. Nothing alarming. "I'd be interested to get all that in writing so I can check it out," I said, and covered half the distance to the corner of the house.

"You took my future." You said it in that interview. You said, 'I like to think I would have found running, but it found me.' Well it was supposed to find *me*."

I turned at the corner and walked half backwards to the porch.

Nicholas didn't follow and I entered the house. Tuesday came home from school. I stood at the front door with a baseball bat. He nodded at her and she gave him a wide berth.

He sat out front for another half hour while I debated dialing 9-1-1 and ate peanut butter and jelly sandwiches until I couldn't hold any more. Lisa asked who the guy out front was. I just shook my head. Tuesday pretended to pay no attention.

Nicholas moved out of my vision. I looked out another window and he was waiting for me, standing right outside the window in the hedges. I started. He shouted, "I'll make you give it back!"

I didn't want to call the police because I didn't want the publicity and most of all, I didn't know how to handle it. If I had the medal I would have given it to him. If he wanted something to stroke while he sat on the couch and pitied himself, so what. But I didn't have the medal.

••

He ended up going away, and the next morning when I woke, I had my food to prepare. Stretches and cross training, then my run, and then a telephone discussion scheduled with one of my sponsors.

Nicholas Fister went to the back of my mind and stayed there for two months.

*

I brace myself for each stride. I alter my form, elongating my footfalls. I shift my landing from ball to side, then side to heel, then lengthen the stride, then shorten it. When my stride is short I land almost on my toes, forcing my injured ankle to act as a spring, absorbing shock in a way it doesn't want to do. Hobbled by pain, I instead stretch my stride and land on my heel. This is better—a jolt of real torture that blasts through my bones and only fades when the next jolt replaces it. Somewhere exists the right recipe of pain that will be endurable and tantalizing, a fuel for the rage that compels the next step.

Although my ankle injury is serious the swelling will eventually help it stabilize. My ankle is messed up and my leg, where it was broken last year, begins to throb. A normal person experiences pain and reads the message nature intended: this is no good for you, stop.

I've learned to hear a different message: Pain keeps you from having all you want. The achievement, the respect. *Keep fighting because pain gives up.*

The first mountain I will climb comes into view. This before the descent that leads to the second mountain, after which, the real climb, Mount Whitney. How will it be possible on a twisted ankle?

I think it through. Why is it any less possible?

After winning a race one time I spoke with the man who finished second. He said the pain was even coming through the opiates.

"The best pain will do that," I said.

Pain is a signal the brains registers and accords reality. My brain says the pain is real, but no one else feels it. I run on the same ankle as a mile ago. Granted, this ankle is torn whereas the former was not. This ankle protests; the other did not. But if this ankle was dead flesh that did nothing to propel me forward; if the Achilles stored and released none of the energy of each stride; if the ball absorbed none of the shock of each contact; if the toes were limp and did nothing to usher me forward— I would finish the race. And the fact that only I feel this pain indicates it does not enjoy the same authenticity as the road or sun.

I can make it go away.

The question is whether I will demand my mind work for me, or allow it to work against me. Ally or enemy. The brain is never neutral.

After Salt Creek, Devil's Cornfield, and Devil's Golf Course comes the 42-mile mark at Stove Pipe Wells. I now run at sea level.

A comfort being back to sea level, as I'm not a strong swimmer.

Stove Pipe Wells marks the start of a seventeen-mile non-stop ascent of the four thousand, nine hundred and fifty-six foot Townes Pass, the exit from Death Valley and the first of three major ascents of the race.

As I near the next rendezvous with my crew I consider possible steps to deal with my ankle. Should I tape it? Tape ice around it until the ice melts and the tape falls off? Do

••

nothing—allow the swelling to immobilize the torn ligaments?

My Garmin says I'm almost thirty-five-miles into the run. I'm still mentally clear. I've been consuming fructose and don't have to worry about not being able to think. No reason to doubt myself yet. Later it will get difficult to know anything but that I have to keep moving forward. The harder I push, the sooner my body will direct sugar away from my brain. I've been in races where I've forgotten my name. I've woken from dreams with my feet still pattering along the ground, miles after the last thought I recollect.

A brain bonk is like a disembodied state, and if you run far enough... it's what you want.

The van resolves ahead. Floyd had gambled that my accumulating local fame would help drive members to his gym. It is the unusual fate of the ultra-runner champion that he can win almost every major race that exists and his fame will remain limited to a narrow bandwidth of running enthusiasts. Running for twenty-four hours doesn't provide the same density of spectacle as a three hour football game.

The ultra-runner fan is a fan because he runs, and looks to his champion to indicate his own potential, should he work as relentlessly as his hero... should he press beyond what God graced him in his genes and what Nurture provided in experience, coaching, environment. Every ultra-runner is an agent in his own fate, and until he breaks into the realm where no man or woman has before gone, he looks to the champion to point to his next dream.

My ankle is dead, as it should be.

Thoughts elsewhere, as they should be.

••

Floyd is dead. As he should be.

Lisa exits the passenger side and walks between scrub and van toward me. The back of the van opens from inside and Mary studies me. Now that I'm arriving I allow myself to hate the heat I've been immersed in, and to desire the ice bath that waits. Twenty yards to the van my feet decide they're on a different project. They don't answer to me. I slow to a walk and notice I've given up my stride, control over my motion. My toe drags. I stumble.

"I want you to drive the back route and find the chick with the bare legs and the yellow van. She's wearing a UV top. White. She was hitting it hard and if she pulls her head together she'll be a threat. Give me a drink. Where's my mix? How many are ahead of me—and what are their paces?"

Lisa places a bottle in my hand and I gulp. While I drink she rubs the mangle of my right calf muscle and her mouth contorts with revulsion.

I think of our wedding day and an image jumps into my mind as if it had been sitting on my shoulder waiting the right moment. I see her in her wedding gown, kneeling in front of Floyd Siciliano. Did that actually happen? "Have you heard any details of how Floyd died?" I say.

"No." She rubs my calf. I drink. "No, I just heard it was bloody. The hotel can't move people to other rooms because they're booked full for the race, and so the police are escorting people to their rooms."

"Bloody, huh? A true shame. Are we checked out of the hotel?"

"The police won't let anyone check out until they're cleared. Floyd was murdered, Nick. Really murdered."

"So we have everything we need in the van for the race? We should have only left a couple of bags in the hotel—stuff

••

you and Mary were going to grab on the fly. Hell, we could probably just leave it and tell them to give it to Goodwill."

"You don't seem very upset about this. He was only your crew chief and best friend for three years. Oh, I know. Some pain doesn't matter. It's all about the run. Well I'm tired. I don't know what I'm going to do. I'm sick of this heat."

I reach to her and take her chin in my hand. Hold her face so she can't evade my eyes. "You can quit our lives together whenever you want—but not today. You and Floyd weren't going to make your move until after Badwater anyhow, so don't pretend."

Her eyes remain fixed. I've never called her out.

She bats away my hand. "Did you do it?"

"Do what?"

"Did you kill Floyd?"

I laugh; I think of the letter. Of Tuesday's death, the flight to Vegas. Of Floyd Siciliano's toothbrush left at my sink.

"Lisa—get yourself together. You only have one present right now. Your past is gone and your future isn't promised. You got one present, and this one right now in the middle of Death Valley is more important than any of the moments you've ever lived or will live again. You better get it right. Pull your weight. Do your job. You can cry over Floyd when you bury him."

"Did you kill Floyd?"

"No more than you."

Lisa stares.

Mary stands to my right, quietly taking us in, a hydrocodone glow to her eyes. She says, "The chest is ready. Be careful. It's thirty-eight degrees."

"Clock it—give me four minutes. That's all. I'll want more. Listen—look at me. Get me out in four minutes."

••

I try to swing my leg into the back of the van and can't lift it.

Mary places portable steps below my feet and I climb, swing my backside around, sit on the edge of the giant plastic cooler. I peel off my sun jacket and pants, slip backward into the pool.

The water shocks. They've filled the cooler too high and water sloshes over the sides into the back of the van. Air rushes into my lungs and my body engages behaviors without me knowing, gasping, shrinking, convulsing. Shock, wonderful shock. My insides rattle in terror. My skin moves on its own like a heavy fist massages it.

In a moment the shock is over. The ice cools my chest and back and thighs. The pain of my submerged body disappears and in its place creeps numbness. In four minutes the cold won't penetrate so deep that I have to worry for my life, but it will cool my muscles back to where they were when I was in the air conditioned hotel at four a.m. I slip until my chest and head sink below the surface. Ice water seeps into my ears and nostrils.

"Three minutes," Lisa says. "Hold steady."

I raise my head out of the water, leaving my torso submerged.

She goes to remove my shoe.

"No! Not that one. I twisted it a mile back."

"We've got to change your socks. Treat the hot spots."

"Do the other foot while I think."

Mary emerges from out of sight, outside the rear van doors. In the distance beyond her I see a shimmering barelegged ghost.

••

"Nick, we can bandage your ankle," Lisa says. "We need to treat for blisters or else the twisted ankle won't be your biggest issue."

Lisa removes my other shoe, peels the sock from my foot. She separates each toe looking for skin that has swollen, become discolored, or slipped from the subcutaneous flesh. "This one looks fine. How's it feel?"

"Fine. The other foot feels fine too. Leave it alone for now. We'll check it later if it starts to hurt."

Mary steps to me from the open van side door. "If it hurts," she says, "you've already done too much damage. Besides, with a twisted ankle you'll alter your stride and cause more damage, more quickly. We need to lube your foot."

"Do it."

Lisa grabs my shoe by the heel and pops it from my foot, releasing a ripple of agony from my twisted ankle that disappears somewhere around my hips at the bottom of the ice bath. She pulls the sock at the ankle and drags it over my heel.

She pulls apart my toes one by one. "You've got the start of a blister on your pinky toe."

"Lance it."

She sticks a pin into the flesh and I don't feel it go in. She presses out the fluid, collecting it in a paper towel, then covers the blister with antibacterial ointment. She slicks the rest of my foot with petroleum jelly and then slips on a new five toe Injinji sock.

Beyond Lisa, the shimmering ghost has become the Barelegged Nova. She's puked herself back to zero, filled up on my water and aid from the van I dispatched to her, and chases after the lead.

••

I don't discount the possibility she could take away my victory and unset record. I have come back from moments of crippling despair and listlessness so severe I wanted to find a rock and beat my head in with it. I have ridden my legs from abject failure to record-setting victory in the space of a few hours. And in a long race she has every right to expect to win. The longer distance gives her female advantages more time to equalize the contest, and she has the determination of a champion.

I emerge from the cooler and shed water to the back of the van. My legs have lost their ability to obey.

"Dammit, Nick. What the hell? You have a minute left and I don't have your sock on!"

I slip down the inside of the van and sit on soaked carpet, swipe the sock and my foot cramps, splaying my toes like someone put a hot poker through the ball of my foot. Lisa grabs the sock and somehow massages the cramp out while slipping it on.

"I don't want Nova to pass me. It's psychological—not for me, for her. I don't want her to get ahead of me. She needs it."

Mary unlaces my right shoe while Lisa slips on my left.

"Quick, where's the tape?"

Lisa looks around her and Mary looks blank. "Shit," Mary says.

"Floyd."

"Floyd didn't bring the duffel."

"So we have no tape? What else don't we have?"

"You need to get some calories."

"Put on my shoe!"

Mary holds the shoe open and guides my foot by the heel.

••

"Mary, in twenty seconds I'm pounding that foot to the pavement for eighty miles. Going soft now won't help. Lace it snug."

Mary gets vicious in her hurry, slamming the back of the heel forward, lacing tight. "You're turning blue on the side," she says.

"It'll swell on its own and immobilize. Meantime, go back to the hotel and get the duffel."

"How? Floyd's dead. They have his room closed off."

"Then buy some tape. Go to Stove Pipe if you have to."

"We can't leave you alone that long."

"Give me a second water bottle and three extra Gu's. Let's go."

I swing my legs from the back of the van out into the heat and for a tiny moment, frozen and slow, I want to walk. The heat scorches and though water runs from my back down my crack to my legs, the water is no longer cold when it reaches my feet. Only wet.

Mary slaps my water bottle in my hand, then gives me a second before taking off. I swallow until I feel an inch shy of queasy, and see Mary's eyes flicker to the road behind me. I turn, and the Barelegged Nova is twenty feet away, stone faced, angry, pain free and rocking.

I spin to launch—and collapse on my bad ankle. Neither my legs nor my heart are taking orders.

"You're bonking. It's the cold. It'll just be a minute," Mary says. "Clear your thoughts. Watch that pretty girl from behind."

I'm aware of the burning heat of the road under my butt. New sweat seeping into my eyes. I wipe my brow, breathe slowly.

"Did you hear how they found Floyd?" Mary says.

••

I look up to her. Lisa is in the van, shifting a box near the front. I shake my head.

"He was killed in the hotel. Stabbed. In his room."

"Who do they think did it?"

Mary shrugs. "They have the whole floor closed off, and escort you going to your room. We went back for ice—it was chaos this morning after Floyd didn't show. We left our bags to take you to the start and went back to the hotel to get them."

Her mentioning Floyd focuses me. I see his face and Tuesday's, and I think of Tuesday in her grave, and with my eyes wide open catch a vision of my baby girl in decay. I twist to the side and a tidal percussion of spasming stomach muscles leaves the electrolyte drink I just consumed splashing on the pavement.

"There you go. Let it out," Mary says. "He's dead. Drink this," she says, and pushes my arm with the second bottle to my face. "Drink it and then you get up and reel in that pretty girl Nova."

I gulp and the cool fluid soothes my acid throat.

I see Tuesday as a young girl, giggling. Lisa slips into the embrace of a Corvette driving bodybuilder. I drink, and roll sideways to my feet, and press up with hands on the burning pavement until I'm on my legs. I toss the empty bottle to Mary. Lisa emerges from the driver side.

"Give me three Gu's."

"We're meeting again in five miles." Lisa says.

"Give me three. You're going to Stove Pipe."

Mary places them in my hand. "When you pass her, hit a seven-minute pace. You'll break her."

I take my sister's head in both hands and kiss her forehead. Twist on my good ankle and set off. The first stride sends a

••

brutal stab through my twisted ankle but the second is dull, and within a dozen steps I find the electrolyte and glucose mix are already resuscitating my frozen muscles. Barelegged Nova has me by a minute. I tear open a Gu and squeeze the energy into my mouth. Gulp water and suck down a second Gu. Ultra-running is ultimately about body attrition. The few minutes in the tub have given my cells recuperation. But as I look ahead to the shimmering Nova, I sense the distance growing. And though I had the energy to launch well, a hundred yards into the run I find I'm on dead legs.

The Barelegged Nova won't slow down.

*

I had suggested to Lisa that I wanted a Bowflex or some free weights to add a dimension to my training. Our basement was finished and there was room. Lisa reminded me Floyd owned a gym. She gave me his card, explaining she'd run into him at a fundraiser for sexually abused girls who needed legal help. Small world. They knew a lawyer in common who was starting a nonprofit.

It turned out Floyd's gym—the Bench Press and Pound—was only a couple miles from our house.

Floyd stood behind the desk and like all men of his size, he seemed to regard me on that first day with a mixture of contempt and mirth.

"How can I help you?"

"My wife gave me your card."

"I know lots of women. Who's your old woman?"

"Lisa Fister."

Something flickered in his eyes. "You come to the right place. Put some meat on you."

••

Floyd looked like a man who didn't merely enjoy conflicts, but sought them like rags to stuff in his gaps. The hard angle of his jaw and the glare in his eyes said he couldn't turn away from even the slightest challenge.

I'd arrived at the gym thinking I was going to sign up. Once I decide to do something I prefer as little extraneous information as possible—just complete the transaction and let me get to it. I handed him my credit card.

"Your wife said you run a lot."

"Distance."

He grinned like a kid with a bucket of diarrhea peering over a garage fan. "Yeah. Well, you'll find everything you need here to man up. Maybe with forty pounds on your arms and chest you'll find a new sport."

He ran my credit card.

I leaned closer. "Floyd, I've changed my mind. I'm going to buy a Bowflex."

He returned my credit card. "Well, you've already paid for the first month and there's no refunds on that. You might see what you bought before you buy machines for the home."

He led through double glass doors into the gym. It was late morning. A pair of women rode bikes and a few men stood at a free-weight area, stacking metal on a bench press.

One of the women glanced at me and stopped to take in the full spectacle. I stand six foot one and weigh a buck fifty-eight. All spine and legs.

But I can run forever.

"We got the free weights over against the wall. If you sign up for personal training I'll give it to you at my breakeven cost, since I like your wife. We'll spend a lotta time on the weights. You said you run distance, right?"

"That's what I said."

••

"Well, I don't run and I especially don't run from anybody, but I'm a general athletic coach, so I can help you there. The research shows you need to build your core. And you need your upper body to be able to drive your lower body when it doesn't give a damn anymore. You know what I mean? My legs get tired walking around the gym—but I swing these pythons and my legs wake up."

"Yeah, Floyd. That's what I was thinking."

He'd already been a prick. Swiped my card, and then informed me of the gym's no-refund policy. I felt like dicking with him.

"There's a couple of strings hanging from your shorts," I said. "Oh. Sorry. Those are your legs."

Floyd squinted like he'd become aware of a mosquito biting him on the forehead. Finally he gave me an Italian smile—dead-fish eyes, mouth lifted at the edges. "Your whole fuckin body is strings."

"That's why I can run forever and you'd collapse if you walked around the gym."

"Look at this." He flexed like he was looking at his watch and got a cramp. "I could squeeze your head so hard the top of your skull would pop off."

"You couldn't catch me. I don't get it with big guys like you. It takes a lot of work to get your body to look like that. Why? What's the motivation to pump up muscles you'll never use for anything?"

"These muscles could beat your ass to pudding."

"You're so top-heavy you could never catch me. And that means the whole thing is for show. You're a Corvette chassis with a three-banger under the hood. You pull up to the stop and rev your engine and the girls laugh."

His face mangled itself.

••

"I'm serious," I said. "You may as well not have any legs. You may as well lay on the floor and reach out to grab folks, if you ever get into a fight."

His nose wrinkled and his glare hardened. Lightning fast his left hand shot out and grabbed my right wrist. He squeezed hard and pulled me against the desk, then leaned even closer to me. "How 'bout I show you what muscles are for, faggot?"

He bent my arm backward at the elbow.

"You feel the tendons and ligaments starting to pull? Will they rip off? Or will the bone snap between your wrist and elbow?"

I searched the desktop for anything I could grab—a pen to stab him, scissors, a telephone to crush to his temple, but there was nothing except paper and the computer monitor. Floyd grunted and the pain ratcheted higher. I smelled cologne like spiced alcohol. My elbow felt about to fold backwards and the muscles from the point in my arm where his grip immobilized them pulled through my shoulder and back.

I balled my loose hand into a fist and reared back.

"Nah," Floyd said, bending my arm still farther. "Don't be a dumbass."

My elbow was on fire and the pain immobilized me. I couldn't think. I saw myself in a cast, saw my training plan evaporate. I heard ligaments tear, and I thought not all pain matters. I'll get through it. I don't quit, ever. I endure anything. There is no pain so great I can't keep moving forward. I eased into the pain and found it was mostly fear. I located inside me a reserve of thoughtfulness, of awareness. So often we behave like the chimpanzee with his hand locked in the hollowed out rock, clutching grain, so excited by the

••

food, and terrified of the oncoming club-wielding man, that we can't think to release the grain and free our hands from the rock.

I released my hand into the pain. I let it wash through me and when I became okay with the agony I smiled.

Floyd released my wrist. He said, "You get the point."

My lungs heaved and my elbow throbbed. I already knew he'd caused real damage. "Yeah," I said.

"Stick around. I'll get your refund."

I looked out the front window to the parking lot, and then to the sky, where a ball of black clouds had formed. The sunlight fought on, unwilling to cede the day, but as dark clouds rolled in the sun had no choice. I wanted to run in the storm. I wanted to get into my shorts and shoes and head for the trails, fleet between the trees and lightning. I loved to run in storms.

But winter was coming and there would be days when I'd need the miles but with less risk than running on ice, or through a foot of snow. I wanted the machines for cross training, and I wanted to joust with Floyd in a sick way, like when a mean dog is chained just short of you.

"No. No refund. Give me my card. I'm going to work out."

So I started training at the Bench Press and Pound because I already paid for it, and because Floyd liked my wife.

••

Mile 39: 6 Hours, 17 Minutes

MADDY: You were injured last year and a lot of people thought you weren't going to be able to come back to the sport. What happened?

NICK: I broke my leg.

MADDY: How?

NICK: You really won't believe it, but a guy named Nicholas Fister had something to do with it, I think.

TOMMY: What?

NICK: Yeah, a guy with my name. I can say that right? I mean, I'm not saying which Nick Fister, just another one.

MADDY: Freaky. What'd he do?

NICK: Well, he started following me. Showing up at my house.

--DistanceHippy Podcast Pre-Race Interview

I started cross training at Floyd's gym and made certain to mention the strings hanging from his shorts every time I saw him. In exchange, Floyd mocked my biceps.

I carry grudges not because I'm vindictive, but because I value simplicity. Judge a man and be done with it. Don't give second chances. If the asshole has the moxie, he'll seize the second chance and save you the trouble.

I enjoyed sparring with Floyd and he enjoyed dishing it back. I started to respect him.

"What have you won, Floyd?"

"What?"

"You talk shit, but what have you ever won? Ever bench press more than anybody in the world? Ever dead lift more? No, I forgot. You'd need legs for a dead lift."

I kept him frazzled and pissed off whenever we talked— more so as the weeks passed and I added up little coincidences, like how I'd heard Floyd say the word 'wheelhouse' in a sentence that would have been less contrived without it, and the very same day heard Lisa use the term for the first time in her life, commenting on the same news story as Floyd. Not in his wheelhouse the dumb prick, Floyd said. And Lisa agreed, thirteen hours later, except her victim was a dumb shit.

I don't recall the moment the full realization clicked into reality, but the night of the freak snowstorm came shortly after.

I antagonized Floyd in the manner of a little boy who's learned he's smarter than a dog, so he taunts it. But I always made sure to keep my arms away from his grasp, and to never mess with him after a forty-mile run.

I knew from the beginning that long ago, something broke Floyd. Guys with healthy egos don't pump their shoulders into eighteen pound hams. He went to the gym because he was sick of getting his ass pounded by the bigger kids on the playground, or the first girl who grabbed his mess laughed out loud. The gym taught him that if he endured enough suffering of his choosing, he wouldn't have to endure quite as much imposed by others. One empathizes. But with Floyd, no matter how much his chest grew, like his skinny legs, his ego never built out.

While at the gym I avoided free weights and kept to the machines, never needing a spotter, coming and going as my training schedule demanded. I'd exchange a fuck you with

••

Floyd at the front door then get to work. A quick fuck you at the end would sate us until the next time.

The firmer my belief grew he was bedding my wife, the easier the greeting was to dish, and the more I anticipated hearing it in return. A runner doesn't respond by provoking a showdown. He keeps his legs moving, keeps his mind nimble. Keeps his routes open so somewhere ahead he can swing a text book from a blind spot.

After I'd been trading barbs with Floyd for six months, using the gym for cross training with weights, a freak snow storm dumped a foot of powdered snow and covered it with an inch of ice. I'd never set foot on a treadmill at the gym, and Floyd had to this point never seen me run.

I don't like the mechanics of treadmill running, especially for durations. But it would be better than snow, ice, and frost bite.

I brought a bag of Gu's, a water bottle, a canister of electrolyte mix, an electric fan, and my mp3 player. A big girl toiled on the runner's treadmill, a nice setup with a wooden springboard. I tried to remember Rodney Dangerfield lines while I waited.

I met her at the Macy's Parade. She was wearing ropes.

I was in a strange place: running from Lisa's unfaithfulness, down-spirited from having won another 100-mile race a few weeks before. A little raw inside, wanting the cover of sweat and exhaustion. As the girl wound down I wanted to give her some pointers about avoiding carbs, keeping her insulin low so it doesn't trigger additional fat stores... maybe urge her to consider a forty-day water fast, but couldn't think of a polite way to do it. I kept my mouth shut. She vacated at ten p.m. after a mile of fast walking.

••

Floyd didn't leave until midnight. He was covering the shift of a girl he'd fire a few days later. His mood was foul. Unaccustomed to seeing each other at this hour, we'd fumbled our initial exchange. Neither having anything shitty prepared, we defaulted to friendliness, and were immediately uncomfortable.

Me, because he was screwing my wife. I imagine the same for him.

"Uh, hey! What you got in the bag?"

"Gu."

"Why not eat a banana?"

"I got a banana. But I can't eat twenty bananas without shitting myself. So I eat Gu."

"You got twenty Gu?"

"Nineteen."

"Shit. How long you working out?"

I can run forever. The whole world is miserable and ugly but when I run I'm not a man or a machine, I'm a soul, and when I start I don't ever have to stop, and there's beauty in that. But no matter how long I run you're still so wrong I should lead you to an empty field and put a bullet in the back of your head.

"All night. I'm probably going to run all night."

Floyd walked a circuit of the gym before leaving two hours later. He stood by the treadmill, leaned in close enough to see the mile count.

"You run seventeen miles already? That thing right?"

I was listening to my mp3 player on low volume and in a zone and though my pace wasn't setting any records it was faster than I usually run. The treadmill was level; I didn't set it to a hilly workout, just a speedy flat, and I wanted to see what I could do.

I'd just come off a hundred-miler victory three weeks before, and I was in a funk trying to figure out what to do next. I'd been toying with running a twenty-four hour race, a different concept in ultra-running—instead of covering a fixed distance in the shortest time, the contest determines who can run the greatest distance in a fixed time. There are road races and track races; one race loops around a city block in Brooklyn for three days. My preferred race is point to point, followed by loops, and then specified duration. It had been years since my last twenty-four hour and I thought the change in training might keep it interesting.

Mental recovery after a race has always been more difficult for me than physical recovery. Proper training depends on urgency and meaning. No one will sacrifice and endure without attaching profundity to the outcome. When I ran thirteen miles as a kid, I hung on through the torture because of the moral battle with my father. The miles themselves had no meaning.

The young runner finds meaning in his passion for the sport, for the conquest. But the career runner perceives a question at mile forty that the young runner blazes past without hearing—

Why?

No race has intrinsic worth—only what the athlete convinces himself is real. Through focus and desire I create urgency for an event until it is a sun burning on its own significance. Then I bask in the heat. Win the race. Afterward, the illusion of accomplishment, of importance, fades. The sun was manufactured. The pain, ginned for the occasion. The past is no longer real. Only the present exists,

••

and the significance of a past achievement pushes out like a trace, deferred to other races yet to be run. It's like looking for meaning in a dictionary and finding words, and more words, and no meaning in any of them. The past is nothing, the future the same. Only the moment and especially the running moment matter.

I'd won a hundred miler and hadn't found glory. So I spent hours on the internet looking for something new that would take me higher, define me narrower, expose my core. I sought a race that would chisel away everything that wasn't my rawest, most essential self. I wanted to cleave away all but the very muscle, sinew, and spirit that defined me.

I wanted a race that would excise my cheating wife like so much dead flesh.

I was running astraddle my lactic threshold. I've always pictured perfection as an edge, something seen only when passed, firmly planted in excess. You go beyond, then scale back. The goal is to realize absolute potential. Not the mere potential God gave or nature nurtured, but the potential you decide as a self-creating agent.

Floyd said, "You run seventeen miles already? That thing right?"

I had never tested myself in a perfect setting—low impact treadmill, cooled by the fan, glycogen drip. I had my mp3 player feeding me and I wasn't of the mind to banter.

Floyd said, "Looking strong, Nick," and turned away. I watched through the mirror as he left and he seemed like a regular man, at ease with himself and gracious enough to wish another well.

Maybe he'd swing by my house, bid goodnight to my wife.

••

I ran harder. Adjusted my glucose and electrolyte intake.

Night is magical for running. I tuned out the world and turned the mp3 player off and just listened to my body, my feet, my heart, my lungs. My hate and pain and resentment. My failing as a husband. My uselessness as a father.

My body worked perfectly, nothing out of place or wrong. On a long run, a small pain eventually becomes large. Ignore it or not, there's a real progression. A hundred miles will exacerbate a mosquito bite. But that night I was fresh and the scene was new.

Floyd returned late the following morning.

I was still running. The treadmill showed sixty-three miles and 9,938 calories. I had a pile of empty Gu foils and had consumed half a pound of electrolyte mix. I was tired. The treadmill board bowed to each impact. I'd been tearing up the miles and sustaining a faster pace than I would in the wild.

The night clerk was a little guy named Toby. He'd spent the hours from two to four a.m. pounding barbells like he wanted to be a big guy. I watched Floyd through the mirror as he came to the front door, spoke a few minutes with Toby, looked into the gym and saw me. He pointed. Said something.

Like the muscle-bound man who flexes his arm to check the time for somebody, I run faster when people stare at me. It's why bullfrogs bloat and bighorns clash. When road running and I come to an intersection lined with cars, passengers looking my way, I surge without thinking. Onlookers give me ambition.

Toby and Floyd started watching me. I tapped the button and bumped up the speed to accommodate my surging energy.

Floyd entered the gym and approached with the clerk until they stood beside me, saying nothing. I upped the speed again. Sweat dripped from my hair like rain and pattered my arm and the black treadmill belt. As Floyd stood beside the machine I thought of Lisa wrapping her arms and legs around him and I turned all that hate inward. I increased the speed again, maxed it out. My left leg cramped. I fought it.

"Shit," Floyd said. "Sixty-three miles. You're kidding me."

I slammed the down arrow until the speed dropped to three and I was limping along. "I'm extending my run. Hand me my phone."

Floyd swiped my cell from the top of my throw bag.

"Dial Lisa for me, would you?"

He swiped open the phone and paused. "What? I don't know her number. Shit." He shrugged.

"Gimme the thing." I dialed Lisa. "Hey. I'm at the gym on a long run. I decided to add a few miles. No, the treadmill. Bring me some PBJs, my spare canister of electrolyte mix, and my bottle of Salt Stick. Get here quick."

I ended the call and pitched the phone to my duffel.

"You seriously ran sixty-three miles?"

I stared ahead. Nodded.

"He was on the mill all night," Toby said.

"And you just told Lisa you're running longer?"

I connected with his eyes. "What did you think an ultra-runner was?"

Floyd stared at my legs as if he might address them directly. "Shit." He shook his head, took in the Gu foils. "Clean this shit up, Toby. You need a hand, Nick? This is unreal."

"I'd like quiet."

Floyd and Toby moved to the front. Toby went home at shift end and Floyd started telling everyone who entered to look at me. They looked at me. He pointed to his watch. Gestured about the gym.

••

The gym rats kept an eye on me as they worked out. Yeah. Pay attention while I define *fanatic*.

I almost bonked by the time Lisa arrived with a duffel in hand. She entered through the front and stopped to talk to Floyd. I watched through the mirror. She put her hand on his, or close enough it was the same, before bringing me the electrolytes. She mixed a few bottles and left.

Later in the morning Floyd approached me with speed. "How many miles you do so far?"

"Eighty-five."

He shook his head, smiled, rolled his eyes. "Can you keep doing that?"

"I am."

"The world record on a treadmill is a hundred and sixty."

"Yeah."

"So are you going for the record?"

"No."

"Why not?"

"Floyd. Let me run."

By four in the afternoon Floyd had called the local television station's news team—EyeWitness 5—and a blond teenager in a suit tried to put a microphone in my face.

"Piss off."

"Give me a chance to talk to him," Floyd said to the kid. "Stand over there a minute." He faced me. "You got a lot of nerve doing a stunt like this in my gym."

"What are you talking about?"

"All this baloney. Going for the record and not going for it. You got everybody riled up. Won't talk to the people who want to wish you well. Tell a kid reporter to piss off. This can help the Bench Press and Pound. It can do good in the community. And you're just interested in yourself."

"I didn't call the reporter."

"No, I did. That's good business. You don't know anything about business. You don't even know what you don't know. But you talk to that reporter and it helps me a lot. And that's how you make friends, least in my world. My people. You know what I mean? Talk to the kid. Tell him you want to run a hundred and seventy miles. It don't matter what you do. Just let him put the Bench Press and Pound on television."

I drank from my bottle. Listened to my heartbeat amid the steady rap of my feet on the mill.

I ran one hundred and fifty-nine miles and quit with twenty-two minutes remaining. My pace was eight minutes and fifty-five seconds per mile, and because I run largely even splits no matter how long I run, I could have easily passed the record.

In the last minutes, Floyd, Lisa, Tuesday, and about twenty people stood around the treadmill. I ignored them and stayed in my zone, an aperture of exhausted awareness bordered by a haze that captures sound and energy so in the midst of cheers and chants, I was aware but unobligated. I watched the circle of lights on the treadmill dashboard and when the circle was complete, and the odometer changed to one hundred and fifty-nine, I rapped the stop button, stepped to the gym floor, and fell to my behind.

The zone vanished. People gasped. "What? I thought he had another twenty minutes?"

"Get back on the treadmill. You can do it! Woo Hoo!"

I knew well what I could do. I was on my ass because of vertigo from leaving the treadmill, not muscle failure. I could have run two additional miles in the last twenty minutes. I chose against.

The television reporter again put his microphone in front of me, and asked what had happened. Was it an injury? I climbed to my feet and carried my duffel to the locker room. The reporter followed me inside, tailed by Floyd and Lisa.

"You could have had it," Floyd said. "I don't get it."

"Floyd, it's not that simple. To take a record you need witnesses start to finish. You have to follow procedures. The whole thing would have been disallowed because I jumped off the treadmill to grab my water bottle at two in the morning and didn't stop the mill first."

"But, you would have finished. You could have shown you could do it."

"Shown who?"

He gawked.

"Who, Floyd?"

When I got out of the shower the television news crew was gone. Lisa was gone. Tuesday had school in the morning.

Floyd sat on a bench.

"You ran longer than people can sit. Or lay down." He spoke like I was the Grand Canyon and he stood at my edge. "Your wife and sister—they crew for you, right? When you go on a race?"

I nodded—without questioning how he knew.

"So what do you do for wheels?"

"If it's a road race, I rent a van in the city we fly into. For a trail run, a car. Whatever."

"What if we used the gym's van, and put your picture on it?"

••

"I don't follow."

Beside him on the bench was a printout photo of me from a website ultra-runner story. I didn't recognize the background, just the mug.

"We could use my van for your crew. And in return, we get your face on the side and you endorse the gym. Maybe do a radio spot for us. Maybe do a clinic for the high school track kids or something. This city's got people running all over the joint. People would pay to have you show them how to run a hundred and fifty-nine miles."

The offer came at a moment when I didn't need the money or the help. I'd just signed with the biggest two sponsors of my career and I could afford to be picky. But something about Floyd's transformation from asshole to awed made me a sucker and without thinking about the ramifications, I shook his outstretched hand. "We'll work something out."

"Lisa runs your crew?"

"That's right. I guess. Sometimes. No, I run my crew and Lisa drives the car and gives me water."

"I'll take it up with her."

"Sure Floyd. No, Floyd. Take it up with me. Call me later."

*

The day Tuesday died I saw her at the mailbox. I was leaving on a run. I'd broken my leg in an ambush in New York and I'd been fighting like hell to recover. I'd quit going to physical therapy because the rubber-kneed therapist kept reminding me not to hope for too much—as if hope had anything to do with the outcome I was bent on creating. Many people fail at their objectives and easing a man into acceptance that he will fail might seem a kindness. But for the person who makes a career of always going farther, anything less than absolute faith is insanity.

Never work under conditions designed to make you feel like less of a loser when you fail.

Choose the environment that insists—and will insist even when you no longer have the strength—that your success is possible, probable, necessary, and if you believe and work hard enough, inevitable.

To overcome my shattered leg, I'd needed to work harder than any runner had ever worked. An entire year I'd spent utterly self-absorbed. Every minute. Leaving the house for my last long run before Badwater, I saw Tuesday standing at the mailbox. She seemed to have been there a while. Her posture slouched, uncomfortable, tears on her face and unable to look at me.

"You're okay, right?"

She nodded.

I ran.

••

Mile 43: 6 Hours, 54 Minutes

MADDY: So this guy who uses your name—
NICK: No, his name is the same as mine. It's equally his.
MADDY: —so this guy's a stalker? Like a real-life stalker? Why don't you call the friggin police or something?
NICK: Well, you see, he listens to your shows, so I need to be careful here. But my sense is that he's a coward at heart. He's a failure in life because he's never taken complete responsibility for himself. He's suffered—but all people suffer. His failure is that he's never willingly suffered to make himself better. That said, he's a military trained assassin, so I should probably cap my remarks with that.
--DistanceHippy Podcast Pre-Race Interview

Just passed Stovepipe Wells, elevation five feet. There's a general store—named *General Store*. A campground. Dunes to my right.

My first steps after a hose-down or ice break are tentative, as if my body has a veto on the next ninety miles. I let it believe that. I set out with my ankle throbbing and ice water dripping from my shorts and top. My feet report a dull ache with each footfall, a light burden that will become sharp as the miles pass. For now my right ankle, which feels like a sock of broken glass, overshadows. The body naturally wants to make small adjustments now, shortening the stride on the weak ankle, shifting the hip to lessen the impact...but those alterations have ripple effects that will manifest a dozen new catastrophes in the miles to come. To forestall them, I fight to keep my stride the same as before I twisted my ankle. I land mid-foot and force my ankle to bend.

The pain now will prevent ten times the troubles later, and truth is, soon I will ignore it. Until then, I picture things I hate.

Running on a twisted ankle and formerly broken leg, and less prepared for the heat as I'd have liked, I succumb to visions of a Barelegged Nova victory. Somewhere beyond me the blonde from Sweden races against time and history. The only female to win Badwater 135 is Pam Reed. To prove it no fluke, she did it twice in back to back years. You can never anticipate who will have the ultimate mettle. The great thoroughbred Secretariat, upon being autopsied, had a heart twice the normal size. Does Nova?

My mind is into the pain, dissociating, evaluating. After a quarter mile I find my stride, rejuvenated from three minutes submerged in ice. Pain dissolves under the bombardment of unrelenting footfalls.

To my side I hear the sticky crush of tires on hot pavement.

"Need you to stop for a minute so we can have a conversation."

It's the female deputy who walks like she has a pool cue screwed to her spine.

"About what?"

"We need you to stop running, sir."

"Drive along like you did the last time. We can talk all day."

"Stop running. That's an order, sir."

"You don't have the authority. I'm running a footrace."

..

The brakes squeal and the vehicle stops. Both doors fly open.

I increase my pace. They've sat in their seats the last sixty miles. Part of me thinks I can outrun them if I make it past them. The rest of me thinks I can't outrun a car—not a V8.

The younger deputy—Edgerton—wobbles as she exits the cruiser.

"Twist your ankle?" I say.

Edgerton runs beside me. Her pudgy partner races around the back of the vehicle to the driver's door.

"You need to stop running," she says. "This will go a whole lot easier if you just let us ask some questions."

"You can ask from the car. You lose nothing by working with me on this, but because you're the law, you have to boss people around—"

"There's a man dead—a man you know, and we're trying to learn who killed him. Sooner we can clear you, the sooner we can focus elsewhere."

"There's a man dead who ought to be dead. That's what you should have said."

"You didn't care for Mister Siciliano?"

"I just want to run my race. I'm not the person you're after. I'll answer questions as many miles as you want to run—or drive alongside and ask. But I'm not stopping. This race is my *career*, lady."

"I know your professional reputation, Mister Fister. But you're a person of interest in a homicide. We've shown a lot of grace in not hauling you in already. And you're not helping your own cause." She settles into a rhythm running beside me despite the uniform and heat.

"All right. I'll tell you who you ought to be looking for. Two years ago a guy started stalking me. He's from New

..

York, and his name is the same as mine. Nicholas Fister. That's who you're after."

Deputy Edgerton looks through me, then registers on my eyes.

"He accused me of having something that belonged to him. He wanted it back. Since then he's stalked me and he's why I have this mess of scars on my right shin."

A car engine roars. I look. The pudgy deputy races by with engine blasting. He swerves twenty feet ahead, blocking my path. The door flies open and he bounces against it on his way out, fury crumpling his face. His hand finds the pistol grip protruding from his holster.

"I'm ordering you to stop!"

I glance for traffic and swing onto the road to avoid the car. The older deputy pulls a square nosed pistol.

"Freeze!"

In that moment I know who I am. I've spent so many years pushing myself to the limits of my existence that having a weapon drawn on me is almost familiar ground. I'm used to staring at pain and not flinching. I wave him off.

"I'm talking to the lady. Don't be a dick."

I swing around him and the pudgy deputy fires. Two darts trailing curly fish line flash toward me, biting into my chest and arm. Wet from the ice bath, instantly, I control nothing.

My body is rigid and pain and fear are palpable as turds or toenails. I drop on the blacktop and my body burns. I can't breathe or control the spasms. My elbow flashes white in my brain and the electricity from the taser manipulates me like a marionette strung from a jackhammer.

Another engine roars.

My crew van swerves to the curb and bounces to a halt in a cloud of dust.

●●

"Bastards!" Lisa screams from the window.

The taser launches me to another place, an electric rage like an amplified version of what I try to accomplish with pre-race meditation.

Finally the electricity stops.

I collect awareness like parts of my soul have scattered in the wind and each one I grasp informs me a little more about who I am and what just happened.

My right elbow is radically wrong; my heartbeat triggers a jolt of agony that cuts through my misery. A wiggle reveals a shard loose inside the joint.

My face rests against hot pavement.

My sphincter has released run-softened stools into the compression lining of my shorts.

I'm unsure if my body will obey when I command. The squirt of shit in my shorts humbles me. The vibrating shock in my mind subsides.

Anger washes in.

Lisa erupts from the driver side leaving the door rocking on its hinges. She runs across the road and lands on her knees beside my head and lifts my face from the searing asphalt. "What are you doing to him?"

"Stand back miss, this is a police investigation. This man is under arrest for obstruction of justice, attempting to flee an officer of the law, and murder if he gives me half a reason. Now MOVE!"

"You tasered him? Where was he going to go?" She waves to the desert. "Out there? You know he's running a race! This is *the fucking BADWATER!*"

"Well I appreciate that but everyone got to respect the law." The stubby deputy lingers near my head as if to kick it.

••

Meanwhile my body vibrates inside and as I attempt to frame complex thoughts my words scramble.

Deputy Edgerton looks up the road as if longing to run it.

I'm regaining my wits and body control. Though I cannot see her miles ahead, the Barelegged Nova adds yards and miles between us. I try to relax and let my body benefit from the moment of repose demanded of me, but saturated in adrenaline, the mind wanders. I've broken my elbow and shit myself. *Minutes will be lost.* Although there is no way I'm *not* finishing this race, I see the Barelegged Nova running away with victory. I see my final record disappearing, one last violent theft perpetrated by Floyd Siciliano and a vast, *vast* conspiracy of mediocre people.

I stop shaking and roll my head and observe my sister Mary on the opposite side of the road with the van. I remember her bringing me Coke and jerky, how she has always been willing to do good but never while anyone is looking. And then I see I am wrong, that through her opiate haze she is more clever than the fevered runner and his cheating wife. She holds her cell phone horizontally, capturing everything on video.

Her eye flashes with a wildness that was not present earlier today, as if my spastic body on the pavement brings home the reality of Floyd's death in a way the earlier police questioning did not. She looks troubled for me and for herself and without dwelling on it I realize my race will be forfeit if I they move my body and I cannot resume from the exact location I left the field.

"Get the stake!" I yell to Lisa. "Get the stake from the back. Get the hammer! Now—before they move me. You!" I yell to Edgerton, "Stand at my feet. Mark the ground where my feet are in the dirt. DO IT NOW!"

••

The plump one rubs the side of his nose. "You're under arrest. You have the right to remain silent."

Lisa runs to the back of the van.

"You! Stop!" he shouts.

Lisa ignores him.

"You want to taser one more, and have that on video too?" I say.

Mary remains across the road with the cell phone framing us, her lips a flat line.

Adrenaline brings clarity. "You know I hate to think of what it would do to the sheriff's department. That video going up on Facebook and YouTube."

"How much did she get?" He removes his hat. Wipes his brow. "Dammit I ordered you to halt and you didn't."

Deputy Edgerton stands at my feet and says, "Deputy Bly, what if we ankled him?"

I am silent. The deputies converse with scowls and stares and raised and lowered eyebrows. The pudgy one is invested. Pride and authority on the line. A wife back home that beats him. He's loath to reverse himself.

"Deputy Bly," I say. "This is your show and I won't argue otherwise. You have the power to cuff me and give me a bad day, or to give me grace. You, the law, justice, lose nothing by letting me finish the last race of my career. I mean, look at my leg. You see this scar? That's where they cut out three pounds of meat last year. And see the blue of my ankle? I'm running through all the hell I can to win this race and finish well. But I can't run through you. I admit that. I should have stopped and I didn't. Please let me finish my race."

His face is matte, his mind slow like an old sawmill hit-and-miss engine that only fires every fifth stroke. He glances

••

at Mary, still training the cell phone on us. He says, "A tracking bracelet?"

Edgerton nods. "It's not like he could go very far. His crew can't follow him through the desert."

"We don't exactly have one in the trunk."

"We'll have one at the Lone Pine substation. I'll stay with him until you get back."

"That's two hours there and back."

Lisa arrives with a hammer and stake. She squares herself with my feet, squats, slams the hammer and the stake bounces. She replaces the point into the quarter inch divot and readies the hammer.

"Miss—" Edgerton says. She gives a curt sideways head shake.

Lisa rests the hammer on the dirt but keeps the stake planted, ready to demark my progress the instant they haul me away.

I shift to my side, then a sitting position. My elbow flashes pain sharp enough to register through the thousand other torments I block.

The stubby deputy looks at Mary with the cell phone, then his watch. Then Edgerton. "You in uniform. You're going to run alongside him for two hours?"

"Or I'll question the crew, in the van. Both."

"This suspect gets away, it's on your head."

"Person of interest," Edgerton says. She smiles but even with forty miles in the bag I could leave her far behind. She knows it. She smiles because she outwitted the pudge.

Edgerton follows while I stumble to the van, fingers splayed as if directing comic book electricity to ten divergent points on the terrain in front of me. My heart rumbles and flips inside, an arrhythmia that would trouble me if not for

••

my sudden commitment to never again lock horns with a taser.

I keep my butt cheeks and 'nads gooped with Vaseline and Glide so the chafing rubs off petroleum and wax instead of skin. But during the race I've been anxious to resume running at every stop, and have neglected to recoat as frequently as I ought. The women don't know to remind me to goop my scrotum, and the layer I applied after showering this morning has worn off, and because I've been thinking about running the last race of my life, or wondering when I'll be arrested by the police or shot by a psychotic ex sniper, I haven't reapplied Glide or petroleum jelly in a couple dozen miles. My ass is raw, tasered, and the liquid defecate in my shorts tells me exactly where I've lost skin.

I laugh, almost giddy.

"What?" says Edgerton.

"That burns my ass." I cough. My throat is dry. I drink. "Lisa, get me a washcloth and soapy water. I don't care if it's warm. And I'll need another pair of shorts."

Mary finally turns away and places her phone in her pocket.

I drop my shorts, step out of them, and gingerly stoop. I pick them up and stand erect. Use the shorts to wipe myself, trying not to smear, and chuck the shorts to the berm.

"You going to cite me for that?"

The deputy holds my look but betrays nothing of her thoughts. A normal woman would turn away. Edgerton does her best Clint Eastwood squint.

"Mary, they broke my elbow. I'll need an ice pack and an ace bandage."

"Broke?"

••

"Just a little piece. The bone that comes around the other. I can feel it in the joint."

"You should seek proper medical attention," says Deputy Edgerton.

"What's your name?"

"Deputy Edgerton."

"Well, Edgerton, I'm going to be a few minutes. Enjoy the shade. Help yourself to the victuals and sundries."

Lisa arrives with a frothy washcloth.

"What's that?"

"Facial cleanser. It's all I have."

"Mmph. Good idea." I hold my injured elbow at an angle away from my body and take the cloth with my right hand. "Get me tomorrow's shorts. I'll wear them the rest of the way through."

A vehicle approaches and I wait before scrubbing myself as if it's a courtesy to the driver. It's a truck, driving slow. Inside the cab a man turns to watch me. He has longish hair and dark glasses. A ball cap.

The truck passes and I'm suddenly angry enough to run naked.

Deputy Edgerton clears her throat. "In another minute I'm going to cite you for indecency."

"Watch this."

I scrub with the washcloth, triggering a burn here and there but mostly delighting in the feel of frothy cleanliness instead of searing acid burn. Offsetting my delight, my elbow sends a jolt of electric pain with each stroke. Lisa arrives with a plastic bag in one hand and my running shorts in the other. I drop the washcloth in the bag and Lisa kneels before me so I can step into my running shorts. I wonder what she thinks— my unit, fully informed of her deeds—hanging next to her

••

face. She keeps her eyes on the task at hand, helping my mangled ankle through the shorts. Edgerton seems interested in anything but the drama playing out between my mess and my wife's face. I'm delirious with pain, dehydration, heat, infidelity.

A few feet away, Mary stands with ice and an ace bandage.

"Bring it. I've already lost ten minutes to Nova."

"Nova?" Edgerton steps toward me.

"The runner ahead of me. Nova Bjorkman, the one who plans to embarrass all American men at the same time."

"I didn't know Nova was running today."

Mary arrives beside me and places a small oval icepack to my elbow. "Can you straighten your arm?"

"No, I need to run with it bent. Just put the ice on as is."

To Edgerton I say, "You passed her the first time we talked. She was puking." I think on it. "So that means you haven't yet had the opportunity to taser Bjorkman?

"She's not under scrutiny."

"Well, I'm not suggesting how to do your job. But she'd stand to gain by having me taken out of the run, wouldn't she? If she's second most likely to win, after me."

Edgerton lifts her brow. "Except there's no prize money. No motive."

"You know what endorsements are worth to the Next Real Deal?"

Lisa snaps the elastic of my shorts. I nudge my nuts to seat them in the lining. Mary wraps my arm too tight with the ace and I take it from her, unwrap the last three loops, and redo them so the blood will circulate. "Need your mind in it, Sis."

She nods and looks to the distant gray.

"Lisa, top off my bottle and bring me a Gu." I turn to Edgerton. "Ready? We got some catching up to do."

••

I kiss Mary's forehead, look down the road to where I want to be. And run.

*

After the one hundred and fifty-nine-mile treadmill run I took off a few days for recovery, and since I'd only been using the gym for cross training, it was easy to avoid going there so long as the freak snowstorms didn't compel me. Truth was I didn't enjoy cross training. It felt like work. I didn't feel alive like I was setting records, but instead like I was in a sweaty gym doing workouts I'd never needed to contemplate when I was young.

I spent a couple days focusing on diet, stretching. Got a short massage to release a nest of toxins—not enough to make me sick, but enough to ensure my recovery led to a new height.

Three days after the long treadmill run I went out for a quick twenty miler. Running in the winter is the same and it is different. You start out cold and run until your body and the environment reach equilibrium. But cold forces different clothes, different rubs, different callous. Different risk of injury.

Five miles from home I saw Floyd Siciliano approaching in his white van. He slowed beside me and the electric window descended.

"You ain't been to the gym. You rather run in the snow and ice?"

"Doesn't smell like sweat out here."

"You got a lot of people talking."

"I did?"

••

"Well." He smiled. "You know Louis, from the paper? He wanted to write you up. And did you see the spot they ran on the news? Everybody wants you to try again. For real."

"I've set records on a dozen courses. More. Seven of them still stand. I don't think the local news folks have done a single story."

"There's no local interest when you run a race in California. Locals want to know about local things."

"That why you searched me out?"

I glanced at my Garmin and waited for the screen that shows average pace, 7:10. Not bad on a recovery day, clothed in layers, running on snow. I wanted to bump down the average but the coach in the back of my mind told me the point of a recovery run wasn't to break down muscle, but to flush toxins, pump in new nutrients and oxygen, restore.

"You're dicking up my tempo. What's up, Floyd?"

"What if we go for the record again?"

"We what?"

"Let's set it up for real. I been reading. We'll get two-three observers. The gym is local and public. We'll run an ad so people can come by, get a tour of the gym, and see you setting a world record. It'll be great."

"I don't like treadmill running."

"But you could set the world record."

His voice carried a note I hadn't heard before. His earlier story was promotion, the business man dreaming ways to create more business. Prodding an associate to go along with his terms. But he now sang a different refrain. Awe projected in his voice, his motions. It was the only humility I ever saw in Floyd Siciliano.

"I'll put your face on the van," he said.

I shook my head.

••

"We'll use the van for your next ultra. Your last trip to California, Lisa complained about the rental. The cost of the car, the condition. Not enough space. We'll use the van. The gym will be a sponsor."

"I'm not interested."

"Why not use some of that talent to help someone else? Your community? You could put us on the map. And the gym—we could be the place you go, your hangout. Next time that running magazine interviews you and does a cover, it could be on my Nautilus. Hell, we got a nice place. And you want to do the ultra in Tempe next January. That's the desert. More like running on a treadmill in the gym than out here in the snow."

I'd only mentioned the Tempe ultra to one person—and not seriously. I had been watching a western. Lisa walked by and said, "That looks like the rocks at Sedona," and I remembered reading about a desert run in the winter.

"You saw Lisa today?"

Floyd looked blank. Twitched his head sideways like I missed the point. "Of course I saw her. She comes every morning."

I shook my head. "I'm not a treadmill runner." I waved him away. "I need to focus on my run. See you, Floyd."

I stretched my stride and looked forward. Let my arms get into it. Set my jaw. Small things runners do when they want people to know they're running. Floyd sped away and I relaxed back into my too-fast recovery pace.

I thought on it. No way. But before I arrived home big flakes fell from the sky and covered the sidewalk. I thought about setting another record, claiming one more victory before I could no longer sustain the pace or muster the endurance. Or desire to win.

••

By the time I arrived home I decided to set a world record. I told Lisa so she could pass it along.

*

I launch fast and Deputy Edgerton works hard to pace me. Feels like an eight-minute pace, probably is nine. Her stride begins wobbly, but evens out quickly. She wears a tight grimace and narrow eyes, runs in tan pants and shirt, black belt, with a holster and nightstick rattling at her hips. The temperature is still a hundred and twenty, even in late afternoon—but to its credit, the heat is dry. Edgerton has already sweated enough to darken her armpits.

"What's your name again?"

"Deputy Edgerton."

"And what about your corpulent partner?"

"Deputy Bly."

"I want you to run with me, Deputy Edgerton, but you're slowing me down. Think you can keep up?"

She removes her nightstick and holds it like a baton. "Long enough to ask what I want to ask."

"What is it with you two and violence?"

She leers. "I know about your win in Western States two years ago, running on a broken foot. But now you've got a busted ankle and maybe elbow too. Then there's the injury from last year in New York. A lot of people think you should have retired."

Her tone is different, tinged by the enthusiasm of a fan. I say, "Yeah."

"I had a broken elbow in high school. That's a different kind of pain. You think you can finish? Or is this a DNF?"

"I've had one Did Not Finish in my life. I'll finish."

••

"So how well did you know your crew chief? Were you close?"

I exhale. Slow the conversation.

"Not particularly. Pick up the pace. I don't like holding back so much when I've got terrain to make up and Nova's running strong."

"How long had Mister Siciliano been chiefing your crew?"

"Three years or so."

"But you weren't close?"

"It was a business arrangement. He had a gym back home. I helped him get some publicity and my family got use of the gym and the van. Expenses paid on trips like these."

"But you didn't particularly care for Mister Siciliano?"

"He and my wife—"

Edgerton is silent.

"They got along better with each other than me."

"So why would you have him chief your crew?"

"Because most athletes have to pay for their expenses. It's worth twenty grand a year to have Floyd run the crew."

"But he was with your wife?"

"Yeah. Well, that's on the outside."

"Of what?"

"Me."

Edgerton labors beside me. If I was more aware, if this had been the beginning of the run, if she didn't have such a pert derriere, I might have thought to keep that information to myself. My objective is to keep them at bay until the race is over—and I've hurt that objective. Because Edgerton is a fan and has the ass of a distance runner.

But sooner or later they'll learn my full history with Floyd Siciliano.

••

"What are you going to do for the last fifty miles, without your pacer?"

"Muddle through. I only liked running with Floyd because he pissed me off anyway."

I drink from my bottle, rip open a Gu, squeeze the hot syrup between my lips, careful not to let the foil edges rip my mouth.

"If you've got official questions I'm happy to answer them. But otherwise, this is a long race and every word costs me energy I'll need down the road. Why don't you talk to the ladies for a while so I can make up some distance? Make a list of questions for the next time?"

I pull away from Edgerton.

When the van passes me a moment later, Edgerton is in the passenger seat.

I open my elbow and an intense burst of agony enrages me.

Looking down the road, I see where I want to be, and run.

∘∘

Mile 59: 9 Hours, 5 Minutes

TOMMY: Playing off what you said a minute ago, a person has to suffer to improve. So what is there that's actionable for—
MADDY: Actionable? Big word.
TOMMY: So what is actionable for a regular runner who dreams of doing what you do? There's considerable separation between your talent and mine. And age. A lot of people feel they started too late to ever fully develop their potential.
NICK: History answers that. In nineteen twenty-two, Arthur Newton was thirty-eight years old. He was an English man in Africa, and he thought the politics of the day prevented him from making a living as a farmer. So he thought he'd draw attention to the plight of farmers by excelling as an amateur athlete. A show of character, you know, to get his voice out there.

So thirty-eight year old Arthur Newton went for a two mile run. He wasn't a runner and it hurt him. But he did it again and again. That's what you call actionable. Twenty weeks later, he ran in the second Comrades Marathon. You familiar with that race? It was started to celebrate mankind's spirit over adversity and commemorate South African soldiers who died in World War One. That's in the charter.

Arthur Newton, with five months of training, entered the second Comrades Marathon. It's a fifty-six mile course. He won, and ran another thirteen years. In that time he set just about every ultra-distance record there was. He trained a hundred miles per week. Now, at thirty-eight, running in South African heat, without technical t-shirts, finger socks and Hoka shoes, tell me whether this man chose suffering? Of course he did.

No one has any excuse. It all comes down to a judgment. You see it's going to hurt. You're willing to pay the price or you're not.

What grabs my balls is that someone like Nicholas Fister from Greenville, New York could have been a good runner. We'll never know because of his decision to sit on his ass. Yet he wants to blame other people for that. Go figure. He should have went for a run.

--DistanceHippy Podcast Pre-Race Interview

I'm strong. I wonder what muscle damage I'm causing my elbow. The joint wiggles with each stride and feels like a corkscrew going in slow. By the time I finish, maybe the bone shard will work up a pool of puss and cut its way out like an infected splinter. One can hope.

Since Edgerton joined Lisa and Mary in the van I've made great speed. I've always tried to maintain level splits but I've never dealt with as much ambiguity and challenge in a race. It's been an hour and a half and I've run eleven miles. I'm not depleting my resources or building up lactic acid faster than I can clear it. I ought to be able to sustain the pace until I make up lost time.

As afternoon grows late and the sun is no longer blasting directly overhead, my perception of heat has decreased whereas the temperature probably has not. My skin remains dry and hot. Grainy from sweat and dust. The repeated hosings with ice water and subsequent drying have become frustrating. I'm tired of seeing Lisa.

When Deputy Bly arrives I want him to strap the bracelet to my ankle and be done with it. I'm at the top of a knoll and can see Barelegged Nova in the distance. I want to run her down and pass her at a six-minute pace. She's taking my race

..

from me and the frustrating part is that without the small accidents, Floyd's death and its repercussions, Nova Bjorkman would be worrying about me.

I hear a vehicle and it is beside me almost in the same moment. Deputy Bly rolls down his window. "Where's Deputy Edgerton?"

My neck cramps. I roll my shoulders. "She's in the van you just passed."

"You aren't going to give me shit about this are you?"

"Strap it on and let's roll."

Bly gasses the engine, cuts in front of me and parks. I slow to a jog and stop. Stretch backward and sideways as much as I can without stressing my twisted ankle. Bly emerges with a black device in hand. I look ahead to Barelegged Nova in the distance, then to the device in Bly's hand, a large, clunky square wristwatch-looking device with a band large enough to fit around my ankle.

"Let's get this thing on. I'm in second place and it's time to reel in the leader."

"Answer my questions and you'll be on the road in no time."

The van stops behind me and when Deputy Edgerton arrives, Bly kneels before me. "Damn son. What the hell?"

"What hell?"

"You're ankle's about to rot off."

"Sprain and strain makes it bruise black. It'll ease up later."

"You can't run on that."

"Kindly put the bracelet on my other ankle. It'll fit."

"You want my advice—"

"No."

He snorts. I laugh.

••

"Here it is anyway. You're hurting yourself. Outside of my investigation. You can't do this to your body and get away with it. Not for long. Says the old fat man."

"I guess we all have our crosses to bear."

He opens the device, inspects the inside, closes it around my ankle. The band fits snug, but it is going to mean problems. Bly works it up and down, makes sure it is locked. He looks up to me. "I understand your daughter killed herself a week back."

Lisa moans.

I glance from his hands about my ankle and see him watching my face.

"Just wanted to ask what the cause of that was?" Bly holds my look.

"The cause of my daughter taking her own life, you mean?"

Bly nods, returns his full attention to my ankle.

"I don't know."

"You're a sick bastard, you know that," Lisa says.

"It's just strange when a family experiences so much of life's ills so close together."

I close off my mind, redirect it to the run. I'm sick of distractions; I'm sick of Floyd and his stealing.

"I'm the connection," Lisa says. "I'm the one. I'm the shittiest mother that ever lived and the shittiest wife. So why don't you leave your little mind turds with me, if you have to be such a jerk."

I shake my head. Lisa sounds like the girl I loved, long ago and irretrievably lost.

"Did you see Nova Bjorkman in the distance when you crested the hill?" I say.

••

Lisa shakes her head. "But I wasn't looking. The deputy was talking and I was talking."

"I wonder how much time I've lost."

Bly stands, places hands on hips. "I have a feeling you're going to lose more before this is over. Not much adds up until we look at you, and the harder we look the better the math. What time did you go to bed last evening?"

"Nine."

"Go straight to sleep?"

"No. Not for a couple of hours."

"Nerves?"

"Travel. Body clock messed up."

"You live in Saint Louis, right?"

"Outside Saint Louis. Close."

"And we're in California. So wouldn't you be sleepy two hours earlier, not later?"

"Airplanes mess me up. I nap. Can't sleep later."

"And where were you at four a.m.?"

"In my room."

"How many times did you leave your room over night?"

"None."

"And when did you first leave your room?"

"I made a trip to the van because I left the bag with my sunscreen in the back."

"What time was that?"

"Six. About six."

"Did you go to your crew chief's room at that time?"

"No."

"When were you in your crew chief's room?"

"I wasn't."

••

Bly glances at Edgerton. Edgerton wrinkles her brows. Bly turns to me with a new glow. "You weren't in his room at all? Zero times?"

I'm suddenly tired. My mind isn't as sharp as it felt when I started. Keeping the brain fueled well enough to oversee running is one thing. Well enough for dancing with two deputies, another. My thoughts are in a long hallway filled with fog.

"No."

"Are you absolutely certain?"

"Yes."

"Yes you were in his room, like the evidence says?"

"To hell with your evidence. I wasn't in his room."

Lisa steps forward. "He wants a lawyer. You have to let him get his lawyer."

"He wants a lawyer he can call one at the station. The only reason I'm going along with this charade is so he can answer my questions without delay."

"I wasn't in Floyd's room. Lisa, get me fruit juice."

Edgerton's eyes shift to my face. Bly doesn't know that fructose, because it is processed by the liver, cannot be routed directly to the muscles. Some of the energy gets to the brain. Edgerton knows.

"You didn't particularly like your crew chief, did you?" Bly says.

"Not particularly."

"Do you own a knife?"

"Uhh. No. Yes."

"What kind of knife?"

"It's at home. Gun cabinet. Used for gutting deer."

"And that's at home? Not in the hotel?"

••

Lisa gives me a bottle of juice. I chug it. Feel queasy, but in moments my mind starts to clear.

"I wasn't in Floyd's room. Not during the entire trip here. If your interest in me comes from something suggesting I was in his room, double check it. I wasn't there. As to the knife—it's an old thing handed down when my grandfather died. Still has blood on it because he was a dirty son of a bitch. You'd probably find chunks of deer meat in the thumb guard—but it's at home."

"Could you describe the knife?"

"It has a bone handle. Brass rivets. A grungy gray blade. Not stainless. Very sharp."

"How long would you say the blade is?"

"Six inches or so. I don't know. I inherited it and put it in my gun cabinet."

"So, uh, how many guns you keep in your gun cabinet?"

I shake my head. Weigh protesting the stupidity of the line of questions, while Nova widens the gap between us. I decide these moments spent with Deputy Bly will be my rest break. I'll skip the next and sort it out later, when I'm falling apart.

"I have a couple deer rifles, also inherited. A pistol, inherited."

Bly nods his head slowly as if my words are relevant beyond the context that is open between us. "So," he says, "Were you ever going to mention that you and Floyd Siciliano were business partners?"

I look at Lisa and she turns from me.

"I'd just like to get back to my run. We can talk for six months if that's what you like. Just let me get back on the road."

"You took a loan out at the bank for a forty-five percent interest in Floyd's gym. The Bench Press. Not getting along?"

••

"I don't kill people I don't like."

"Yeah. So what led to that? Buying half his company?"

"I was looking ahead."

"Yeah." Bly wipes the side of his nose with his finger and wipes his finger on his pant. "Yeah, well, I think it's interesting your business partner just died. Means we have a lot of other stuff to look at. You know that, right? You could make this easier on yourself if you just tell us what you did."

"I got up this morning and went for a run."

"Yeah. Well I been doing this a long time and every instinct I have says you're good for this." Bly steps close enough I can smell his breath, feel his belly on my arm. In a low voice he says, "You keep running. I seen how dumb you dipshits get by the end. So just you run."

I step backward. I want to hold his eyes without blinking but mine are dry and I can't do it. I turn to Deputy Edgerton. "If it's all right with you I need to talk to my wife for a minute before I resume my run."

Edgerton nods. Bly turns to his vehicle.

I follow Lisa to the van. Mary is in the driver seat, again with her phone recording video. Lisa opens the back doors, withdraws a foam mat. Her face is flushed and her shoulders slump. She looks like a woman capable of driving a van over a cliff.

"You want to rub my leg? Give me a hand. I can't do it."

Lisa unrolls the mat, folds it into half, and kneels on it before me. I think of a time long ago when this pose would have been interesting, but the ugly in her eyes is soul deep—the story on Lisa is yet untold—and I wouldn't put my dick in her mouth if my goal was to choke her to death.

"It's cramping low, right below where the muscle groups split. Can you feel the tightness there? Do we have a roller?

••

Or was that in Floyd's room? You think it was in Floyd's room? Did you see it? Maybe if you used a rock or something to bust up the cramp."

She exhales hard, leans, grabs a rock.

"Not that one. Look at the edges."

She pitches it and resumes with her weak fingers.

"Nevermind." I pull my leg from her and lean forward. "Another thing. Why'd you tell them I'm a cuckold?"

"You are."

I watch the ground and almost savor the insult, the penetrating bomb of ugly she just planted. When a woman says without remorse that she's a cheat, she's locating blame, she's making a statement about the size of my dick or what I did with it. She's saying that even the humblest definition of man is too big for me to fill. Like her vagina.

"You know what?" Lisa says. "I'm done. This whole horseshit game is up. You and me—this is a business deal and I'm pulling out. I'm going home."

"How?"

"I'll drive the van. I'm driving it anyway. And you know we were getting the papers together, Floyd and I. We were just waiting for this whole farce to end."

I look at her.

"Whatever. Just don't be so vocal in front of the deputies." I see my race disappear. "Regardless of how you and I end, you'll be better off with me winning today."

"We buried our daughter two days ago! What kind of asshole are you? It's over."

I let her rage puff by. She stands. Looks to the vast expanse of land unmarred by human deeds, as if it's possible to outdistance an event and no longer be within the grasp of history. I look with her though I don't know what she seeks, or what happiness would look like for either of us, except to be done of the other.

"Mary can take you back to the hotel. It's a half hour in the van. You can call a cab."

I drink from my water bottle, reach for a foil of mashed potatoes, olive oil, and salt, and ingest the contents quickly. I knead the muscle in my leg. Lisa still stands with her back to me.

I leave her.

I run a half mile immersed in my thoughts, wondering where I found the word *cuckold*, wondering how I happened to store it away, how I recalled it so aptly when my reserves are low.

The van has not yet passed me on its way to the next rendezvous.

On a slight uphill turning grade it's easy to twist and look behind. I do so. Lisa remains at the edge of the desert, back bent, head low, hands at her face.

I look ahead to where I want to be and run.

*

Nicholas Fister wore on my mind. I'd see him when he wasn't there. I thought about Tuesday being so naïve and sweet she'd make the mistake of being nice to him.

Like the time I burned my father's bowler, given a gorgeous opportunity to respond to angst, I seized it. I needed to convince Nicholas Fister his intimidation left me unconvinced, and his attempt to shackle me to his failures was a nonstarter. I'm not afraid of legitimate guilt—I enjoy a romp with genuine guilt as much as the next person. Guilt means you did something nasty and got away with it, and conscience, as the last bulwark against rampant evil, on behalf of the species, makes a stink about it. You got away with it, but don't do that again. It's bad for humanity. Right. Cool.

But illegitimate guilt is manipulation.

I usually choose to compete in races based on the advice of sponsors who want maximum exposure. I'll run a race to best the reigning course champion, to see a new location, or measure myself against a new terrain. A lot of courses claim to be the most difficult in the world—and that's as good a reason as any to run a course. On the other hand, as ultra-running surges in popularity, small events put on by local running clubs are starting in every corner of the country.

I chose a new hundred miler called the Greenville Hunnert, located a handful of miles outside of Greenville, New York.

The small Greenville.

The course was in a state park and consisted of two laps around a twenty-five mile trail for the fifty-mile race, and four laps for the hundred.

I wasn't aware of the Greenville Hunnert until I came home from a run late one morning and saw a truck in my driveway.

The scrotum rolls. The stomach seizes. You measure three hundred and sixty degrees of surroundings in an instant. Adrenaline fireworks through your veins and you think, how do I take this guy out with minimum ancillary damage?

The truck was a plumber.

I loathe fear so I faced it. I went inside the house and a half hour later found the event I was looking for—three months out. I checked my race and training schedule, registered and volunteered to help with publicity. One of the organizers was a marketing pro and jumped at the opportunity to cash in on my name. I did three local radio interviews, a couple radio spots, and an interview for the local paper. The race club hoped to accomplish the same annual tourist windfall as Leadville and other towns, by creating a hundred-mile run and calling it the world's toughest. I was all for it. My excuse—it was the closest race to where I grew up. I missed the terrain.

And salt-of-the-earth people.

Smaller races usually attract only local talent until they are established. But as the sport grows and more runners seek big-name events, organizers have shifted to a lottery or invitation system, leaving scores, hundreds, or thousands of runners without their chosen event. The overflow circulates to less-known events, and over the last few years top talent commonly graces small races.

I always check the registrations to see the competition. For the Greenville Hunnert, the only racer I knew was a kid who will one day surpass most of my records, a skinny, pale, bearded and bald force of nature named Kevin Amory. Batshit crazy, he always ran with the same batshit pacer, Jean Stanley. Kevin ran like an LSD burnout, tapping electron energy and cosmic good humor for infinite mojo. He'd jaw with runners, trees, butterflies, whatever.

We decided to have some fun with additional promotions. The organizers had no money but I paid to fly us both there a week early. We hosted several running clinics, events at three High Schools—Including Nicholas Fister's alma mater, and were photographed nose to nose, like boxers, which became the next month's cover of Ultra Runner's World Magazine.

All that media was like me going to Nicholas Fister's back yard, popping the clutch and doing donuts.

••

I thought of everything, even the possibility Nicholas would sneak to St. Louis to harm Lisa or Tuesday. Two factors combined to tell me to leave the crew at home. First, the course consisted of four laps on a trail. I'd be passing three aid stations four times, and would have the ability to leave drop bags on the course as well. Second, and more important, Floyd would be around to look after Lisa and Tuesday. One of the rare perks of your crew chief bedding your wife.

I kept a lookout for Nicholas day and night the entire week. I rented a car, found his address on the internet, drove by his place. His house was a small gray square with a four-sloped roof and a garage that stood separate, a ragged yard and a bent flagpole with no flag and two-foot weeds growing in the white limestone circle at the base. I pondered how he could have bent the flagpole and the only thing I could come up with was that it was bent before he put it up and he didn't care.

On the night before the race I stayed in the hotel room and went through my pre-race routine, memorizing the course map, reviewing and doublechecking the contents and placement of my drop bags, planning my calories, liquids.

I was in bed at eight for a six a.m. start—but couldn't sleep. I wrestled the sheets off my bed so I turned on my tablet, opened a browser and searched, "Nicholas Fister Greenville."

One hit. I clicked the link and the Greenville Democrat newspaper popped on the screen, LOCAL HERO COMES HOME. I scanned for a date: November 2004. According to the short news story, Nicholas Fister graduated from high school, joined the Marine Corps, served six years, most as a sniper in Iraq. Had forty-eight confirmed kills before being medically discharged. Welcome home.

••

He looked in perfect health and the story didn't mention the nature of his medical problem. From the stark stupidity of his gaze, I suspected a mental hiccough, and I lay on my back wondering about that.

Race morning I mulled around with the guys and gals in a showy good mood, but I watched the trees.

The horn blasted and I set off as I always do, at the pace I'd decided to maintain the entire race—knowing that on a new course I was unlikely to do so. I wanted the win badly. I wanted Nicholas Fister to know I would travel any place I wanted, kick ass, and I didn't owe him a damn thing.

After the first mile I was in my groove, comfortable with the terrain. I settled into an easy rhythm that felt sustainable forever.

Night fell on my fourth lap. Dark hits hard and fast in the woods. I ran until my eyes couldn't discern rocks and roots, then turned on my headlamp on the low setting to conserve battery power. The organizers had marked the trail with green and pink chem lights so it was easy to stay on course. The single track was narrow enough that passing another runner required his participation, but a hundred runners spread over twenty-five miles allows for long stretches of solitude. As other runners slowed I basked in the illusion of picking up speed and strength as I lapped them.

No hundred-mile race ever unfolds as planned. A few miles into the fourth lap I was running a little hot, making up for an earlier slowdown caused by not anticipating my calorie burn correctly. I'd bonked and to get back to my needed average, I hit a downhill hard, joyful with caloric excess and the sensation of controlled recklessness that attends hitting speed in the dark.

••

The single-track carved in and out of a ravine, each time crossing a miniature escarpment of limestone that forced runners to leap or step down. My headlamp flashed to the escarpment and I extended my front leg.

Light blasted from the darkness.

I was blind.

The light extinguished and though my headlamp remained on, I saw nothing. I missed my landing; my ankle twisted and I collapsed full speed into jagged limestone.

I writhed and growled and cursed and tried to run but the pain was so great I could not convert it to ambition. I screamed obscenities into the darkness and heard feet crashing away through the woods.

Propelled by shock, I crawled up the ravine, cussing myself forward, pumping myself to never quit. Elbow by elbow I dragged myself along the trail trying to figure the math in my head, how many miles remained, and the pain came in waves as if coaxing me to a new reality as a shattered runner. My right leg was numb and slippery.

After a few yards my tibia—dragged like a hook—snagged a root.

The section of trail where I broke my leg was near a dirt road, and sometime after the attack, Kevin Amory and his sidekick tripped on me a quarter of a mile farther down the trail. They'd smelled my blood and wondered what sort of animal had been wounded.

They crossed arms, made a seat, and carried me to the dirt road near the trail. Kevin went on to win the race, while Jean stayed behind to dress my wound with his sweaty shirt and wait with me for a ride to the hospital.

Mile 62: 10 Hours, 2 Minutes

TOMMY: You said at the beginning that you want it more. Good luck, I'm sure there are a handful of runners who think they want it as much as you do. How important is that, really?

NICK: I read something and committed it to memory a long time ago. Herb Elliot was one of the greatest runners of all time, undefeated in the mile, and he ran sub-four minute miles seventeen times in two years. What he said stuck with me. If you emphasize the physical side of training, your body gets strong. But maybe not your mind. But if you emphasize the mental part of training, the body will inevitably follow. The first muscle to train is the mind.

--DistanceHippy Podcast Pre-Race Interview

I turn from looking at Lisa staring into the desert with hunched shoulders and a broken soul and question my role in her cheating, and Tuesday's death.

Pressing my fists to my eyes brings elbow pain. And clarity.

Whooping loud enough for the Barelegged Nova—still miles ahead—to know I'm after her, I launch forward. The sun occupies its midafternoon slot, sending light that lays heavy like ten feet of water; air so thick with heat it suffocates.

With each stride my elbow jolts me; pain creates a mental lattice that holds ambition together.

When Deputy Bly tasered me I recognized a startled implicitness in Mary's eye. A look I'd seen before.

We grew up with little family around. Our grandparents lived a mile away but my father's siblings all moved to different parts of the country. "Never let Grandpa take you on a walk," my father told Mary, much as a dog will mark its territory with piss.

My father's brothers moved from New York to Florida and Spain. One joined the Army and moved from base to base. I only saw my uncles once during my teen years, right after my grandfather died. They hated their own father, and behaved as if my father was heir to his evil. I noticed when they spoke to him they had difficulty locking eyes, mostly preferring to look at anything else.

On holidays Mary and I watched parades on television and listened to our father's running commentary. The goddam this. The fucking that. Politicians. Sluts. Silver spoon assholes. Floats and football, cheaters. Until as a teen I disappeared on long runs at every opportunity, jaunts that lasted sunup to down. During extended months I didn't keep track of miles or times. The *doing* of it was more important than the *achievement* of it. I'd pack a peanut butter and jelly sandwich or four, a couple pears, and drink stream water from cricks I discovered along dozens of miles of road.

I'd run until I couldn't, and timed every day so I collapsed in bed right after I got home.

I used to question why Mary never took up volleyball, school plays—some activity to absent her from our father. I wondered if it was because he was never as mean to her. She never spent time in the potato cellar—you don't punish girls that way, my father said one time. Mary had burned a six-dollar roast. Not a four dollar or some other denomination.

••

She'd burned a damned six-dollar roast. He brought his fist to the table. No it's not the potato cellar for you. Not the cord. Carve off the burnt shit for the dog.

I'll square up with you later, he told her.

When I ran my half marathon on the driveway, and decided I would die to prove my will more powerful than my father's, I learned a greater lesson, the will is more powerful than self. Separate the will, and feed it, and it overpowers whatever it encounters.

I look back and see not the hand of God but something less personal, synchronicity. Things that move without compulsion, fit together, tumble one event into another, and in context seem impossible but from a distance reveal themselves as unavoidable. My father learned nothing from his defeat, or even that I'd defeated him. The lesson was mine. I could drive myself as far as I chose, and my body would perform whatever I demanded.

My fate was subject to my will. The more profound my desire, the more my body answered and the more the world yielded. And more importantly, awareness of the dynamic between will and fate, between cause and effect, creates responsibility. Awareness creates choice, and doing nothing is choosing mediocrity by default.

An even greater truth revealed itself to me. Because complacency and status quo go hand in hand, destiny is forged at extremes. To arrest control, one must be willing to live at the edge, to break rules, to risk all. And again, awareness creates responsibility. The aware person has no choice but ruthlessness and risk. Otherwise: be a victim of someone else's forces applied for someone else's purposes.

I grasped my responsibility to make my fate yield to my mind.

Mary did not.

I spent time in the cold potato cellar while Mary was warm upstairs, subject to a different kind of suffering I never fully suspected. Virgin, early-teen boys have great imaginations, but because desired experience and personal experience are so far removed, they have zero belief that sex actually does happen—for anyone. The stork makes more sense than the belief that some lucky people actually get laid.

I never fathomed why my father was equally happy with me on a ten-hour run as locked ten hours with the potatoes.

Mary has been a strange sidekick. Her misguided choices have never led her to learn that being ready to die for something only rarely requires us to die. Most obstacles yield before we do. Learn the lesson once; the benefits accrue forever—but learning it the first time requires the moment of rebellion Camus said entails embracing any future, no matter how bad, over the present. Mary never reached the point she'd prefer oblivion, so she never held power over her present.

Mary's husband Darrel used to sit in a squeaky rocking chair. Before he claimed disability he bounced from job to job until he scored the perfect gig at a debt collection agency. "Think of it," he said. "*I get paid* to call people up and be a shithead." But after he got a doctor and the Social Security Administration to agree his bad back wouldn't allow him to sit at a desk on the phone all day, he instead spent his days sitting in a recliner eating TV dinners, piling empty Lite beer cans on the floor. One time he got up to drain his last six pack and I saw a V shape of ham gravy, smashed peas, butter stains on the cushion. He left the cans on the floor for Mary to pick up and his sloppy dinner trays in the sink, instead of the trash. One time when we were watching football Mary

••

didn't notice him wave an empty beer can at her during a sixty yard touchdown run. "You're about a shitty beer wench," he said to his wife, and threw the empty at her. "With a fat ass, too."

A man that'll cuss his woman in front of company leaves little doubt what he'll do behind a closed door. They'd been married two years when I noticed her cheekbone was puffy. I looked closer. "What's that makeup caked for?"

I took her wrist and held her from turning away. Mary craned her neck and pulled from me.

"Let her go," Lisa said. "Christ, you're scaring Tuesday."

"Get her out of here for a minute. Mary, what is this?"

Mary jerked her arm and faced me, eyes shiny, bloodshot.

"Darrel do this? Darrel?"

Head cast downward, Mary nodded. I raised my hand to touch her cheek and she shrank. "Easy Sis. I just want to see."

I pressed her cheekbone and it was a hard like a swollen ankle. Mary winced.

"What are you doing?" Mary said, following me. "You can't—no Christ no—not a gun. Don't do this."

I pulled a Winchester .30-30 from the cabinet and a box of shells from the center drawer. Lisa grabbed my arm. I faced her.

She said, "Nick, it's none of your business!"

Tuesday wailed.

"No. It's everybody's business."

I spent the twenty-minute drive to Mary and Darrel's place pre-living scenes, testing language, each iteration advancing my fury until I sat in the driveway slipping cartridge after cartridge into the rifle, looking to the front door, knowing Darrel sat in his rocking chair behind it. Probably in a bath robe, feet on the ottoman. I levered a shell into the chamber, opened the car door, dragged the rifle out after me and had the safety off and my finger in the trigger guard ten steps from the door.

Locked. I beat on it then thought better of alarming Darrel.

"Who is it?" Beer cans clinked on the hardwood floor. The latch clicked. The door opened a crack, stopped by a chain.

I slammed the heel of my foot to the door. It burst open, thudded on Darrel's foot and bounced back to me. I shoved it open again and Darrel was jumping on one foot and holding the toes of his other in his hand. Ambidextrous for a guy with back issues. I raised the rifle to Darrel's belly. Prodded him. He dropped his foot. Stared at me. I stared at his stubble, the oil on his skin, the slouch of his shoulders. Pot belly. The spread of toppled beer cans.

"Strike Mary again, I kill you."

I held his look until he trembled. But when I lowered the muzzle a smile flickered at the edges of Darrel's lips. He doubted me.

I jerked the rifle to my shoulder and pointed at his head.

His nostrils spread.

I raged at the bully's precept that whatever you can get away with is moral, that big animals eat little animals, men beat their kids with telephone cords and grandfathers take little girls for walks in the woods. My fingers pulsed with adrenaline and my brain spazzed. I couldn't finish a thought or frame a word.

I just wanted Darrel's brain on the wall.

Three feet away, I aimed for his ear and pulled the trigger figuring I'd turn it over to fate. The bullet zinged from the stone fireplace and a splot sound issued from the wall. Darrel jumped and winced, his reflexes delayed by a tide of beer splashing in his brain. He wiped his face of the burning

••

powder residue, brought his hand to his ear and screamed, "My ear!" He danced and each circle he turned the wet spot at his crotch expanded.

I levered another shell, leaving the brass where it fell. Jabbed Darrel with the barrel and he stopped hopping.

"Touch Mary—" I couldn't form another word and stood trembling.

Darrel said, "Oh Christ above."

I barked a war cry, a single vowel of wrath that left my throat raw but formed no word, and left.

Mary stayed at our place that night and Darrel was gone, along with his beer and the television, when I escorted Mary home the next morning.

"How will he get by?" Mary said.

"The government will send his disability check where ever he tells them. Meantime, close every joint account you have."

Mary said, "Can you stay and help me with something?"

I looked at my watch.

"Please?"

"Okay."

"Move your car. I want to make a pile on the dirt."

Mary went into her house and was ready to drop an armload of frozen TV dinners onto the drive when I backed away.

"Park at the neighbor's," she said.

I drove across the street. Mary had placed Darrel's rocking chair on the porch. "Tell you what, she said, "will you put everything I leave on the porch on top of those TV dinners?"

I nodded. "I could haul some of this to Goodwill. I'm sure someone could use it."

••

"I don't want it to exist," she said.

Mary gathered everything Darrel had left. From the size of the pile I suppose he vacated with a change of clothes, his television, and his beer. I carried jeans, shirts, Playboy magazines, empty beer cans, frozen dinners, boxes of papers I didn't look too closely at, everything about him that touched Mary's life, every residue of his existence—the soap from the shower, his towel, razor, everything. A radio and a hack saw. A push mower. When the pile was six feet square and three high, I said again, "Why don't you go inside and rest. I'll haul all this away and you won't have to look at it anymore."

Mary opened a bottle of isopropyl alcohol and dumped it on the pile, then emptied a two-and-a-half-gallon container of gasoline as well. She tossed a match.

Six years ago, Mary hunted Darrel on the internet. He'd moved to Seattle and was living with a woman twenty years his senior with three sons his age. Mary divorced him, and I wondered for three years if she'd ever pair up again. We had her over for dinner one night and afterward watched a French movie about a pair of lesbian bank robbers. I can understand that, Mary said. Then she asked if Lisa or I would mind if she brought a guest to Thanksgiving dinner.

"Uh."

"Of course not, Lisa said. Who is... she?"

"He? He owns a gym. His name is Floyd Siciliano."

For Thanksgiving Lisa ordered a turkey cooked in an oil vat. She swung by Kentucky Fried Chicken for a monster tub of mashed potatoes and gravy. She couldn't equal their gravy if she poured their gravy into a saucepan and stirred. With mac and cheese we tested the bounds of Fister decadence.

••

Mary was late and I sat around grumbling at the game. Every time I gave a damn the Jets rewarded me with a stupid play or the officials with a bad call. I tossed haphazard cuss words at the television while Tuesday thumb-typed on her cell phone. Lisa sliced a can of gelled cranberries into medallions in the kitchen. Finally the door opened and a giant New-York-looking thug stood looking at me. Longish hair with a half tube of Bryl Cream. He was big like the ass of a seventies Cadillac.

He adjusted his mess and stepped inside.

Mary squirted through the doorway beside him.

"—you doin?" he said.

"How? Fine. Come in. Hello Mary."

Mary carried a casserole that turned out to be canned green beans and mushroom soup, stirred. I watched Floyd for a minute and had a difficult time seeing her attraction. He had a massive chest and arms. His face was rugged as if hacked from wood—giant features that would look grotesque on a face with less acreage. Brow high, a street cool to his eyes, like he was sizing up every human near him for a fight or a fuck.

"Aw Christ the Jets," he said, sitting on a lazy boy. "You got beer?"

Mary went to the kitchen to help Lisa dish mashed potatoes.

"Did you see that shit ten minutes ago—that call at the two-yard line? That was bullshit."

"Weren't you driving ten minutes ago?"

"Yeah but you could see that shit on the radio."

Floyd predicted each play for the next quarter, and broke down winners and losers for the remainder of the season. Finally, "So what do you do?"

"What do you mean?"

"For a living?"

"Mary didn't mention it?"

"Nah. We barely talk, you know?"

"No," I said, "I'm not following."

He looked to the main kitchen entrance, not seeing that Mary had poked her head around the corner of the hallway entrance. She smiled at me and gave me a big thumbs up. Floyd was a winner. The one.

"All we do is fuck," Floyd said.

Mary dropped her head.

"Your sister's a freak—I tell you what. You couldn't pay a girl, shit she does."

Floyd grinned like I was on the team.

Mary backed into the kitchen.

*

Though I could have run enough treadmill miles to set a record at the time—the record moves a lot—preparing for an official attempt requires planning. I had to fit it around important races, ensure I had two unassociated witnesses, certify the treadmill, and think through the logistics. Last, to minimize the risk of unknown unknowns, I also wanted to train more on a treadmill.

Floyd and I set the date for the record attempt six months out. I phased in changes to my routine and saw Floyd more frequently. He'd comment on every woman who walked past, but under the hyper-masculine front he started seeming like a tolerable guy—someone to be pitied for his cosmic lack of social awareness. You don't hate a dog for sniffing your neighbor's nuts. You just realize he's a dog.

••

The more time I spent at the gym, the more opportunity Floyd had to update me on how the record attempt factored into his business. He had media and advertising contacts, and his stroke of genius was recognizing he wasn't personable, didn't like the people he was trying to attract—the wimps and slobs who needed his equipment—and would be better served hiring a consultant to manage the event.

In the gym office I joined Floyd and Mitch McMann, a marketing wizard Floyd found by referral from a gym member. McMann stood as tall as Floyd but his shape was far different, leaving no mistake his brain was the most powerful muscle on him. He wore denim frayed at the legs, a Mardi Gras t-shirt and flip flops. He carried a Mac by the corner, no computer case, and moved in a jerky, one-too-many-Red-Bulls style. Every turn forced him to push his glasses back up his nose.

He started before any of us sat. "I've distilled the problem into a three-prong attack to create maximum buzz. See, your problem is different from creating an ongoing campaign because everything centers on a focal point: a single day that a champion runner will set a world record in the gym. I get excited thinking about it. Generating the right kind of exposure and publicity—a high proportion of locals who will consider joining the gym—is a separate marketing objective from creating the ongoing media and advertising presence that will capitalize on you two's business relationship, your sponsorship of his running."

I flashed into an alternate universe where the New York Marathon medal never arrived, and instead of running, I'd focused all my energy and pain into academics or business. And committed suicide.

••

McMann said, "I recommend using a threefold approach to generating maximum targeted exposure for the record attempt." He raised his fist and stuck out his thumb. "First, make attendance of the event by twenty-five-dollar ticket only—and give away most of the tickets..."

McMann raised his arms behind his head and inhaled. Exhaled. "That's the first part. The second is how to ensure you get maximum future exposure from the event. There's one critical aspect we must manage at the same time."

Floyd looked at me and grinned.

"What's that?" I said.

"Video. I presume you'll want to record the entire twenty-four hour event. That only makes sense for proving the record. But we'll also use the video on your website, YouTube channel, and in future electronic advertising. You'll want a special video that shows the crowd, the Guinness people—they'll be here right? —and the treadmill. The ups and downs. Training montage. Strain on the nuclear family. Candid bathroom shots. Nothing adds reality like a bathroom shot, right? Everything. We'll shoot enough video for a dozen small ads, and combined with the twenty-four hours from the record, we'll have enough context footage for a sixty minute documentary. We'll get it on YouTube, Netflix, Hulu, all of them."

I pictured everything McMann said, the media circus and spectators stopping by to chat, how we'd time it so the finish was most convenient for maximum cheering carnage, and a hollowness grew in my stomach.

••

Hindsight: I sat next to Floyd Siciliano, the man tapping new energy fields in my wife, helping him plan the perfect carnivalization of my career.

I picked up a great sponsor, a sports clothing and accessory manufacturer, during the prelude to the treadmill record. This presented synergistic opportunities, McMann explained, because my sponsor would capitalize on the event as well. The more the world heard about Nick Fister, the more it reinforced our efforts to create publicity for the gym.

The sponsor deal also provided Lisa with a flush checking account.

I don't know exactly when her extracurricular sex life started. I'd been suspicious for a while and by the treadmill record attempt it was an open secret. When every "good morning" concludes with a "go die somewhere," you know the tension isn't merely about who's screwing who on *Days of Our Lives*. Important as that is.

I assumed even Tuesday had figured it out.

One day I returned from a photo shoot of my new running shoes to find Lisa swaddled and recovering from plastic surgery. She looked odd from the first moment and before I isolated the difference, I thought she looked disproportionate, sickly. Top heavy. She sat on the sofa in shorts and a sweatshirt, her face bearing a pressed smile, set firm below hard eyes.

"Who'd you get those for?"

"Me."

"Right."

"Well I'm going to be off for a week so I can heal."

••

"Off what? You haven't had a job since Tuesday was born."

I went to the kitchen to cook greens and rice.

She said, "Can you bring me a glass of water and the pill bottle on the counter?"

I looked at it. Hydrocodone. Fake tits and dope. Next, blowjobs for meth. I carried her fix to the living room.

"So let's see the tits. I want to see what I just bought."

"Go to hell."

I tossed her the pill bottle. Put the glass of water on the table. Walked away.

"You didn't pay for them," Lisa said.

Meanwhile I trained. Stride mechanics are different on a treadmill. On a road, a runner pushes off with quad muscles and finishes the stride as the hamstring pulls up the leg behind. But on a treadmill, the revolving belt carries the leg through the cycle, and the hamstring is less taxed. The runner's job, on the road, is forward propulsion. On the treadmill: preventing a face plant.

At ten miles a week, who cares?

But twenty a day, it's a different story. The trail presents constantly changing terrain: avoiding a pine cone changes the dynamic for the entire body. But unless someone drops hazards on the belt, treadmill record attempts take place on a perfectly flat surface, zero incline, constant speed, and the runner repeats a narrow range of motions for twenty-four hours. This stresses certain muscles and atrophies the rest.

I didn't want the record attempt to disrupt my normal race schedule for the year, so I balanced my focus between two objectives. First, I wanted to maintain parity between my treadmill and trail abilities. That meant strength training for my hams and other muscles to make up for the lack of workout they received on the treadmill. To mitigate muscle boredom, I used a rocker board and did other training to retain foot and ankle strength.

The second objective was to prevent boredom. Lincoln would forgive Booth after ten hours on a treadmill. Running outside, the view is different every instant. I lobbied Floyd to place the treadmill on the sidewalk in front of the store. We set up a garage fan and Floyd scheduled a chili dog truck for the following afternoon.

When the day came I was ready.

I hit the treadmill start button and was running. Two reporters arrived, one with a television cameraman, the other writing notes on a smartphone the size of a legal pad. Tuesday live tweeted the event, which was retweeted by a handful of running enthusiasts, and then Rory Mitchell, the editor of UltraRunningWorld.com. By the four-hour mark Tuesday had hundreds of retweets and new followers. A few were close to St. Louis and swung by.

By nightfall I'd drifted into my own world and the darkness was refreshing. The hoopla, the constant faces of the observers, plus Lisa, Floyd, and McMann grew wearisome. But as night quieted my surroundings and others grew tired, I remained strong and alert.

I remembered a dream I had as a child, before my mother left and my father stole my marathon medal. I think of it rarely but when I do it is stark. I see vibrant fall browns, oranges and reds. Yellow leaves on a blacktop road. A man—the future me I dreamed as a boy—walking hand in hand with a woman, towing a wagon with a child. That was the future I imagined before my mother left. I fell asleep wondering what I would be when I was thirty, if I lived that long. A boy at school had died of cancer and another lost his head on a snowmobile, driving through a barbed wire fence. If I lived to thirty, would I be the man with wife, child, and wagon, slowly walking through perfection?

At thirty-five years, my wife was a cheater and my daughter, maybe like all girls, scarily precocious.

In the middle of the night, ten hours in, the MEANING questions arrive.

Why am I doing this?

So what if I run longer on a treadmill than anyone in history? What's it matter? I'm sure a hundred thousand years ago, Xinquan was the greatest living spear chucker. Who gives a rat's rear?

If I'm so wonderful, how come my IRA has thirty-two dollars?

Is it time to think about a new career? A real career? Real profit from my reputation and records?

By dawn I was sleepy. Only twelve hours into the run, I had been awake twenty-two hours and had twelve remaining. The evening had been cool and aside from a scare when the treadmill seemed to short out for a split second, the night passed quietly. McMann woke Floyd, sleeping inside the gym office. The observers agreed it would be acceptable to bring a second calibrated treadmill outside in case the short matured into something more serious. So long as we accurately recorded the mileage from the broken machine, we could add it to the next. McMann moved a camera that was recording

••

every minute of the run so it caught the treadmill dashboard, and a half hour after the treadmill's brain fart, I was in position to keep running should a more serious malfunction render the treadmill incapable of completing the run.

At dawn I started smelling sausage from the McDonalds a hundred yards down the road, and when Tuesday arrived I asked her to buy me four breakfast burritos. After consuming sugary gels and drinks all night, my mouth was a sticky paste and my stomach was so empty it felt like a claw was scraping the inside. The smell of sausage and eggs was maddening. I ate two of them and almost vomited.

I ran.

Lisa walked by and I noticed she looked nice from the side. I wondered what her rack cost—and since I didn't buy it, I mused that this record attempt would likely drive enough business to the Bench Press and Pound to cover a facelift.

I ran.

As the clock counted closer and closer to twenty-four hours it became apparent that unless I sustained an injury I would set a record. I passed my earlier mark of one hundred fifty-nine miles with forty-five minutes remaining, and realized with a little grit I could pad the record.

Seeking the fury of a twelve-year-old boy with a rifle trained on him, I consumed a gel, pint of water, and Salt Stick capsule. In minutes the elixir breathed oxygen to my weary rage. I dropped to a seven-minute pace, and after a few minutes, realized I could dig deeper. I shaved thirty more seconds off. Wobbly without sleep and beginning to feel friction in my left hip, I sustained the pace through the finish.

Floyd slapped the treadmill stop button. The odometer read 166.54 miles, surpassing the old record by six miles. I was unsure whether I wanted to walk or sit or crawl to the floor

••

and sleep. Instead I wandered to the locker room and sat on the commode. I urinated from the seated position, braced my head in hands and closed my eyes.

Floyd stood outside the stall.

"You okay in there? You're the new record holder. Can you believe this shit?"

Floyd's been rethinking his life. He's been training on the treadmill. He's been sleeping with my wife while I've been thinking about anything and everything but her and him. I've been keeping it for fuel, saving it for when my father would not be enough. But it's beginning to feel like a commercial that used to piss me off every time I saw it, but now only produces bored frustration.

"I'm going to do the spring marathon," Floyd said. "It's coming in March and I want to prove it, you know? Then I figure I'll maybe pace a couple with you."

I exhaled hard. Thought about sleep, about escaping to dreams.

"I dunno, ya know? I just feel better getting some miles, losing some pounds. And sponsoring you's gonna be good for the gym. You see the people here? Been signing new members all day."

He was silent and I didn't say a word.

Mile 65: 10 Hours, 28 Minutes

MADDY: Any preparation in particular for this race that you didn't do for others?

NICK: I ran a hundred and twenty miles a week for three months leading up to Badwater. I spent a couple hours a day in the sauna. I did some of my running on the treadmill, which I put in the laundry room with the dryer exhaust hose duct taped to my raincoat.

MADDY: You've been outside the, uh, studio. Did the training get you acclimated?

NICK: You know, if you smoke a cigarette or something, you can feel the smoke in your lungs, right? It burns and doesn't feel normal. Well, Death Valley air is like that. You feel it killing cells in your lungs. This place reeks of death.

    --DistanceHippy Podcast Pre-Race Interview

During the Greenville Hunnert a fifteen million-candlepower spotlight blinded me and I fell five feet into a rocky gulley I was trying to leap.

I'm a pain connoisseur but I'd never mixed a compound fracture with an ambulance ride on a dirt road. The paramed shot me full of dope and soon I felt nothing.

The fall broke my tibia and fibula—the bones of the lower leg. A skin break exposed my tibia, which I dragged through the mud in my fifty-yard attempt to crawl the remaining twenty miles to the finish. By the time I arrived at the hospital, muscle had died and needed cut out. Other tissue was dirty from leaves. The doctor found moss from the rock that broke my leg.

I said great, we can use it to identify the rock.

"Painkillers make people funny," Doc said.

"Did it make your hair purple?"

"Yeah, that's the drug."

He cleaned up the mess and put me in a cast. Since I'd run eighty miles before snapping my bones, the doctor insisted I stay at the hospital a full day afterward, to ensure all my body functions returned to normal and the additional trauma hadn't disrupted my recovery.

I slept—and later woke up screaming, "Arrrgggghelp! Shit!"

I couldn't think. My calf felt like it was a slow-motion explosion confined by the cast. The pain was devastating. Mind stealing. I couldn't think to find the button the nurse had said to press if I needed anything.

A nurse burst into the room, saw me trying to tear my leg off at the hip. He called a doctor—different from the one who'd first helped me—and in twenty seconds she was wheeling out my bed, barking commands to prep a surgery room, and ten other orders I don't remember or couldn't understand.

We arrived at surgery. The doctor said something in Latin. Turning to another she said, "Compartment syndrome."

Compartments are cozy. Safe. How bad could that be?

An angel behind me with a delicate wrist placed a hand on my shoulder and covered my face with a mask.

··

Humans fill their internal monologues with the same repeat stories—a default mindset framed in words that hum in the background and provide the architecture of our conscious experience.

No one in my family achieves anything.

You have to be connected to make money.

I can't be good.

I deserve the potato cellar.

Except—through the accidental discovery of willpower—I became a distance runner.

But I still hear the voices, and although my need for self-worth has compelled me to excel at running, relapse to worthlessness is always a lost race away.

Winning is everything, thus the fuel that motivates my training, my focus, and my ability to claw deeper and fight harder for every second of pace during a hundred-mile run, that fuel is sacred. I store it like so many barrels of diesel. I keep the depot hidden so no one knows my reserves. I guard it so no one can destroy it.

In my hospital bed, they fed morphine into my IV for my leg. But the rest of me... heart and soul...

What if I'd have chosen something other than running? I used to study science just for the enjoyment. I read a lot, before I started running all the time. What if I had become a scientist?

Would I be whole, by now?

During the publicity before the Greenville Hunnert I met a trooper from the state police stationed near Greenville, ten miles down the road. I'd stopped at a coffee shop for an early afternoon caffeine jolt before meeting an Albany newspaper reporter. The trooper sat at a table talking with a local mom with two kids in a double stroller.

He recognized me as I waited for the reporter. He asked what it was like after twelve or fifteen hours. Where did I get the desire to continue? We talked about the weather too.

He said my name was uncanny, and I shrank from saying, yes, I know there's another fellow here with my name. I'm here to dick with him.

I didn't say that and the mother with the kids interrupted us to tell the police man goodbye, and I gulped my coffee and stood. It was good meeting you. Thanks for the support, and all. I waited for the reporter outside.

I recognized the state police trooper when he stood at the entrance to my trauma unit room. He hesitated to enter.

A device made of stainless steel tubing suspended my leg by a nylon strap. My foot felt numb but I couldn't tell if it was cold or not. The sensation was like trying to parse a foreign word in the middle of an English sentence. I knew it was significant, but couldn't register the meaning. I was trying to think of the right context when a nurse opened the track-roller curtain that split my half of the room from a kid who'd shattered both his elbows on the basketball floor during Friday night's game. Earlier I'd asked how he wound up with two broken elbows and he said he was so high he didn't feel it until the next day. He'd smoked a ziplock with his team before the game and when he dove for a steal, drove his full body weight into his elbows. It was miserable, not knowing how far he'd be able to open his elbows when they healed, and the more he thought about it the more he wanted to break the casts and straighten his arms.

I said I hope I never break an elbow.

The trooper at the entrance opened his mouth.

••

My surgeon was a woman younger than me; she wore thick glasses and yellow hair in a short braid. She looked at the policeman, at me; closed the curtain to the pothead kid, and said, "Do you feel good enough to talk? Can you think clearly?"

Her question struck me funny. At least her hair didn't burn in purple flames.

"The emergency surgery was caused by Compartment Syndrome, which occurs when pressure builds up in a compartment—a muscle group—and the pressure has nowhere to go. Lymph and blood flow become restricted. This damages—and then kills—muscle."

"What causes it?" I said.

"Pressure buildup."

"What causes pressure buildup?"

"Your leg break damaged tissue."

"I know a hundred people who've broken their legs. I've never heard of compartment syndrome. What was unique in my case?"

The trooper looked at her.

The doctor looked upward, away.

"Are you going to make me Google it?"

She smiled tight. "You're not going to be able to run a hundred miles on that leg. Compartment syndrome is like a pressure cooker. The cast on your leg gave the swelling nowhere to go. The front of your leg absorbed a lot of energy in the impact. Like a train wreck. Plus you twisted your leg. The calf muscle groups are compartmentalized more rigidly than, say, your thigh. In the calf, the other muscle groups don't yield, and the cast holds everything in place from the outside. Increased pressure from the injury, the swelling, started a kind of spiral. The more pressure, the more pressure. Finally blood flow stopped and muscle died."

"I'm stuck on the part about the cast."

"During the surgery, I removed the tissue that was dead. The alternative would have been the ultimate loss of the leg. No choice."

"How much tissue did you cut? Filet or roast?"

"Sixteen ounce. When fully recovered you'll have impaired motion control, a reduction in strength and stamina, and the injury will force other muscles to work harder, in ways they're not used to. The human body is adaptable, but unfortunately, your days as an elite athlete... This isn't the kind of injury that allows you to return to one hundred percent. You'll be lucky to get fifty percent—compared to where you were yesterday."

"Yeah, I got all that. Anything else?"

"Well, yes. The death of muscle tissue results in the release of myoglobin, which is processed by the kidney. We've completed tests and your kidney function is fine, given the stress you were under at the time of injury. The stress from running eighty miles."

The policeman nodded, reassured.

"How long does my leg have to hang in the air?"

"Three or four days. Your leg is immobilized right now with a splint. In three days, we'll need to operate again. You see, treatment is two-phase. First, I made two incisions in the calf, the first—" she reached to demonstrate the location on my leg, "was in this area, on the medial aspect, and the second, here, on the lateral. These gave me access to remove dead muscle."

"How did you know it was dead?"

••

"It was purple. After relieving the pressure that prevents blood flow into and out of the muscle, it will either revert to a redder, healthier color, or it will remain purple. If it remains purple, it is dead. After waiting several minutes—ample time—I removed the tissue. The second phase of your treatment will be after the swelling reduces. Right now, if we closed the wound and put you in cast, you'd possibly develop the same problem again."

"Yeah, there's that cast again."

The doctor waited. The trooper in the doorway coughed and we both looked at him.

"Any other questions right now?"

"If a cast is the wrong thing now, why was it the right thing when the other doctor worked on me first?"

"I can't answer that."

"I bet."

"Any other questions?"

"I don't want any more pain killers."

She studied me, slowly nodding her head. "You have a very serious injury, and I've given you bad news. I'm explaining in depth so you understand the gravity of what has happened. If you don't heal properly, if you re-break your leg, or there is more damage, you can still lose your leg. Just try to rest, and trust me that I'm not going to get you hooked on narcotic pain killers. But for now, to heal, you do need to take what I prescribe."

No, doctor; I need the pain.

She left and the state trooper lingered at the door. He shuffled his feet. I wanted to process the doctor's words but instead I said, "You get the bad guy yet?"

He crossed his hands at his belly like a vertical corpse. "We don't have very good news either, I'm afraid. We recovered a car battery and a spotlight. Anyone with a workbench and a pocket knife could have rigged it."

"Dude, that so sucks," said the kid with two broken elbows.

The trooper shook his head.

"You want to open the curtain? Me and the kid are friends."

The trooper dragged open the drape. "Your attacker wasn't there waiting for you. Assuming it was a man—he set a trip line so you turned on the spotlight right as you leaped the rocks. It was a fifteen million candlepower spotlight, like to illuminate a hill, spotting deer."

I reached for my Styrofoam cup of ice and the police man delivered it to me.

"It was attached to a car battery with a spring-loaded switch. Maybe you don't remember feeling it, but you triggered a fishing line strung across the trail. It was a couple inches from the ground, located where you'd step on it as you leaped across the gulley. You activate the switch, create the flash, then dark."

"So how did he know it was me?"

"The perpetrator... This looks like random violence."

I take it in. They aren't going to do anything. I twist my head to the kid. "What do you think?"

"Whacked out."

"I agree. Any fingerprints? Anything?"

"No prints on the battery, spotlight, nothing. No guess of where he fled—he or she, except the forest road that your friends carried you to. But we've got no way to guess which tire tracks are his."

"This isn't your job, is it? You're a trooper?"

••

He swallowed while nodding. "The incident is being investigated by the Durham chief. I just wanted to come by and check on you."

"But I can tell you who did it," I said. "The guy's name is Nicholas Fister—"

"Nicholas Fister?"

"Yeah. You know him?"

The trooper's head shifted back on his neck. "Guy's a war hero."

"Strikes me as a kook."

"That too. You've had a run in?"

"He's been stalking me for years. He showed up out of the blue one day when I was running in St. Louis. Him and his John Deere ball cap. He's stalking me because he thinks I stole his destiny as an ultra-runner."

The trooper looked to the window. Minced sideways. "I went to high school with Nick. He was mostly normal. Kept to himself—but when I heard he joined the Marine Corps and became a sniper, I thought, *that makes sense.*"

"What happened? Why's he a nut?"

The trooper's brow wrinkled. "When he came back from Iraq, the VFW give him a homecoming, grilling burgers and hotdogs down at the pavilion, you know."

"Yeah?"

The trooper hesitated.

"So?"

"I was just going to say I noticed how different he was. You know, in geometry class, I remember he'd do proofs in his head. He'd rattle off thirteen steps, postulates and givens and all that, like he could see the logic unfold in his head. Spooky smart, you know? But when I talked to him at the

••

pavilion, it didn't seem like the same guy. Like his wires were messed up."

I closed my eyes. "Great."

I stayed at the hospital three days for the surgery to put my leg back together and another four days to make sure there were no further complications. Tuesday flew to New York to help me make the trip home to St. Louis.

The police never discovered evidence linking Nicholas Fister to the battery and spotlight.

*

Floyd said we should be in business together. My career and reputation already exist. May as well create synergy and make more money from the same training and triumph by emblazoning my face on the gym.

It would be a good deal for me.

Floyd's accountant walked me through the numbers. They were sound. The gym was profitable—but not too profitable. It could do better, and that's why Floyd was so keen on creating a partnership. My presence would elevate the gym's prestige. I'd hold clinics for area champions-to-be. My capital—from a bank loan that would be repaid from my share of company profits—would allow the Bench Press and Pound to find new members and open new profit centers from the existing. It was an equity play, like borrowing money to buy a rental house, and the renter pays the mortgage. Same thing, the accountant said. Except only a person with some fame to exploit could pull it off, this particular way. I'd become the face of the gym, and in a few years, we'd franchise it.

••

I trained like mad to run a hundred miles again. But my contacts at each of my sponsors seemed less sure. "You can do it!" became "You know how it is with the bean counters upstairs..." My agent said not to think about contract renewals, new sponsors, or promotions until Badwater. Had I considered writing a book?

The gym could provide a backup plan.

On my third day of being part owner of the Bench Press and Pound I was warming up for my leg exercises. I studied a nautilus machine for a long moment, running my hand over the smooth metal, pushing the bar through an easy motion, no weight, just the fluid perfection of a well-designed machine.

My leg still looked like a fistful of hamburger was missing, but my daily stretches, weight lifting, nutrition, and massages were stimulating healing. I felt like a young man daring himself to take a big bite and chew like mad.

But another part of me remembered James Bliss, the old man from my youth who'd ripped a tendon from his hand and been deformed with a claw the rest of his life. It never slowed him down, he'd said with a creepy wink.

My thoughts drifted to the quality of the gym, the newness of it, and the thrill of business. The fear of knowing if anything went wrong I'd be selling the house and looking for work at a sneaker shop.

I couldn't give up running, but I had an exit. Maybe a smart exit.

Floyd strutted from the office and sat on a weight bench a yard from my Nautilus leg extension machine.

"You getting that meat grown back?"

I grunted and maintained rhythm with my repetitions. Floyd waited for me to finish the set.

"I got a guy coming here in two hours you gotta talk to for the business."

"Aren't we done with everything?"

"The paperwork, yeah. But that's just the start. The business is everything else. It's no biggie but it's important, yeah? You be here in two hours?"

"I be here."

The incongruence of being a business partner with Floyd was still fresh. Sometimes when I looked at him I thought about my wife's legs wrapped around his back. I hadn't slept in the same bed as Lisa since I'd found a couple of black pubes on the sheets. Though to be fair Floyd had enough testosterone the hair could have come from his ankles.

I thought the whole thing would end with a divorce and everyone being two-faced, modern, spiteful friends. If I had seen another solution, maybe I'd have chased it. But outside of pitching a reality TV program based on our lives, I was blank.

We only learn about the opportunities we learn about; life isn't constructed so a person can jump entirely out of himself and land in a different awareness of what's possible. I liked the gym and the idea of a career fallback, and maybe in the back of my mind, I saw myself running out Floyd, rather than the other way around. If nothing else, the gym was an insurance policy in case Nicholas Fister from Greenville came back and ruined my left leg.

Or if my rehabilitation failed.

I became more cognizant of my age—and decay—every training walk, then every run. When I first stretched a jog into a sprint for a few yards, it didn't taste like running used

..

to taste. No explosive power. No lightness. It didn't feel like I was able to glide above the earth forever.

It felt like being subject to gravity.

Recovery from short runs took days. Fortunately, although *I held my heart in my hand and ate of it*, as Stephen Crane said, I never finished. There was always more bitterness to consume. More miles of road when I stopped, more brokenness fighting into my awareness.

I lifted weights until the meeting Floyd had arranged. I showered, threw on jeans and a marathon shirt. Floyd hurried me from the locker room to the office.

Behind the desk: a leather executive chair on rollers. Floyd put me in it. At first if felt like I'd invaded another man's home, but I adjusted.

"It's as much your desk as mine," Floyd said. "I want you to feel that way. We're business partners now. What's mine is yours."

Yeah, likewise.

"This is Frank Gillespie," Floyd said. "He's an insurance broker."

Floyd and Frank sat in metal chairs opposite the desk and I was oddly in the position of being the businessman evaluating both.

"Insurance. I see."

"I axed Frank to come over. He handles all my—our— other insurance for the gym. The van. I have my home and Corvette insured through him. But I wanted him to talk with us about a buy-sell agreement. Kind of give us the outline, ya know."

"Buy sell agreement. Right."

"Right," Frank said. "Now that you're business partners, you each have a great deal of insurable interest in each other's

••

lives. If something should happen to either of you, it would put the other in an awkward position—of being in business with the other man's heirs. I don't know about you, but I wouldn't want to be in business with my friend's wife..."

I watched Floyd.

"No shit," Floyd said. "My heirs are my brothers in New York. You don't want to partner with them. I tell you that." Floyd said.

"Two things," Frank said. "Life insurance. You each own a policy on each other, and when the first of you dies, the insurance company pays the death claim, providing funds to buy out the heirs' interest in the business. Second thing is a buy sell agreement. I can recommend an attorney. It's a legal document that delineates how each of your interest in the business will be appraised, and how the transaction will occur at either of your deaths. Naturally, as the company grows, the document will need to be amended."

I met Floyd's eyes. "Sounds like a good idea."

*

We planned to fly into Las Vegas McCarran International Airport on Thursday, five days ago, to have plenty of time to acclimate and prep for the Badwater race on Monday. But my daughter Tuesday died on Wednesday. We hunkered as deep into our lonely souls as we have ever been, held her funeral, and flew to Las Vegas on Saturday. I was numb and irritable at the same time, clinging to my focus.

I should have been happy for the pain, but the mad completeness of death was like a noise so loud, it left a vacuum. I couldn't think. My guts vibrated. There was nothing good in it. Talk of heaven sounded like fraudulent bullshit. The fabric of day-to-day life was turned upside down and I clung to the nylon mesh but questioned how gravity changed sides. Nothing made sense and the only sane response was to hole up in my head.

Then we flew to Las Vegas.

Floyd had calculated we'd have a great payoff if any race videos or photos included the van with the gym's logo and my face, and since I'd told him I planned to announce my retirement after the race, he drove the van from St. Louis, loaded with our gear plus a digital camera and enough batteries to record twenty hours of bootleg video for an unauthorized Badwater 135 documentary.

We filled the van with a giant cooler, drink mixes, everything we didn't want with us on an airplane. I hoped to avoid waiting for luggage at the airport. That changed at the last minute when Lisa decided she needed an extra suitcase.

Lisa, Mary and I flew from St. Louis. After landing we walked to the luggage claim area, and Lisa and Mary visited the restroom. The baggage claim was desolate but for the folks on our flight. The area seemed vast compared to the people in it. Some played airport slot machines.

I studied the flight boards to see which carousel to watch for our bags. It wasn't spinning yet. I looked around. Suspended from the ceiling and hanging twenty feet above was an airplane that looked like an old Piper.

I noticed a figure on the upper deck, fifty feet away, a man leaning forward on the guardrail. He wore a dark green hat. We locked eyes. He grinned with Ted Bundy confidence and waved by opening and closing his fingers like a five-year-old.

In the two seconds I flashed a look right and left, seeking an escalator to the upper level, Nicholas Fister disappeared.

••

Mile 70: 11 Hours, 13 Minutes

TOMMY: So we mentioned Nova Bjorkman. You said you wanted
to win more than her. But isn't she a threat?

NICK: Of course she's a threat. You already mentioned Pam
Reed. The longer the race, the better women do.

TOMMY: Why is that, you think?

NICK: They have better control over their egos and make fewer
mistakes of aggression. And they have a superior ability
to burn fat. Take two athletes, male and female, with the
same body composition, the woman will burn more fat
and less muscle than the man. She'll also run better in
colder weather, and swim farther in cold water, like Loch
Ness. The world record is held by a woman there, I
believe. Same with the Irish Channel.

MADDY: So, what about Death Valley heat? Would fat be a
disadvantage?

NICK: Well, from what you're saying about this Bjorkman gal, I
better hope so, right?

--DistanceHippy Podcast Pre-Race Interview

My Garmin tells me twelve miles. I try to remember
what the last Garmin said when the battery died.
Fifty-eight. The number arrives not as a
conclusion, but a possibility.

I hold the first number top of mind, and while staging the
second for addition to the first, the first disappears and the
second is top of mind. Finally, I become aware of seventy,

and am satisfied. It takes a mile to do the math. Should I add the mile or subtract it?

I've run seventy miles, plus whatever I ran without knowing my Garmin was dead.

Regardless, I'm about to arrive at a new difficulty. Mile seventy-two begins a twelve-mile climb. A brief respite then another climb to mile one hundred, then a decline, a flat, and the final ascent, a five-thousand-foot climb in the space of a few miles.

I'd rather have the heat.

My ankles are disasters.

The right is swollen and tight, a club I wield against the ground. Do your feet hurt baby? Because you've been running through my mind all night.

Ha!

I always know when I need fructose because I get happy. When I notice, it never pisses me off that I didn't plan better... because I'm happy. And I never remember it happens until the next time I am caught happy by surprise.

My left ankle is functional but the pain is dizzying. Magnificent. The tracking band, although smooth, has bounced with thousands of strides, abrading away the skin below. The plastic wears against ankle meat, and although the sun is halfway to setting and the air is oven-dry, sweat somehow manages to trickle into the open flesh.

The sharpness keeps my mind from going other places, like Floyd Siciliano's hotel room.

From elapsed time I expect to see my crew again soon. I'm cresting a small hill and because they are not waiting on this side of the slope they must be on the other.

I wonder at the relative coolness of the night, now that the sun isn't direct and the air temperature is a few degrees cooler.

••

I suspect the time is around six pm but time isn't worth knowing. The temperature is still a hundred and ten, I bet, but its number doesn't matter either.

I shift to avoid an uneven road surface and my right ankle stabs upward like a knife going into my calf. The sharpness keeps my thoughts congealed around the happy task at hand. It surprises me for a moment when I realize the task at hand is keeping me performing the task at hand, and that pain is somewhere irretrievably in the middle of it.

Nick, get real.

The task at hand is winning this race and being done with the insanity of ultra-distance running.

The task at hand is making sure I don't go to prison.

Nearing the top of a knoll, I am ready for a break. My heart beats thin and woozy with utter candor: *ease up a minute. I want to check something out. I'll tell you when you can run.*

I walk.

Think.

From here to finish, my body will tell me every reason it cannot comply with my demands. My job will be to not listen.

Run.

Cresting the hill reveals an expanse, patterns of dusk, brought early by rare clouds and high mountain walls. A set of revolving red and blue strobes throws the peacefulness of the entire valley into disarray. Ahead of the lights is a white van.

Under the cardboard taped to the side with my race number, the size of a door, is my angry face.

●●

Floyd Siciliano had a photographer stop by the gym right after I signed. The shutterbug aimed the camera and clicked and flashed and Floyd said, "Nah, this is shit. You got the look all wrong. You're a champion. You got to look focused. How would your face look if you learned some guy was boning your daughter? You got a look for that?"

The mind works for you or against you, but sometimes when you've pushed the body too far, it reminds the brain that self, identity, the part of me that is me—is a projection that'll decay a hell of a lot faster than muscle and bone, when the blood stops pumping and the electric sizzles out.

I stop and almost topple forward. Now that my legs are motionless, they feel incapable of bearing me. Hands on knees, vertebra pop beneath tight muscles. I arch my middle back outward and wonder.

Now what?

It's difficult to think. Are the police holding the van, waiting for me to arrive?

To arrest me?

They could have tracked me to this square inch. And if they lost the signal they could have driven the route. I look forward down the road, then behind me. See other athletes in the distance. No, the route hasn't changed.

I walk my hands up my thighs until I stand, and step forward, and ease into a slow jog. I count thirty paces and the impact pain in my soles is manageable. Like magic. A few seconds of rest is sometimes enough.

Down at the van, their eyes will be jaded by the flashing light, their day in the heat and glare. When I get close, I'll sneak into the desert and circle around. Low crawl through weeds and rocks, snag some Gu. A jug of juice.

••

I progress down the slope with my gaze on the revolving lights and the varying edge of road, picking up speed until the fronts of my legs again begin to feel like shattered glass. It is frighteningly easy to back off. I'm capable of stopping altogether. Am I capable of quitting? To avoid another ankle twist I shift toward the center of the road. The colorific chaos of the red and blues threatens to end my run, and career, right here.

Somewhere ahead is the Barelegged Nova. Pretty name, Barelegged Nova. Pretty legs.

Tonight, when I catch her, I will propose marriage. What sort of thousand-mile runner would come out of it? I imagine a doctor set to deliver my baby, crouching at Nova's crotch, starting gun in hand.

It is only the earliest onset of dusk but I can't see Barelegged Nova's lights. The rules state a blinkie light must be worn, but strategies vary. Most race leaders prefer to keep their adversaries unsure of their location, so they carry headlamps and blinkers but turn them off when they can see well enough without. Likewise, runners stalking the leader prefer to keep her unaware of their gathering proximity. Except when the pass is imminent. Then you want the leader to know you're coming hard and there's nothing she can do to stop it.

Regardless of strategy, the rules say lights must be worn and turned on.

The back doors of the van are open. Figures move between the lights but I can't determine perfect shapes, only colors, and from them I expect two deputies and one crewmember. The deputies search the van.

What does this mean? I replay the questions in my mind. Was I in Floyd Siciliano's room?

••

No. I'm certain I wasn't. We had a beer, all of us. But not in his room.

And the knife question. Siciliano was stabbed. Do they assume a man killed him, and since I knew him, it must have been me? Why search the van to find the knife that's in St. Louis?

They couldn't have gone to St. Louis, searched my house, taken my knife, and planted it in the van?

Has enough time passed for them to do that?

Nothing is worse than thinking with a fuel starved brain.

Fifty feet from the van I walk, remaining on the same side of the road. If I cross to the other side and somehow make it past without being seen, my crew will search toward the starting line. And without replenishment I will be at my end. I could give commands for five hundred more miles but without water, salts, my body will not listen.

I walk wide of the cruiser. Mary emerges from a shadow beside the van, moving quickly toward me. I hold out my empty water bottle to her but she takes my other hand and says barely above a whisper, "They're searching the van."

Methodically so I can remember what I am doing I remove her hand from mine, take her Gatorade bottle with my left hand and place it in my right. I drink. Breathe. Drink again. "What did you say?"

"They're searching the van."

"I'm bonking hard. And I need a sponge. Where's the tall one? The deputy gal. Is she the most beautiful thing you've ever seen?"

Mary takes my hand in her other hand and squeezes it. "I'm sorry."

"Sorry for what?"

∙∙

She emits a half-second squirt of a cry, chokes it back. "Life is so shitty for us."

"Are you drinking enough water? Electrolytes? You need to look after yourself. It's hot out. Where's Edgerton?"

Mary turns from me, her hand trailing in mine until I release it. At the back of the van she calls to Deputy Edgerton. I sit in a foldout chair that's presumably been waiting for me since before the deputies arrived. I throw out my legs as straight as I can make them without spasming my thighs, then fold them beneath me to stretch my knees.

"She'll be here in a second," Mary says. "You want new socks?"

"Yes. But I want Edgerton to remove the ankle bracelet for a few minutes so we can treat it."

"Treat what?" Mary squats. "Oh shit, Nick. Oh shit."

"It's just skin."

"No, it's not skin."

"Well, if we cover it with antibacterial ointment, a dressing, then a sponge, I'll be able to wear the bracelet and be protected from the rubbing. Find ointment and a sponge."

I feel my brain coming back.

Mary places her hands on my knees. I hear shuffling behind her. "You should quit. DNF. Everyone would understand. You need to take care of yourself. This is serious. And with all the other things you're dealing with—"

"It's a flesh wound. Can you get me the other Garmin? Is it recharged yet?"

She turns from me. In a moment she hands me a Garmin with a full charge. "They think you killed Floyd."

"Of course they do. Now please go find the race we finish so I can need this shit."

Mary shakes her head. "Say that again."

••

"Please go find the shit I need to finish the race. Now!"

Deputy Edgerton steps into view. "How you holding up?"

I study her face for a moment and my prior words slosh against my memory. I hold up one finger, a confused delay. Looking straight into her face I see a human being that can't hide her genuineness. I see a kind of beauty that never finds words, one that resides in a person like cicadas buried deep until after thirteen years they cannot be denied.

Deputy Edgerton is in love with me.

I think out my words before I say them. "Need you to take off the bracelet for a minute so we can treat my leg. The skin's rubbed off."

She shines a flashlight. "Ah, Nick. Nick."

"You mind getting the key off your compadre so I can get it fixed up?"

"You know this isn't looking good for you. We got you for motive. Floyd Siciliano was having relations with your wife. Plus you being business partners seems like a good place to dig. We have you at the scene of the crime. You're staying in the same hotel and you left a beer bottle in the victim's room. We find the weapon—"

"Hold on. I said I wasn't in his room."

"That's what you said." Edgerton exhales. "Did you drink beer last night?"

"What's that—"

"Did you drink beer?"

"I had a Sierra Nevada. It's a tradition."

"Well, we have a Sierra Nevada beer bottle with your fingerprint, left in the victim's room. He was stabbed about the groin—so many times there wasn't any groin left. That implies rage, such as a man would have after learning his wife was unfaithful."

..

"Bah. I knew that a long time ago."

Mary gives me another bottle. I drink. Orange juice. Perfect. I chug it knowing I'll throw it back up. I want the time it buys me. I want my brain back. Somehow the stakes have escalated and while I'm flirting with Edgerton, she's being a cop.

I shake my head. "No. You've got it all wrong. I feed on that shit."

"And you never told me you took a last-minute trip to Albany, a few days before your daughter committed suicide. You visited the man you accused of killing Floyd Siciliano a week before Floyd Siciliano ended up dead."

Lisa must have told her.

"I went there to explain I didn't have the medal he wanted. I took my first Western States belt buckle as a peace offering. I wanted to make sure he'd leave me alone here. I needed a Badwater win and I didn't want him to attack me again. Look at my leg."

"Be that as it may. If I go to Deputy Bly and ask him to remove this anklet, he'll put you in cuffs and Mirandize you. We'll be driving to jail. The only reason he's holding back is because of the video your sister took. From this point, you've got no margin. If you start pushing, that's intimidation of an officer of the law, and we'll pull you from the race. You'll trade an ankle bracelet for handcuffs."

Mary arrives with antibacterial ointment and a dressing.

I'm awash in fructose. I twist. Look down the road.

"Come here, Mary. Closer. Here, right here." I kiss her forehead. "Can you give me some water, a couple Gu, and refill my bottle with Endurolyte?" I take the ointment and dressing from her. Squeeze a clump onto my finger and struggle to bend to my feet.

••

"Let me," Edgerton says. She holds my hand and wipes the glob my from my finger to hers, and sits at my feet with her legs extended. I study the shape of her thighs, the swell of muscle that belies her athleticism. The soft paradise where her legs meet. I watch the corners of her mouth, the set of her jaw as she lifts the bracelet as high on my ankle as it will travel, exposing the circle of wound around my leg. I take in her neck, how it disappears into her uniform blouse and gently inflates it. She wipes the ointment on my skin, then releases the bracelet and squeezes a goob twice as large to her fingers.

"You're like Jesus," I say. "Washing feet."

"No," she says. "I'm not the one who's condemned, and you're not forgiven."

Mary arrives with another bottle and I lean back and gulp while Edgerton dresses the wound. When I look down again my stomach feels close to rupture, but my legs start to feel alive. If my brain is convinced, my body knows not otherwise. I look down the road.

This race is in the bag.

"How far ahead is Barelegged Nova?"

"I didn't see her," Edgerton says.

"She passed twenty minutes ago," Mary says.

"How'd she look?"

"Strong."

I nod, though I wanted to hear something else.

Using my arms to push erect, I stand, fill my Gu belt from a box in the back of the van and carry several more in my hand that I plan to consume. See if I can break the rules and catch up calories. As biologically impossible as a sparrow

••

shitting an elephant, but I will try. I pass the empty bottle to Mary.

"Your leg," Mary says. "Let me rub it down real quick." She kneels and works the muscle. "I can't believe he's dead. You know that time you met him and he said that stuff about what kind of a freak I was in bed?"

"Mary—"

Edgerton cocks her head sideways.

"He was making fun of me," Mary says. "I never slept with him. I hadn't slept with a man since Darrel. He was testing you to see how you'd react. Didn't you see the way he was watching Lisa from the moment he walked in? You know Nick, I used to think about killing him. No, I mean that honestly. I'm glad it happened. He's in a worse place, and I'm glad. Most people hope God is real so the person they love will go to heaven. I hope God is real so Floyd Siciliano burns in hell. I really hope there's a God."

Edgerton studies Mary.

Mary looks into my eyes and I realize she stopped rubbing my leg a moment ago, and that something in my sister is desperately broken. The heat has melted the glue holding her together.

Or is she cleverer than I, buying me time to finish the race?

I must return to my run. Extract myself.

I check my body like a pilot doing a preflight inspection. Nothing beyond salvage, but I better stretch my IT bands before setting out.

I place my right foot over my left, kick out my right hip and lean to the left, stretching the outside of my right leg until my knee feels about to snap sideways and the muscles in

••

my ass feel ready to tear. I switch legs and repeat, this time less forcefully because my right leg bears all my weight.

Straightened, I bend forward at my hips until the tightness in my lower back releases with a pop. I stand and touch Mary's shoulder for balance. She turns her face and presses her cheek to my hand. "It's almost over," she says.

I hold Deputy Edgerton's look for a long while. Something lurks in her that I haven't fully fathomed. I don't know that I want to put my animal in the same zoo where she keeps hers. She blinks, curtly smiles, and I take my cue.

I kiss Mary on the cheek and feel the wetness of a tear I had not seen. I look down the road. It's where I want to be.

"You run, Nick. Dammit you run."

"Deputy, you know how to find me."

I shove off and my feet land like concrete, but as my shuffle converts into a run, the hurt diminishes. I even out my stride and think of the mechanics of running. I see da Vinci diagrams, arcs, legs, a film of runners in the 1936 Berlin Olympics, that hungry scared glare on Jesse Owens' eyes at the start. That hunger for so much more than a fast run.

I pull myself into the semblance of good form and tell myself the finish line is near, and crossing it will transition me to a new kind of being, with a new life. I'll take time to learn my lessons. To face and deal with things. I'll rest for a month and grieve.

*

I spent a lot of time around the house after I broke my leg. After two months I couldn't stand myself, the sounds of domestic life, Tuesday and Lisa fighting. Respite didn't come until Lisa discovered new errands that required her to leave the house for most of the day.

By my first recovery run I'd had enough time as Floyd's business partner to want to suspend my business career. I couldn't fathom how to be a paid ambassador for the sport. When I tie my shoes and toe the starting line, I am *part* of the sport. How could I retire from that, and from the *outside* pretend to speak for the sport?

I needed to return to racing. Running is who I am and what I do. Why couldn't I be the guy who runs hundred milers at eighty years of age faster than the best twenty-five year olds? I had to rehabilitate back to one hundred percent—I couldn't be one of those guys who kept doing it long after no one took him seriously.

I ran up Olive, like usual, a simple out and back route I can extend to fifty miles if I like. I'd test my leg a few miles, then give it a couple days to see if anything developed. But the pain encroached on unbearable and instead of running two miles and turning around, I kept going. At fifteen I turned. I'd lost tremendous stamina, and controlling pace uphill was impossible.

I wanted to pull out my hair. As the pain of each stride shot fireworks from ankle to groin, I mouthed my mantra: I will not stop. I will not fail.

Eventually I believed it: I would recover and announce my comeback at the most impossible course, the Badwater 135, and set a course record.

Re-convinced of my destiny, I quit. At twenty miles my right leg radiated the kind of pain that signifies honest disaster. I pulled my phone out of my pack, called Lisa to come get me, and started shuffling home.

••

When we first got serious I told Lisa my concept of marriage: during grade school recess the teachers appointed two dodge ball captains. Each took turns choosing teams one person at a time. Captains had to balance their desire to build a winning lineup against their wish to include people they most enjoyed. If your best friend was captain, being chosen first ostensibly demonstrated athletic ability. But inside you celebrated the tightness of the bond. Your friend was loyal because your value extended beyond mere athleticism. *You were a valuable person.*

As the pool of Unchosen shrank everyone feared he'd be the one to leave the bleachers last, and walk uninvited to the captain who ran out of options.

In life we all expect to be chosen last. Life is a dodge ball in the face and no one does it well enough to merit being called before anyone else. But being married means if chance makes either of you a captain, you call your spouse first. The game could be bocce and you could be the worst player since the Roman era, but your wife always, no matter what, calls you first.

That ends when she beds other men.

I started and stopped running three more times before Lisa arrived a half hour later. If she had left within a few minutes of my call she would have arrived in roughly thirteen minutes. Any minute beyond thirteen she spent on other priorities, other guys for her team.

The kid chosen last owes no loyalty.

Seventeen minutes doubting your marriage is enough to derail it, when you have new questions and they all point to the same answer.

••

I usually ignored the mail and most everything about the day-to-day operations of the house I lived in. Laundry, groceries, vacuuming, repairs. I was either running or recovering from running and I've earned a good enough living the last few years with the endorsements to gain the efficiency of paying other people to do the things I don't like to do.

I don't often see the mail but one day during my recovery, when Lisa was away, a letter caught my eye. At first I thought it was a credit card offer but as I looked again I found it was a bill. I tore it open. Chase Visa. Nine thousand, three hundred, forty-eight dollars and forty-one cents. I flipped it over and searched the fine print. Twenty-two percent interest.

I'm not a real businessman but I know something about making money work for you instead of against you and I couldn't fathom why—if we had forty thousand in checking at First St. Louis—should we pay Chase twenty-two percent interest to borrow their money? I flipped through the rest of the mail and then ventured into Lisa's room and rummaged through her desk.

I found six similar envelopes, took them to my room, opened a spreadsheet and started inputting numbers. Lisa had charged forty-eight thousand dollars on six cards. The weighted average interest rate was nineteen percent.

I couldn't remember a single thing other than her chest that she bought within the last few years—and no store-bought rack is worth fifty grand.

Looking deeper, one of the cards had been open for a year, and she'd been using cash advances from the newest to make the payments to the rest. After a couple hours of forensic math, I deduced the initial charges were about thirty thousand dollars.

A part-time assistant who cooked, cleaned, made the bed and crewed ultra-marathons might expect about thirty grand a year.

Lisa sleeping with Floyd had never signified our marriage being over, somehow. I thought of her infidelity as an unmeasured, undefined event whose full significance had yet to be revealed. A disaster rolling out in such slow motion, I beheld the future with more curiosity than dread. But running up debt simply to have an income outside of her dependency on me seemed a Rubicon decision, with a resulting insult more profound than the one given by her faithlessness.

I asked myself where love fits into that kind of realization.

How long has it been since I even pretended I knew what love was?

The facts of my life swirled around me like fists and feet on a marionette, God jerking and pulling the cross. Forty thousand in high interest credit card debt. My career stuttering to an end. My business partner nailing my wife. My daughter slutting up to Doors dork Thornton. My sister in an opiate nosedive.

Who was this Lisa-woman living in my house?

And who was I, but a coward staring at a far-off victory while under my face arose the stench of absolute domestic defeat?

Lisa flashed her headlights as she approached, pulled to the right and waited on traffic, then looped a U-turn and swung behind me. I climbed inside, sat on a towel she'd used to cover

••

the seat. Clicked my belt. She glanced to the side mirror and pulled into traffic.

My leg throbbed. Now sitting, I sensed other things were wrong. I'd compensated for the leg's weakness by adjusting my stride, placing more demands on other muscles. I'd rubbed the underside of my left arm raw against my tank top, meaning my entire form had changed. What other stresses would emerge? I unclicked my seatbelt and leaned forward, rubbed the area around the front scar, then kneaded my calf. Weight training, again?

"Put your seatbelt back on."

"I'll put it on in a minute."

"Put it on. I don't need another ticket."

I rubbed my leg. Closed my eyes. Remembered the Sam Kinison joke about needing a six-pack just to keep from cutting off his wife's head.

Lisa swerved. Braked. Slammed the shifter into park before the car stopped, sending my forehead to the glove box.

"Don't be an asshole. Put your belt on!"

I stared at her. She waited. I put on my belt. Inhaled carefully.

"You told Tuesday she can't date Thornton. It doesn't matter if you don't like him. She likes him."

"Stop talking."

"It's a new age, kids are doing what they want and there's nothing we can do about it but try to help her understand—"

I unfastened my seatbelt. Opened the door and exited. "Go home. Or wherever. Goodbye."

I walked, then ran, and five minutes later she drove by with her middle finger framed in the passenger window, shouting syllables that didn't make words.

••

By the time I arrived home the pain in my leg had progressed from refined to exquisite. I stopped several times and massaged away some of the swelling. In a couple short months I'd crossed over from young athlete to old man. I had faced crises in runs before, once running a sixty miles on a broken ankle. I knew how to find my inner grit and use it to grind the problem, instead of me. But with my leg I sensed I was up against a hard edge of reality that would not give no matter what I believed, no matter how far I pressed. I didn't know what to make of it.

Every other challenge in life had yielded to fanatical applications of belief, will, and willingness to suffer greatly. But I stood looking at my right leg as if I was at the outer perimeter of the universe, confronted by a brick wall that extended infinitely in all directions. Well, shit. I was wrong.

And then I started running beside the wall, because if it goes as far as it looks, that'll keep me going a long while. If I had to change course then so be it, I'd run with a broken leg. I'd run hobbled. I'd press harder than ever. I'm conscious, after all.

By the time I entered the house through the back door and arrived in the kitchen I was jumping on one leg. I hopped to the cupboard, took a horse pill from a prescription bottle, and downed it in a mix of water, chia seeds, and L-glutamine. I pulled a PBJ from the fridge, struggled to the living room, stretched out a mat and sat.

I folded my right leg with my hands and pulled off my running shoe and merino wool sock. Gouged the ball of my foot with my thumb, urging the muscles to loosen. In a moment the sideways pressure on my leg created a new dimension of discomfort.

••

I looked up.

Lisa stood in the aisle, her face flushed, shoulders squared.

"You're not the person I want to see right now."

"Well you're going to see me. I gave Tuesday permission to date Thornton. If you contradict me on this, I'm not going to put up with it."

"That's nice. Now piss off."

"You don't even care about your daughter."

"No, I'm just skeptical of a boy who only wears Doors t-shirts."

"How do you know anything about him? Until this accident you were never here. You train more than workaholics work. Everything is training to you. You run ten hours at a time. Then two hours in the kitchen because every calorie has to be grass fed free range organic! I'm surprised you even remember your daughter's name."

I removed my second wool sock. "I don't trust Thornton... because I *was* Thornton."

She stomped away. From the bedroom came a crescendo of curses until she again stood in the hall entry, shouting full voice, "...something you can do about it? Like this obsession of yours?"

"What—"

"This obsession! You've been lifting weights with a broken leg! You're running on a treadmill with a broken leg! You can't rest for six weeks so your body can heal. But stuck in the house like a broke dick you can't have dinner with your wife and daughter. Can't slow down to know what's happening around you. You're just off, all the time, all about your running, all about your career. We get it! We know we don't mean anything to you. Fuck me I don't get you." She turned again. "You want out? I'm done."

••

She pointed at me until her hand shook. Her mouth parted, but for the first time ever no words issued from it. She dropped her arm and her face contorted in rage. Or sorrow. Who gives a shit. The bedroom door slammed and until Tuesday killed herself, Lisa and I spoke not another word except as malcontented business partners.

She lived in my house and hated me but couldn't live without me. As I trained after my injury, I realized I couldn't live without her either.

I needed all the torment I could get.

I picked up the shoe closest to me and studied the sole. Ran my fingertips across the chipped and feathered tread. I brought it to my nose and inhaled the scent of rubber, the road, the miles, the residue of living in an ugly world and doing what it took to get through it. I thought of the peace that enters my brain when I've beaten myself down to nothing, and simply can't go on.

I brought a wool sock to my cheek. Felt the dryness, the texture. Closed my eyes and meditated on the torment inside my leg, focusing until the pain gave up, and it was just me and my body.

Anything more was illusion.

●●

Mile 89: 14 Hours, 20 Minutes

MADDY: What's your strategy for having a pacer with you? When do you bring him in? What do you want out of a pacer?

NICK: Well, I don't often use one, and that speaks to what the pacer's job is. They can't do anything to make the race physically easier. I mean, they can't lower hills. Their job is to help the runner keep control of his mind. When you're out there seventy miles you start to ask the same questions every time. The pacer is there to take control of your mind when you can't. That's the bottom line. When your brain doesn't work, your pacer's better.

MADDY: Your pacer is your crew chief of a couple years, right?

NICK: Yes.

MADDY: When do you think you'll bring him out of the van to start running with you?

NICK: Depends. I might not run with him at all. Truth is, we don't much like each other.

--DistanceHippy Podcast Pre-Race Interview

For ninety miles I've been fighting through every kind of pain, turning it around like a judo move, taking the force that is meant to destroy me and instead using it to drive me farther.

How does it work? The mechanics? Extraordinary suffering forces the mind to travel elsewhere. To sever ties with the body that is destroying it. When this happens, pain feels separated. Somehow distant. Free from pain yet infinitely aware of it, adrenaline results. Train the mind and the body will follow. My mind burns pain and my body runs on anger. Calories, electrolytes, biochemical processes need a master.

My right ankle might have broken bones, judging from the nonstop throb and the stabbing sensation with each footfall. I cherish each. My left ankle is rubbed raw and swelling into the tracking bracelet—hopefully soon it will impede the alarm from its perennial shifting. Even with the antibacterial, the sponge, and the dressing, it rubs. Sweat continues to salt the wound. My elbow is numb on the outside but the shard of bone inside the joint is chopping meat to burger.

And my ass is raw. Abraded by sweaty shorts and cheeks, sautéed in shit, then rubbed with facial cleanser and coated in Glide.

I take in the state of my body and delight in each murderous footfall. My energy stores feel high, but I've been unsupported too many miles to figure the math. I have a hundred complaints, none of them crippling. I relish knowing my energy ebbs and flows but my will is a rock that has never failed me.

I crest a knoll and the terrain flattens; ahead I make the strobe of a runner's obligatory light, demanded by race organizers for safety. Night is treacherous for runners. We tend to be depleted after a full day in the oven heat, baked senseless. I've been interviewed by both Jim Morrison and Roger Waters. We drift from the road to berm, across the road and all over. We sleep while we walk or run, and waken unsure of our identities or locations. We jump when the gargoyles jump.

Only one runner ahead: Barelegged Nova Bjorkman.

••

Racing toward her, each landing foot shoots a stabbing sensation that lifts my mind to dizzying heights, hysterical without laughter, the knifing in my elbow, the burning in my ass. Racing toward Barelegged Nova I muse she must be a cataclysmically good lay. With a name like that. I should tell her when I pass. She'd dig that.

My training has earned a dividend and I'm cashing it. Garmin tells me I'm flirting with an eight-minute pace, insane for a broken body, but it feels good like mouthing off to authority feels good. Speed affirms life. I seize danger because I hunger for the punishment.

Barelegged Nova is down the hill. Lights erupt behind me and pass. The evening air is stiflingly calm. My feet, my breathing seem amplified through loudspeakers. My awareness is crystal—but narrow. The vehicle drives toward Nova Bjorkman and passes her slowly, perhaps exchanging an empty fuel bottle for a full before accelerating out of sight. Against the rules, but it's dark.

My van has abandoned me. Has Lisa gone home? The plan was to leapfrog every two miles. She's missed at least ten frogs. Without the second bottle and extra Gu, I'd have chased a fairy into the dark by now.

I slack from my pace and dust off an old trick to keep the motivation burning hot: I think of the best hand-drawn signs I've seen spectators wave alongside the route. *"Your feet hurt because you're kicking ass,"* held by a white haired, beaming old woman. *"Because 101 miles would be crazy,"* held by a young mother with another on the way. My favorite, by a hippy surrounded by a yellow haze of marijuana smoke in Tempe, Arizona, a hundred yards before the finish: *"Fuck Yeah."*

I back off to a nine-minute pace. I'll resume speed when Nova's a hundred yards ahead, but for now, I conserve energy. I want my pass to shut down her hope. Nothing wastes more of a runner's soul than a back-and-forth battle for the lead, stretched over three dozen miles.

Somehow night has fallen completely. Floyd Siciliano is dead, and now it is night. Stars disappear into mountain. The temperature has cooled enough to refresh me.

As a kid I'd get close to the mirror and stare and after a minute my mind would float above my two heads. A pool of cognitive clarity pops into existence like a parallel universe just long enough for me to question who I am.

Where's my van?

I flop my hand bottles side to side. The first is empty. The second's splash is weak, maybe a gulp of my drink mix remains. I'd guess the air temperature is upper nineties. I'll continue to sweat and lose salts all night, even though the comparative difference in temperature leaves me cool.

I pat the fuel strap around my waist, a nylon band with elastic loops for holding energy gels. I carry six. Each Gu contains one hundred and ten calories, but before I can multiply them, I see the Barelegged Nova's light flash, or a falling star, and have to start the mathematics over. My pace feels fast. I should be holding nine minute miles. I check my watch and observe in near shock that I'm at seven-and-a-half.

It's a flash and crash. The boom before the bust. The body cries, *Alamo!*

I back off, again. Take a tiny swig of water, enough to wet my throat only, and snap the top closed.

In the past if the van had a flat tire, Siciliano would have fixed it. But Floyd Siciliano is dead and my girls are modern women. Lisa would call the Automotive Association. Mary would pop an Oxy.

••

My legs know where to go but without my support vehicle, I'm unsure how to play the moment. If I pass Nova and the van is further delayed, I'll give up what I gained and that'll only encourage Nova.

But... will this be my last opportunity to reel her in? I've done this so many times, fought my way out of second or fifth because I know how to fight harder, how to demand more. One must receive the self-destructive impulse with open arms. I've danced with her. Made love to her. I've pushed myself to collapse so many times I don't fear it, but anticipate it like an athletic orgasm. I'm prepared to demand absolutely everything.

But now? Doubt. I can pass Barelegged Nova.

Will she stay passed?

I look up from the road. Maybe my anguish won't matter.

Nova's shadow and strobe grow larger. She is close enough I see her shape inside the light, like a black hole defined by the brightness beyond it.

The mountain ahead looms forbidding but all races are forbidding at the end. The mountain—all challenges—are nothing but an empty saddle waiting for an ass.

I trust. I run. Think about my elbows, my foot strikes, my gait. My mended right leg aches like no other ache, a bone-deep soreness around a missing filet. The pain isn't sharp so much as nauseating. Like being kicked in the balls. I should have sued.

The ankle bracelet says they think I'm a murderer.

I think about calories. And where the hell is my van?

"Well Babe?" I practice out loud, "Are you a cataclysmic lay? Like having a super nova-gasm?"

Headlights behind me pull my attention. Finally, the van?

I gulp the last from my electrolyte bottle.

••

I've been running straight for so long that looking to the right wobbles my balance and I veer a couple feet toward the passing vehicle. My legs tighten at the surprise motion. I swerve back to the white line and stumble off the pavement. The switch to packed dirt pinches my swollen toes and my elbow bounces from my side.

Headlights cast the entire future in a white glow. I don't turn again, preferring to wait until the vehicle is ahead enough that I can regain the road with minimal change in orientation. A moment ago I was feeling brand new. Now, every muscle is ready to seize. The headlamps illuminate empty distance ahead and somewhere to the left the road cuts hard and heads up a near five-thousand-foot ascent.

The vehicle is not passing. I am aware, but running in the dirt beside the pavement requires more brain wattage than I'm generating.

I've been at zero so many times during my training and racing, I'm cognizant at a chemical-electro level that without intervention, without miracle calories, salt and water entering my system I'll die before the finish line. The thought humbles and exhilarates. Is it time?

Is this where I cross the line and don't cross back?

The vehicle beside me pulls slightly ahead and from peripheral sight I discern it is not a van. It crosses into the empty oncoming lane and when the driver's window is adjacent:

"How's the leg?"

I know the voice and it fires my little remaining adrenaline outward in all directions. Could I outrun a madman through the desert? A sniper man who 'does distance'?

..

Without turning I croak, "You got water?"

"You got my medal?"

"It burned in a house fire." I cough, clear my throat. "Three years after I got it."

"Bullshit! You coulda said that last time."

"In the woods? When you busted my leg?"

I get the sensation he's pointing a gun at me. Knowing I risk a total body cramp, I twist to look in the cab. A cigarette glows and the dashboard casts a pale green hue. He drives a midsize pickup truck and we're close to even eye level.

"I tell you what, Nick. In the bed of my truck I have a case full of tools to make your life look like mine. I could pull over up ahead and just wait for you. Or I could get out and do it now."

"Get out and do it now you psychotic cock."

I haven't seen Mary or Lisa for twenty, thirty miles. I don't know how many, and Nicholas Fister is here, and Floyd is dead, and everything comes crashing into a singular awareness that somewhere up ahead, maybe here, Nicholas is going to murder me like he did Mary and Lisa.

●●

Mile 100: 16 Hours, 9 Minutes

MADDY: Any regrets? About your career? Races you wanted to run? Records you wanted to set?

NICK: That's a tough one, Maddy. I didn't mention this but my daughter... She couldn't make the trip and it's caused me to... think a lot. I said you have to be out of balance to run long distances, and I believe that. Part of being out of balance for me has been the amount of time... it's taken. I've trained more hours per week than most mid-ladder MBAs trying to become the CEO spend at the office.

"That's a big cost to the family. I don't usually think in terms of regrets because they diffuse focus and belief, but if I could change anything, I would go back and spend more time with my daughter.

--DistanceHippy Podcast Pre-Race Interview

W e stand uncomfortable in a Methodist church three blocks from our house. I ran by it every day, sometimes twice a day, for years. I'm numb, wondering which pain is significant and which is not. The casket sits ahead, and in a few minutes I'm supposed to stand beside it and say something about Tuesday.

I fold an index card and unfold it. I don't remember the words I put on it and I can't imagine they will bend anyone's emotions, or that twenty-five years from now Tuesday will be remembered except as some stray thought.

Her immortality will come from her video.

Years and years ago I woke thinking Lisa was crying. She'd had breast cancer and spent a week with a tube inserted into the bottom of her breast. Every day I drove her to the radiologist so he could slip a fragment of radioactive metal inside her to burn the area where they'd removed the lump. Twice a day, I drove her over bad roads in Jeep with a tight suspension, while she had a tube sticking out of her breast, taped to her rib cage.

At night she slept on the couch. I either snored or rolled around too much and she was concerned about my flopping arm striking her.

I worried. I slept with the bedroom door open and told her if she woke up and needed anything to call. Nothing was insignificant. A couple of times I woke up halfway down the hallway, thirty paces from bed, launched by her call. I'd help her with whatever troubled her, and afterward it was good. The moment was silent, internal, and it would never have done to say anything about it. But I was validated. I was working hard to make a living. Working to defend a title and keep my meager endorsements so we could pay the bills. And while keeping the honed mental edge of a professional, record setting ultra-marathoner, I was hypnotically and instinctively attuned to the needs of my suffering wife.

Shortly before Tuesday died I heard something and before I woke, I was on my feet.

My bedroom door was closed and I stopped short of it, not knowing where I was, calm by nature but drawn as if by a siren's sobs. I touched the door, pressed my hand flat, blinked away the confusion. I looked back to the bed and remembered Lisa hadn't shared my bed for years. She slept down the hall. I let my blood pressure stabilize and wondered what I'd heard, or dreamed.

• •

Then I recognized Tuesday's voice—the same sobby world-is-ending woe as when Timmy Smith broke up with her the day after he no-showed a study date.

I eased open my bedroom door. Listened.

Tuesday's door was open. Lisa's door was open. They were together. I leaned against the jamb.

"He made a video," Tuesday said.

Lust possesses a primal beauty, turns sex into art, every meditation into sorrow or passion. But young people hold an incomplete command of emotion and intellect. They make bad decisions to keep their lives edgy and real.

And sometimes they're just evil.

Thornton took Tuesday's Happy Birthday blowjob, given to him alone, recorded it, and shared it, so pedophiles could have her too.

The video she made unknowingly is around the globe, stored in the memories of untold computers and servers. She'll be dust for a hundred years and the image of her will remain, and because it will be seen by people who are removed from the intimacy in which she performed the act, her performance will not portray love or passion. She'll be seen a willing animal. That is young existentialist Thornton's gift to the world: he's taken the image of a beautiful and very young woman and for a few dollars turned her into the hologram of a grunting whore.

We're in church. Tuesday is in the casket, up there. Lisa and Mary lean against each other and I ignore them, and try to get my mind on Badwater.

Floyd sits behind us. I wanted him to be on the road, driving the van to the desert, because the race is Monday. But

••

with true grief in his eyes, he put his hand on my shoulder and said it'd be wrong for him not to be here.

He didn't know what I knew about Lisa.

And I didn't know what he knew about Tuesday.

*

Nicholas Fister keeps the truck steady beside me and I wonder how long this will last. "Come on, you want to damage me? Get out the truck and let's dance."

"You been on the road eighteen hours now, right? You best go easy, you want to get to the finish line."

I lurch to the truck and slam against the door. Raise my folded arm, launch a fist and feel his face on the end. The truck jerks backward and I bang my arm against metal getting it out of the window. Wobble and avoid stumbling sideways. The truck engine roars and Nicholas grunts syllables that come out like twenty cuss words run through a blender. He grinds the stick transmission; the truck bounces forward, rocks. He's again beside me and I'm ready to dive in.

In the green dashboard light Nicholas looks like he smeared chocolate below his nose. He laughs and spits out the window at me. "You know I was a sniper. You looked me up. I know you did 'cause I know I got your attention."

The terrain is flat but leaving the road in the dark invites a million unknown troubles, and as often as I've been face to face with Nicholas, I feel the comfort of an odd détente.

"What are the odds?" he says, and laughs. "Two Nick Fisters in the middle of one big ass nowhere like this."

"Give me water, shithead."

"Yeah, alright."

••

He passes a liter bottle of Mountain Dew to me. It's cold like it came out of a cooler. I twist the cap. Sniff it.

"It ain't piss. Remember I'm your biggest fan? And that's not how I'm going to bring you down."

I sip and the taste is like a citrus fountain burst in my mouth. The fizz feels clean and the sugar coats my throat like syrup. I gulp and gulp. Breathe. Gulp more. Stop and inhale, exhale, let the carbonation rumble from my throat in a prolonged belch. I shouldn't drink more so quickly but I can't help my desire. It feels like salvation. I upend the bottle again and finish it.

"That's damn near a full liter," he says.

"More."

"This is gonna hurt you in the end, Nick Fister, champion of the world. Say, how'd that crew chief of yours die? They got you for that yet?"

"You did it, for all they know."

"Me?" Nicholas laughs. "I don't know anything about it. And I don't know why your crew left you out here alone, and hasn't checked on you in thirty miles. I don't get it—they surely seem devoted to you. But I bet those deputies are all over you. When they put that thing on your ankle I wanted to vouch for you. 'He doesn't have the guts to kill a man outright. Not this Nick Fister. He's a stealth operator. He'll take a man's destiny and sneak off with it.' That's what I wanted to say."

"But you didn't."

"Hell no."

"Nicholas, I'm through with you."

"No you ain't, either."

He spits out the window and the glob lands on my leg. The engine roars and Nicholas Fister is two red taillights.

••

Not a hundred feet ahead is Barelegged Nova, walking with a gait that can be diagnosed from a thousand yards: a cramp seizes her entire right leg.

Strong on Mountain Dew and a circus of emotions I can't name, I draw upon Barelegged Nova Bjorkman. She boosts her pace and works out her limp. Most leaders attempt to match their passer for a short while hoping to shut down the lead change, or if that's not possible, search the opponent's face for strategic insights. But much like a boxer saved by the bell, Nova's van arrives and she slows to meet it. She speaks a fairy language and I realize I forgot to ask her my question.

Fresh on Mountain Dew, I am clear. I drop a gear and try to make a gap while Nova replenishes stores I cannot. That nagging thought creeps up again. I'm willing to go exactly to the ultimate threshold. I'm willing to go until I lose consciousness, and when I regain it, go again.

But will that be enough against Barelegged Nova?

Seemingly a moment after the van takes off she is again beside me.

Although she is exhausted, from her sounds I discern her form is better than mine. Her feet land like flower petals, roll through and push off the toe. No whoosh or zip of her arms, no struggle for wind. Just a light metronomic pulse of hundred-pound comeuppance.

"You'll never win," she says. "It's no shame for an old man to drop out."

She drinks water and I do not. She consumes calories and I am reluctant to give my body what it needs because my wife and my sister have abandoned me or are dead like my daughter and crew chief.

••

I think, for a moment, that I am utterly alone on planet earth. Utterly.

I look down the road, a dark line heading into blackness.

In the worst case my Gu will need to sustain me thirty-five more miles. The remaining calories will have to come from muscle tissue and fat. Though I am gangly thin my fat is sufficient. The average man's beer belly could sustain him five hundred miles, if his body knew how to burn it. I don't have five hundred miles, but I have thirty-five. And I can get more water at the next weigh in. If I gorge myself, I might be uncomfortable, but I will survive.

However, the problem is not the quantity of water. It's the timing. Gu needs a certain osmolality, a certain dilution in water in the gut, to be absorbable. Seven-point-eight ounces of water per one-point-one ounces of Gu. Otherwise it sloshes around, a fuel tank with no line to the engine. The body diverts water from circulating blood, and when that is not possible, the Gu ferments, causing gastric distress. Energy gels without water cause more harm than good.

The tactician in me says I should reduce my pace to burn calories at a more efficient rate per mile traveled. Consume Gu only when I get so stupid I don't know my name, thus allowing my taxed body water volume to remain where it is most needed: in my blood. Without replenishment from the van, this strategy would give me a chance of finishing.

But I haven't sacrificed everything to finish. My inner strategist says I'm here to win and I'm neck and neck with the one who can beat me. And if I don't break her now, I won't.

I need to convince this woman competing with me is hopeless.

I've eaten three Gu's in the last hour, more than normal, none with enough water to assist digestion. Though I gave her water, she gives me none. I want to crush her.

"Where is your crew?" she says. "Have they decided to go home because you are great hero, don't need them? How will they say when you are defeated by woman?"

"How will they say what, Nova?"

"On your best day you still would have lost."

I focus on my ankles, my ass, my elbow. My unfaithful wife and my dead daughter. This woman, the Barelegged Nova, has already crashed once. She is afraid. She pushes hard immediately after coming out of a cramp. She masques her pain and fear behind obscenity. The longer she paces me the more her respiration sounds taxed. Her left toe drags slightly. Her shoulders rotate with each stride as she coopts them to help propel her.

Though I am tired and empty my body insists it has more to give, and now is the time.

"Good night, Nova."

I run.

Casting a backward glance before cresting a small hill, I see I've opened a considerable lead on Nova. She stoops at the side of the road, washed in van headlights.

Returning eyes forward, I see a near-full bottle of Evian water on the roadside with condensation at the top. It spells naïve, backwards. I am game. Because drinking it might not be fatal, I open it. The water smells as if it has been dead a long time, and microbes have lived and died, and plastic has leached its phytoestrogens, but sometimes when you run beyond the pain that matters you find a willingness to risk

••

even more. Especially if it means attaining your goal and ending the misery sooner.

You make decisions as if your mind floats above, between your face and the mirror.

● ●

Mile 105: 16 Hours, 59 Minutes

MADDY: Nick, we're almost out of the time. I just want to tell you you're my hero.
TOMMY: Not very sportsmanlike. For the record, Nick Fister is giving us the bird.
MADDY: I mean that Nick. We've spoken a couple of times and you always seem like a straight shooter, but each time I end up feeling you're not really human. Because what you do is so unreal. I'd rather you were a different kind of animal, or had an abnormal heart like Secretariat, something, so there'd be an explanation. And frankly because if you're just a guy who trains hard, you lift the bar too high for the rest of us.
NICK: Maddy, I'll tell you what it is. Every time I run, I'd rather die than lose. Most athletes say that and it's a throwaway statement. Not me. I'd rather die. It's that simple. A man ready to die can turn the amp to eleven, if you get the reference. We all reach the point we want to quit. Yet we all have strength hidden away when we get there. A death wish is the only way I've found to tap it.
TOMMY: Yeah, wow. Simple.
MADDY: And points for the *Spinal Tap* reference, too…
                    --DistanceHippy Podcast Pre-Race Interview

Five days ago I set out for a run with my mind fixed on last minute details of the Badwater race. Lisa was helping load the vehicle at the gym, and probably getting a last-minute knee trembler with Floyd. He planned to depart for Death Valley with the van later that afternoon.

Lisa, Mary, Tuesday and I would fly the following morning, acclimate in hell for three days, and then race.

Although my leg had not rehabilitated to full capacity, I achieved something far north of the fifty percent the doctor predicted. The months of rehab, then seasons of weight lifting and endurance training, elevated my game. During my training taper I realized, not considering my leg, the rest of me was more race ready than any time in my life. An honest assessment, it helped me believe my body would be able to compensate if my right leg couldn't carry its load.

After Badwater I would retire, focus on building the gym, my running clinic, and maybe write a memoir or movie script, if I could find anyone interested.

Five days ago, my training schedule called for a semi-long run of twenty miles, recovery food, stretches, an hour in the infra-red sauna, light cross training, then recovery. The bright sun promised a hot day when I set out at 9 a.m., and I remember debating whether I should postpone my run until afternoon to get the full benefit of running in the heat. I shrugged off the thought; I'd have all the heat I wanted soon enough, and at this late point there would be no training gain.

Tuesday stood at the mailbox, withdrawing her hand and closing the lid. Her mouth was flat. Two weeks had passed since I'd heard her crying to Lisa about the video. I looked down the road and back to her. Tuesday lifted her head upward with a faint smile. I waived, pressed start on my Garmin and set out.

The last time I saw Tuesday alive I passed her by twenty feet and didn't meet her eye.

Four hours later I returned from my run. On the back porch, stretching beside the picnic table, something seemed out of place. I opened the door and stepped into a wall of

••

noxious air that smelled of burned meat. Housefire! I charged inside, mind's eye seeing a bedroom ablaze behind a closed door and moments to act before the house was engulfed. Breathing hard from the run, I inhaled a lungful of carbon monoxide before I sensed the house wasn't burning.

The silence was eerie.

Gagging and woozy I opened every window I passed, opened doors, and found the bathroom obstructed.

From the thump I knew Tuesday was behind the door. Another cloud of poison rolled out, air that smelled heavily of charcoal grill, burned paint. Kneeling, I reached around the door and moved Tuesday's legs, then rushed inside over her body and two tabletop charcoal grills to the window. I opened the glass and slammed my fist through the screen. Stuck my head out and vomited.

Eyes closed, I saw Tuesday as I had stepped over her:

Flat. Arms crossed. Staged. She'd brushed her hair while she was breathing in the carbon monoxide. The brush lay by her head, as if she'd dropped it when she felt consciousness leaving, and her last act was to lay flat and cross her hands at her stomach.

I carried Tuesday to the back yard, returned inside the house, called 911.

She was long, long gone.

I sat beside her but was afraid to touch her again, having already felt the rigidity of her skin. I didn't attempt to revive her. She'd lain next to two Hibachis for close to four hours. She left the ladder below the smoke alarm so we'd know she disabled it—sparing us the trouble of replacing them all, I guess.

The coroner pronounced her dead before Lisa came home from the Bench Press and Pound and was greeted at the door

••

by police. I'd answered every question and when she arrived they began interrogating her, routine questions that make the innocent feel as if every sign was obvious, and an ounce of empathy or outward focus might have saved her life.

Infinitely true.

When one of the police gave me a final wave off, I left the house. I hadn't eaten, hadn't drank. Again I passed the mailbox, and didn't think that an hour before, the postman had collected Tuesday's letter.

I turned my thoughts to the Badwater 135.

*

Nova's on me. Night tactics. I leave on my lights because I want her to understand I beat her clean, and she should have run faster. And the rules. Of course the rules.

Each time her van stops for her, they are closer behind me. My Garmin is out of charge. I don't know my speed. I've been out of water for a desert eternity. If not for the grounding nature of pain, I might believe I am already dead.

How many miles or minutes have elapsed since I passed Nova? I don't know. But Maddy and Tommy were convinced she was real and every time she pukes her guts out she gets up and keeps coming at me. I have no more calories to consume, no more water, no more chemicals. My body needs chemicals. Calcium. Magnesium. Buncha shit. Nova's van provides her all the chemicals she needs. Her stamina and my rate of decay make her victory inevitable.

Yet I toil on. Everything in the desert... everything in life... *might be illusion.*

One time after I won a no-name hundred miler on a quarter mile high school track, I wanted to know what it felt like to go to the absolute end. After winning I kept running full-speed laps, but stopped taking water, electrolytes, fuel. I wanted to find the brick wall at the end of the universe. The impossible bonk.

I know firsthand the feeling of heightened stress on the heart and lungs. The laboring intensity of each beat, the narrowing of consciousness as it draws the curtains and prepares the burn boxes. I know how pain becomes distant, like it reports through a thousand miles of copper cable. How balance drifts and wobbles. I know what it's like to believe you run on a track, but your body is running down a flight of stairs until you stretch and roll, unconscious.

I remember the gravity-free moment I regained awareness, and the bewitching—totally hot—look on the female paramedic's face.

Today, now, Badwater 135, without additional calories, I have less than two miles in me. When I collapse my body will require a half hour of burning fat and muscle to stabilize and give me the ability to propel myself. Maybe more. I started out in better shape today; maybe I pushed harder, have farther to fall and a steeper rebound.

I have continued this losing battle of attrition for miles. Seemingly hours, buying time for my unfaithful wife and dedicated sister. My mind follows rabbit trails I wouldn't take seriously except for being incapable of serious thought: Did Nicholas Fister really kill Mary and Lisa?

That's a lot of murder going on.

With so little brain power I'm surprised I know how to breathe. I contemplate complex ideas slowly, one insight trailing another like cars on a desert highway at ten-mile intervals. By the time one arrives, the other has left and I know the solution to a question I no longer recall.

• •

42

Or did Lisa break with whatever depraved code she clung to, and set about a series of murders?

Is this her plan for me? If she kills me outright, she won't get the insurance money. But if I die because my body can't handle another ultra, my death will be a profitable accident.

Though I can't string numbers together in simple addition the math behind Lisa as serial killer chills me. I ask questions as an outside observer—such as Edgerton—might. Did Lisa pull strings for the business deal with her lover, Floyd? Plant the seed that he could easily exploit her husband, a celebrity athlete?

Not only does she stand to get the gym, but she's contingent beneficiary on both insurance policies as well.

Is Lisa trying to kill me?

All I know is without my support van, I will lose this race. And with Nicholas Fister out there, maybe my life.

I withstand two more miles of running-as-controlled-fall. When I can no longer control the fall, I reduce my pace to a juddering walk. Each motion cycles through a catalog of pains. Ankle, calf, hip, back, elbow, shoulder.

Inflamed. Swollen. Raw. Ripped.

My mouth is sticky-parched. My temperature soars.

My mind has fallen off a cliff into oblivion. I focus on the side of the road seeking carrion or a cast-off bottle of water, anything I can feed my body and convert into miles.

Then I stop and am still for a prolonged moment of fading balance. I feel a starburst of pain from my forehead then every location of my body that contacts the ground. I roll to my back and the piercings of stones and glass are a pleasant reprieve.

My legs won't move.

My career will be forgotten.

I've been nothing to everyone.

All the hatred and anger and pain I've nurtured has eaten away my insides like so much acid, and all that remains of me will dry in a few days' desert sun.

*

Neither Lisa nor I treated each other with our normal malicious indifference. Tuesday died on Wednesday. We'd planned to fly to Vegas, and then drive to the hotel at Lone Pine on Thursday, but changed our flight to Saturday and drove to the Furnace Creek Ranch, which is closer to the race start, instead. Sunday we attended requisite meetings held by race organizers, for the safety of runners and crews, and the race started in three waves on Monday, at six, eight, and ten a.m.

It struck me on the flight to Vegas that regardless of my win, or completion of the race, I would end my career on Tuesday.

I went through the chaos of speaking to the police, planning and attending the funeral, and changing all our arrangements before the race with a certain kind of distance. Lisa, Mary and I sat in the car with the engine running before pulling out of the driveway and going to the airport. None of us spoke and I sensed it was our only moment to pull out.

"Momentum," Lisa said. "Let's just go."

It would have been entirely natural for her to want to share her grief with Floyd Siciliano.

••

I slid the transmission into drive and as I turned my head caught sight of the mailbox, the lid closed with part of a colorful flyer sticking out.

"Have you gotten the mail?" I said to Lisa.

A single shake, no.

I put the car in park, exited, filled my hands with a pile of junk mail, and noticed one letter addressed to me in a feminine script.

"Pop the trunk," I said, and Lisa did from the key fob hanging in the ignition.

I dropped the mail into a slot of space in the trunk between a cooler and a handbag, and folded and slipped the letter from Tuesday into my pocket. We walked through the airport like zombies and the only words were when Mary said, "I'm going to the restroom," as we waited to board our flight. A half hour later we fell in line, boarded, and when the aircraft was turned to the west and St. Louis far behind, I extracted the letter from my pocket and read.

> Dad,
>
> Mom knows this but you two don't talk much so here. I'm ashamed and can't stand how I've ruined myself. I know this is the coward's way, but I am. But I want you to know something so maybe someone else will be spared.
>
> Floyd is an ANIMAL—
>
> Thornton made a video of me and him. It was supposed to be just for us to look at. When we broke up he said he erased it. It was a bad video and I'm so ashamed. He shared it with his friends and somehow when I went to lift

••

weights Floyd showed the video to me at the gym. It was on a website. Floyd made me do stuff from the video and I can't believe how big a mess I made and I just want to be gone.

I told mom. She didn't believe me and acted like I made the video on purpose. I hope you believe me.

And I hope you have a good race at Badwater. That's what's important.

I cried and left my seat before the pilot dinged the bell granting permission. A stewardess caught my eye and stepped aside. In the restroom I sat and dripped tears to the floor between my feet.

I couldn't stop imagining scenes as they might have played out.

Tuesday had been chosen to be one of three cheerleaders at the bottom of the pyramid. She didn't think she was strong enough—she'd trembled at practice, under the weight. She didn't want the others to know, and started going to the gym for an extra workout on her legs and back three times a week.

My mind reeled. I imagined it: Floyd starts giving her extra attention, showing her technique, teaching her how muscles must be torn down to be rebuilt stronger. Sometimes he stands close to her. Sometimes he touches her gently, to help her get the right form. She can trust him. Technique is critical. Except the video the Doors punk made is on the internet and Floyd finds it. He thinks, why settle for the porn when you can have the star? He corrects Tuesday's form one day and suddenly a hand is somewhere it isn't supposed to be, and she looks around and sees the gym is empty and it's dark outside, and when she resists he says, look at this, and he pulls up a video he has ready on his phone, and Tuesday sees herself as the world sees her, slobbing Thornton's skinny Doors prick like she's an animal in heat, and she knows her world is over. She does the rest in shock. Tuesday does what Floyd says because in the back of her mind she thinks everything is over. She convicts herself: it's her fault, she tells herself, because she's the slut who gave in to temptation, and the only way forward is to do what the guy who could beat her senseless says to do.

And since her life is probably over anyway, what's one last rape?

I told mom, Tuesday wrote.

But Lisa had chosen Floyd. She needed his affirmation because she couldn't have mine. She *needed* her thirty-five-year-old body, her tit job and three hour sweat sessions to compete.

Even against a fourteen-year-old girl with no fat, no sag, no stories, no evil.

Compete, even against her daughter.

Somewhere below us, on some stretch of highway, Floyd Siciliano drove a van with my face on the side.

I decided I was going to do something about it.

••

Mile 110: 17 Hours, 6 Minutes

MADDY: So death… doesn't scare you?
TOMMY: How close have you been?
MADDY: Yeah, has any victory ever demanded you get close to the line?
NICK: If you're doing it right, they all do.
--DistanceHippy Podcast Pre-Race Interview

A slow-motion meteor slices the sky, a slash of light that rips open the star speckled blackness so cognizance can tumble back into my brain. I'm on my back. Rubble presses into my skin. Against my skull. Awareness accelerates. My elbow shrieks at me with the same old agony, only five octaves higher. I recognize the tune but the notes are beyond my range. The inside of my mouth feels like dry sand and an insect crawls on my right forearm.

I said, Is it good friend?
It is bitter, bitter.
But I like it because it is bitter, and because it is my heart.

The simultaneous roar of tires and engine pass me on the road, feet from my head. The van is yellow and I think of

Barelegged Nova. I don't know how long I have been unconscious but if that is her van, she has passed me while I lay prostrate, strobes flashing. Perhaps she was the slow-motion meteor.

I want to close my eyes, but an irritating thought punches through. I'm alive. I'm conscious.

I must run.

Another set of headlights follows the van. I tap a reserve of strength and roll back my head. Is this my crew? Or Nicholas Fister, ready to end our disagreement? The headlights are dimmer than I remember from the crew van, and something about them puzzles me. The shape? Distance between?

The vehicle stops yards short of me, close enough that the engine sound reverberates through the ground and I smell burned oil and hot dirty undercarriage. A door clicks and the engine remains running.

I close my eyes.

I am not ready to end my days here. If my life's purpose was to experience misery, I have misery yet ahead. If it has been to tap depths of despair, there are depths unexplored. And if I was created to work through pain and emerge a whole, self-agented man, something more than God gave through genes or experience through nurture—I have not fulfilled that either.

I can die. But I do not want to.

I crane my neck. A form approaches. I clench my stomach. Push—

And see a sleek, bare, shapely leg.

She kneels beside me and I recognize a smell I had not realized I had noticed before. Soap and shampoo. Edgerton.

"Shorts?"

"Do you know who you are?" She says.

••

"Nick."

"Where are you?"

"You smell good."

I roll, push with my right leg, and the muscles coil around themselves and lock in spasm. The tightness pulls through my wounded ankle.

"My leg," I say, thrashing to my right side. Pebbles impress my arms and left leg but I feel relief on my head as it no longer rests on a sharp stone. "My leg. It's locked up."

Edgerton stoops and I imagine a look of concern on her face that is more evocative than the one formed by harsh headlights and shadows. "Here?"

The concern is real. Wisdom shapes her brow; the smell of soap and shampoo combined with the ground and oily undercarriage make me think of spending an evening with her in a tent, maybe penetrated by faint light from a campfire. She rubs my muscles with her fingers and when I agree she has located the knot, she shifts for balance and begins kneading the muscle with her palms, one hand on the front of my leg for support, the other, crushing into the back.

"How many pushups can you do?" I say.

"Forty-three."

"Edgerton I love you."

"I love you too, Nick. But when you wake up you won't remember any of this."

I laugh and the feeling is foreign but exquisite.

The spasm in my leg abates under her grinding fist. I want to tell her to stop. I am not worthy. I don't want to put her out or take advantage. But I haven't felt touch like this in so long I'm confused by it. I haven't smelled a woman this way for years, and never while she performed a kind act.

••

I'm speechless. She continues. Emotion floods through and I waste water dripping it out my eyes.

Edgerton shifts to a new angle. "I'm going to switch legs, okay?"

I grunt and she quickly repositions herself to my other side, bends my leg, works the calf, the thigh. The other door slams and in a moment Lisa is beside me, maybe aroused by some vague jealousy. She kneels with a bottle of energy drink. "Can you hold down a Gu? A mashed potato?"

"Where were you forty miles ago?"

"You need food. You need calories."

From experience I know being depleted to zero affects not just the mood, but its wellspring, the soul. I've never been out of hate, until now. Only pity remains. I pity Lisa. I'm empty. "I quit," I say. "I'm done."

A breeze removes Edgerton's scent and replaces it with Lisa's sweat and coconut oil.

Edgerton says, "You're still on pace to set a course record."

I sit partly erect, braced on my good elbow. "Lisa—the drink."

While she holds the bottle I see on the ground a metal object gleaming in the headlights, and realize it is Edgerton's lower leg. She is an amputee. I think of the joke I made about her limp upon exiting the cruiser, miles and miles ago. *Twist your ankle?*

"Nick, you hear me? You're still on pace to beat the record. Your original nine-forty pace was to break the record by an hour. You've got twenty-five miles to go. If you can hold twelve minute miles, you'll at least tie the course record."

I gulp cool fuel from the bottle until it is empty. Lisa leaves with the bottle.

Edgerton says. "You got the balls to finish this thing?"

••

"I want some of Mary's dope. Give me a pain killer."

Edgerton is silent.

Lisa returns with a foil tube of mashed potatoes, butter, and salt. She squeezes a glob into my mouth and I swallow without chewing. She squeezes another glob. "That's all of it. Now drink more electrolytes." I take the nozzle in my mouth and gulp, then lean back on the pavement.

Edgerton says, "You'll be better in a minute. Just let the electrolytes wash through you. Right now that calcium's hitting your muscles. Five minutes ago they didn't know how to flex or release. In another five you'll feel like you slept an hour."

"How long was I out?"

"I don't know. I don't think very long, from your pace."

"I haven't had support in forty miles."

"Listen to me," Edgerton says. "You're going to take some time now to rest. You bonked super hard but your body is a machine. The tank was empty—but while you were out your liver was busting ass breaking down fatty acids into glycogen. You know this. You're ready to walk now, and in ten minutes, you'll feel like you rested a week. You have plenty of time."

"What about Nova?"

"She feels as shitty as you do. I promise. Forget about her for now. We'll reel her in together. Just keep putting those calories in your mouth. Liquid first. We'll keep a fifteen-minute pace for two miles, and when you have the energy we'll drop it to twelve. We'll sustain that, and keep putting in the calories, and you'll start to feel alive in no time. You've bonked before. You've bounced before. You're the champ. This is nothing for you."

..

Nauseated from the bellyful of sugar and fluids, dizzy from partly sitting up, I remember Tuesday at the mailbox, sending by post the letter I didn't give her the time to deliver by hand.

And I hope you have a good race at Badwater. That's what's important.

"No, I'm done. I don't give a shit."

"What makes you tick, Nick? What is it?"

I think. I've never said it to anyone. Not Lisa, not Mary. Never Siciliano. But Edgerton compels me to speak because I know she'll hear. "It's hate. I hate all the fucking evil. It's everywhere and I can't deal with it."

"And you don't hate it anymore?"

I laugh. "I became it."

Edgerton holds her fist in front of my face so I can see it. Opens her hand revealing a key. She slips the key into the ankle bracelet, unlatches it and hands it to Lisa. "Bring back a fresh pair of socks."

Edgerton removes the bandage from my ankle, holds my foot and eyes the swelling.

"Not bad."

She places my foot on her thigh and removes my shoe. My toes are a bloody tangle. "This might sting." She peels off my sock. "Bring antibacterial as well." Edgerton prods here and there. "That hurt? That? Yes? Okay." I can't feel anything except the sting of air hitting my ankle where the flesh is gone.

"You've got a blood blister on the outside of your big toe. My policy is to lance them all, even the blood. There's a risk

..

of infection, but you have to get rid of the pressure if you're going to keep running on it. What's your take?"

"I'm not running."

"Bring me a lance," Edgerton says, and Lisa arrives with everything at once. She knows the routine, my faithful, unfaithful wife. Edgerton wipes my toe with an alcohol swab, lances the side. She presses with her thumb and blood drips. I look from my foot to Lisa and her eyes are frazzled red from the long day, the heat, the stress.

"Where's Mary?" I say.

Lisa shakes her head sideways.

Edgerton says, "She's giving us some background on Floyd Siciliano, down at the station. Keep drinking that stuff. Eat more potato."

Edgerton gives the needle to Lisa, wipes my toes in antibacterial ointment and applies a fresh sock. "I thought a high mileage guy like you would have black toenails."

"Nah. I drink plenty of water."

The speed of my response surprises me. The sugar is hitting. I'm almost human again. With awareness arrives a fresh urgency to my myriad aches and grumbles.

Edgerton places my newly shod foot on the ground. "You can get twenty-five miles on that. You've got one marathon to go." She takes my twisted, swollen right ankle gingerly in her hands, bracketing it with interlaced fingers while she maneuvers my foot to her leg. "Give him another tube of potatoes, Lisa, if you've got one."

Many ultra-runners report their organs quit working, such as the pancreas, making it impossible for them to digest anything but glucose. I've never had that problem and the potatoes, salt and butter taste gourmet.

••

"There he is," Edgerton says, looking into my eyes, smiling. "That's good, huh?"

My shoe removed, Edgerton pulls each toe away from the others in turn seeking blisters. "Wow, this one's perfect. No blisters. Must be the swollen ankle, somehow."

"It's because I'm compensating with the other."

She rubs my toes in Vaseline, applies a fresh Injinji five-toe sock. Slips on my shoe. Ties it loose.

"Nick?" Edgerton stands. "I'll make you a deal. You can quit when you want to. But not this mile. Get up." She bends, takes my good hand in both of hers, braces backward and pulls. I don't have the ambition to help and she falters, releases me to a sitting position. "All right, we'll do it this way." She circles behind me, weaves her right arm under my shoulder. I feel her soft against my back, see her shaved leg beside me as she squats to lift me.

"No. You'll hurt yourself. No. Give me a second. Come around front. In a second."

I lean back my head, seeking her, and find the scoop of her collarbone. I rest and she rests into me. Lisa, at my left, twists away.

"I've got you," Edgerton says. "Just test those legs and see. They'll hold you."

"Okay, come around front."

I lean forward until she is before me.

"Lisa, give me a hand," Edgerton says, "Get behind him and lift. Careful of his left arm."

I send hope to my legs and they respond with strength, but half way up my right leg cramps. I stumble forward and Edgerton embraces me, my head at her breast, and I could cry for all her softness and warmth. I could cry for so many living things that have lived and died in darkness, reaching

●●

out to the world with hope and love and finding agony and suffering, the universe's lack of obligation. My thoughts are a jumbled flash. Physical collapse and emotional collapse are intertwined, made of the same atoms.

Edgerton separates from me but keeps a hand on my shoulder. I stand and think with sudden daring that some future I have not considered awaits, better than any I had conceived with Floyd Siciliano's gym.

My legs hold.

"You got it," Edgerton says. "You have an iron will. You decide something is going to happen and the whole world stages where you want. So tell those legs what they're going to do. Get ugly if you got to. Show the whole world that Nick Fister is the greatest distance runner of all time. You got it? You're feeling strong, I can tell. You can do it."

I step forward bearing the full load of my body. My strength disappears, and as I falter it returns.

"The rules say I cannot assist you covering the distance. So I have to release you. Are you going to be okay?"

"I got it. I got it. Let me go."

Edgerton lets go. I'm wobbly like a baby giraffe standing on joints and bones.

Lisa sobs and looks away, wipes her face with her empty hand, and I don't want to know, can't ask, couldn't register the resources to care.

"Lisa, would you refill that bottle on the ground, and bring me a belt full of Gu's. Thank you. Now Nick, remember: nothing sudden, nothing too taxing. In a few minutes you're going to feel like Superman but I don't want you to start acting like him. When you start to feel strong, hold back, don't go all in. You've been through some trauma. Let your body catch up, before you give it more."

••

I nod and as I am about to respond that she makes good sense, my stomach convulses and mashed potatoes blast from my throat. I retch and hunch, splash ankles. Topple forward. Gag up potato and weak bile, land on my left hand and knees on rocks that feel like glass.

"Go ahead," Edgerton says. "Get it out and we'll start fresh. Nothing like an empty stomach to start on. We'll build on that. You got this."

"I said I'm done. Empty. I don't give a shit. I quit."

Edgerton grabs me by the back of the head and lifts me erect. As I take over standing on my own power I hear her beside me, feel her breath on my neck.

"Your sister gave herself up so you could finish this run. Your sister will either face life in prison or the death penalty so you could finish this run. Now buck up. Move!"

Mary?

I think of her standing in the snow when I was twelve, giving me a black knit cap with Coke and jerky. An apple.

Mary.

I think of her upstairs while I was in the potato cellar, the croaking of the bed.

Somewhere deep in my circuitry, a program fires.

I step.

"Move, Nick Fister."

I step. Another.

Mary—her life forfeit. Stolen when she was eleven, so she could endure misery and self-doubt, self-abasement, self-immolation, so a man like Darrel could take advantage of her, and then Siciliano.

I want to scream.

Mary?

..

Mile 111: 17 Hours, 21 Minutes

MADDY: Okay, speed round. This is where we ask ten rapid-fire
questions. Your job is to answer as quickly as possible.
NICK: Okay.
MADDY: Uphill or downhill?
NICK: Uphill.
MADDY: Ball or midsole?
NICK: Midsole.
MADDY: Longest training week ever?
NICK: Four hundred and fifty-two miles.
MADDY: Shit. Are you serious?
NICK: Yes. Is that one of your ten questions?
                     --DistanceHippy Podcast Pre-Race Interview

As we move through the darkness I'm lost in a swirl of
reality I don't recognize. I've been here before. I've
been to my edge and walked alongside it for miles,
but never this edge, where beyond lies all the brokenness of
my life and the people in my life, staring at me.

"I'm tired," I say.

"You're strong," Edgerton says.

I stop walking, place my hand on her shoulder, rest.

"Eat another Gu."

"I'll throw up."

"Eat one anyway. You might absorb something before you
throw up. Drink fluids with it and you'll keep it down."

"I don't want it anymore. Don't need it."

"You know, we didn't tell you very much about the crime scene because we were waiting for you to make a mistake—give us a detail you couldn't have known from media reports."

"Uh-huh."

"The beer bottle with your fingerprints—it also had Mary's fingerprints."

"She took it there?"

"Either Mary or Floyd. Drink some fluids."

I drink from my hand bottle, tear open a Gu and squeeze the slime into my mouth. I've had so much Chocolate Outrage the taste is chocolate awful. "So how did he die? You asked about my deer knife?"

"Handcuffed to the bed, both hands and ankles. His mouth covered with duct tape."

Much as I hate the idea of Floyd Siciliano alive, I don't want the details of his death because they are attached to Mary. The more Edgerton relates, the surer she must be of Mary's guilt.

"If I was half a man I would have killed him. I thought about doing it after the race."

"Mary spoke about finding Tuesday's letter on the airplane. Let's move forward. Just keep moving and it will get easier. Your body is catching up, but you'll feel restored faster if you keep moving."

"What? On the airplane?"

"You left it on the seat. She said you cried, and left her letter on the seat when you went to the restroom."

So now I've killed Mary too?

"There's no chance someone else killed Floyd, and Mary's just covering?"

"Who? You?"

••

"Sure."

"How many times would you have stabbed Floyd Siciliano?"

"I don't think I would have ever stopped."

"Neither did she. The scene was unlike any I've seen, even in the books."

"How?"

"We found his penis on top of the television. The toxicology report isn't back yet, so we haven't confirmed one aspect yet."

"Tell me."

"That's good. Keep moving. You're doing great."

"One aspect?"

"Mary said she seduced Floyd by saying she was ready to get freaky. She cuffed him to the bed, taped his mouth, and cut off his penis. After a while, she opened the tape at his mouth enough to shove in five hydrocodone capsules. She said she told him what they were, and he swallowed them willingly while she held a beer bottle at his mouth."

"She gave him pain killers?"

"That's her story."

"Why?"

"The punishment was him losing his penis, and she wanted him to be conscious during it. After cutting it off, she allowed him time to get used to not having it. After that, she drugged him and stabbed him three hundred times, all around the groin. That was her count—three hundred."

"She wanted him to be conscious at the beginning and drugged for the last? What sense does that make?"

"Was she abused as a child?"

"Our father abused her. I don't know to what degree."

"So maybe it was revenge. Stabbing a man three hundred times—counting each one—"

"I don't get it," I say. "The pain killer part."

"Punishment is for the punished. It inflicts the will of society on the person who has done wrong, but it benefits the punished—by going through it they earn back a place in society. Punishment teaches a lesson, but justice isn't like that. Justice benefits society; we believe in justice and trust if we are harmed it will be made right for society as a whole."

"She gave him pain killers for justice?"

"No. For justice, she would have turned him in as a pedophile. By stabbing him three hundred times and keeping count, Mary went to the third place. Revenge is for the victim, and Mary's attorney will no doubt argue insanity."

"So she cut it off for his benefit and then killed him for hers?"

"Either that, or she's the coolest killer I've ever heard of, and staged the revenge aspect because she knew no court executes people for rape."

I think of Mary burning her husband Darrel's belongings, how casual she was, how absolute. Within a moment of Darrel being absent her life, she erased everything he'd ever touched. She made a permanent judgment. I'm chilled thinking back. She wasn't in a rage, she'd been methodical, efficient, blank.

I keep the thought to myself.

Energy arrives not in waves, but like blood pooling about a gunshot victim. I say, "Let me try to stretch this pace a little." I push off a little harder with my left, then a little harder with my right, and find my legs remember how to run.

"We have some miles to burn," Edgerton says.

••

After a dozen yards I'm okay. The pain of a thousand separate hurts combine into a narrow conscious thought, and I sweep it aside.

This new pain, Mary, is not fuel. Tuesday is not fuel. My broken marriage—it won't convert. I run and none of it is used up, only me. There has to be a better way.

"I really did think it was Nicholas Fister," I say.

Mile 115: 18 Hours, 1 Minute

MADDY: Best recovery food?
NICK: Peanut butter and jelly sandwiches.
MADDY: Shortest race you ever won as a professional?
NICK: Marathon.
MADDY: Cold weather or hot weather?
NICK: Warm.

--DistanceHippy Podcast Pre-Race Interview

W e depart Lisa and the support vehicle.
"What's your name?"
She smiles. "Deputy Edgerton."
"Your real name? First name."
"I don't have one."
"You could make this easier."
"I could." The lift at the corners of her mouth entices me.

Washed in Lisa's headlights I feel like a teen being chaperoned. "So what's your name?"

"Savannah, I go by Annah."

"You got another twenty miles in you?" I nod at her prosthetic leg, a straight one, not a bowed blade like the sprinters use. The device joins her leg below the knee. It is skinny with a blue metallic sheen that catches headlights and throws a curved glare.

"Iraq," she says.

I think for a moment of my experiences lately, how some things matter that haven't for a long time.

Edgerton looks at her watch. "You're on track. Call it an eleven fifty pace to beat the record."

Though I've had a few miles without the tracking device, my leg feels incongruently lighter than before. We face a downhill grade, not yet steep, but sloped enough to challenge the quadriceps, the front thigh muscles. After long, taxing runs, downhill is always where I am most susceptible to cramping. My form has never been perfect and each impact flirts with seizure.

"I need salt," I say. "More than the drink."

"You have it on your belt?"

"Wasn't thinking."

I open a pill dispenser and take two. Drink from my water bottle. I think of Lisa in the vehicle behind us, alone, imagining our daughter in the seat beside her, talking girl stuff. I remember them in the kitchen together. Tuesday cut an onion and her eyes dripped tears and Lisa came in the room and started crying too, and before long they were sobbing and laughing. And now Lisa's alone.

I blink away the thought.

Edgerton has good form. She runs erect, rib cage open, shoulders back. Her arms swing, but the range is short, efficient.

"Doesn't seem like the prosthetic interferes with your form," I say.

"I had to learn."

"You mind if I ask? It's just not what I would have expected. When you ran with your uniform on I couldn't tell you had a prosthetic. And now, without looking at your leg, I still wouldn't know. Your form is perfect."

••

"I was lucky I guess. I survived a helicopter crash and only lost a leg. And the amputation was below the knee, so I don't have as much to overcome, in terms of energy cost."

"Meaning?"

"The more body you lose, the more energy running requires. A double amputee who lost both legs above the knee pays a heavier energy price than a single amputee below the knee."

"So for endurance, is the challenge primarily about energy cost, or are there other effects?"

"There are small differences, marathon length. Different muscles in my back, is where I notice it. The first goal with a prosthetic is to get both legs working the same. My prosthetic is designed with a forefoot strike, and I was a heel striker before. So that took adjustment. And the prosthetic has to be sized perfectly. And one of the biggest things is just learning to trust it. When I started, I didn't lift fast enough and I stumbled. The leg didn't clear the ground, so I compensated by swinging it to the side. But after a while, I started to sense it better and now both legs work about the same."

"What's a long run for you, now?"

"Marathon. I've thought of trying ultra, but I need to clear some time in the schedule."

"Not as much as you think. If you can do a four-hour marathon, you can do a fifty miler, easy. Maybe more."

"Says the guy who ran four hundred and fifty miles in a week."

"That was actually in four days. I took three off."

My stride is short, choppy. My right ankle and foot are like a block of wood. My left is merely stiff, from my brief roadside rest. My elbow ice pack long ago turned to a heat absorbing pad, but my arm remains wrapped and suspended at the angle I would carry it anyway, with minimal stress on the joint. The angle doesn't hurt, merely the wiggling that allows whatever bone shard is inside to slice and dice. By now it must have a little pocket of hamburger carved out because the pain is rather bland.

"How'd it happen? What did you do in the Army?"

"Air Force. I was a flight nurse."

"It shows."

"Lot of training. Most people don't realize. You ever heard of SERE training?"

"Isn't that for Navy Seals, or something?"

"All the branches send people. But it started as an Air Force school in World War Two. Aircrews are at high risk of capture."

"You been there?"

"I been there."

"So why aren't you still a nurse? Why change to law enforcement?"

She looks at me. "I like catching bad guys."

We continue with just the sounds of our feet. In a moment Lisa drives alongside. "Still good?"

I don't like hearing her. A vagrant thought—I imagine myself turning off the road and running into the black distance, away from her. "Drink mix," I say. "Potato. Pull ahead a half mile so you have it ready."

Lisa drives and when the taillights are small, they go out. Before they do, I see the reflection of the yellow van, parked, waiting to leapfrog Nova Bjorkman.

"How far ahead is she, you think?" I say.

"You were down for about ten minutes from when we arrived until you started moving again. Nova passed you right before we arrived."

••

A mile. Picking up one mile in twenty-five is nothing. But Bjorkman is strong, has already proven the ability to run herself wretched, then pick herself up and do it again.

Ahead, the downslope is long and steady, giving the feeling of great elevation. Though mountains loom they are distant and the black sky seems flush with the horizon. A falling star flashes bold across the sky.

"Do you believe in omens?" Edgerton says.

"I'm not sure I have existential beliefs, right now."

Downhill coasting. Aside from a new hitch in my side—something gastric from sloshing fluids seeking entry to intestines and blood vessels—I feel like I'm gliding in neutral.

Minutes pass. The vehicle is ahead. Lisa has left the lights on and the engine running. The exhaust is offensive in the mountain air—after Death Valley, anything else is a mountain.

Lisa greets me with a new hand bottle, ice cold and full of energy drink mix. I consume another Salt Stick capsule and wash it down.

"How's your stomach?"

I'm looking at the ground and shift to her eyes. Her face is querying, motherly, almost invested in me. "Lisa, we good on mix? Enough for Edgerton to drink?"

"Plenty."

"Can you mix her a bottle to carry with her? And do I have another belt? Can you load it with six Gu's, and give it to her?"

Lisa holds eye contact like a perfect soldier.

"One more thing. You look tired. You holding up?"

She cackles. Raises her hands to her mouth and her eyes fold into chicken tracks. "I'm so tired I can't imagine what you feel," she says. She has a foil tube of potato, butter, and

••

salt open for me just inside the van. She hands it to me. "I can't imagine."

And I can't see a single redeeming truth in either of us.

I sense a moment of kindness in her, a neediness. Floyd has abandoned her in death, and Tuesday as well. I'm all she has. But the thought of remaining legally tied to her is repugnant, and after she gets a night's rest and takes stock of me, she'll see the end as clearly as I do.

But for now I touch her shoulder. "Thank you for coming back."

Edgerton steps into the hazy glow of the dome light.

"Deputy Edgerton, we've got a water bottle and Gu belt for you. Lisa was just looking for it," I say. "I'm taking off. Lisa, stay here and get that stuff for Deputy Edgerton. Leap me in two miles. Let's keep it tight. Edgerton, stay with Lisa until you have what you need, then Lisa will drop you off and you'll pace me the rest of the way in."

••

Mile 120: 19 Hours, 3 Minutes

MADDY: Music or quiet?
NICK: Both.
MADDY: Moleskin, petroleum jelly, or powder?
NICK: Vaseline.
MADDY: If you could have been any runner in history, who would you be?
NICK: Pheidippides. The run to Marathon is only the last part of the story. He did that after running a hundred and fifty miles to get to the starting line. Oh, and he didn't die at the end of the run. He got laid.

--DistanceHippy Podcast Pre-Race Interview

The day after I bought into the Bench Press and Pound, I walked out the front door to get a water bottle I'd forgotten in the console of my Jeep. Returning to my weights, the front desk was empty and the phone was ringing.

"I'm an owner," I said—and the thought arrived with special force because for the entire morning I'd been lifting weights with my rehab leg, Badwater was a month away, and the financial uncertainty of retirement was upon me. I lifted the phone from the cradle.

"Bench Press and Pound," I said. "This is Nick."

"Is the owner there? This is Ameren."

The electric company?

"Like I said, this is Nick Fister. One of the owners."

"Yes thank you Mister Fister, this is Jane Lewis with the Ameren collections department. We have not received payment since March and your account is three months past due."

"Wait, this can't be right. There's a mistake."

"No sir, no mistake. The amount owed is three thousand four hundred-nineteen dollars and eighty-nine cents. Last payment—received late—was February nineteenth."

"I'll have to, uh, speak to the owner. The other owner. This is a surprise to me. What's your name and how do I reach you?"

Floyd's newest hire Tim came around the corner as I returned the phone to its cradle. "Tim, who handles the bills for the gym? Does Floyd do all of that?"

"I don't know nothing about that."

"Okay. Fine. When's Floyd here today?"

"Noon."

I went back to my weights, drank from my water bottle. Thought. February nineteenth, she said.

The first time Floyd proposed me buying into the gym was in February.

The late bill had to have been an oversight. I extended my leg straight, allowing the weight to come to rest, then sat on the bench. I drank water again.

How could a business forget to pay the electric bill?

I'd seen the books. The Bench Press and Pound was flush with cash before I bought in, and even more afterward. I walked to the office. The door was locked.

"Tim, can you open this?"

"I don't have a key. No one does. Well, Floyd does."

The next day I called the Ameren lady to see what more information I could learn. But when I reached her the bill had

••

been taken care of—these things happen, people forget, no harm done, she said. Still I wondered how I'd misread the books.

A day later I noticed Lisa's key ring on the counter. There was one I didn't recognize and when she went to the bathroom I swiped it, made a quick drive to the hardware, and copied it.

That evening I went to the gym for a late day workout. Pat was at the front desk, a young newbie hired after my treadmill run. I nodded at him and stuck the copied key into the door as if I knew it would work. It did.

So why did Lisa have a copy of the office key?

I swung open the door.

At the desk I turned on the computer and opened Quickbooks. Floyd had the passwords written on a sticky pad. In a moment the program opened. The numbers looked foreign and jumbled. None of them made any sense. I was crazy to think I could discover something by sneaking around, crazy to buy into a business, crazy to think I could do anything but run away from my problems, forever.

But I looked at the menus and found "Reports" and then "Company and Financial," then "Statement of Cash Flows" and that seemed like a good place to start. The computer hummed. The fan kicked on and a report flashed to the screen with graphs and pie charts. The numbers meant nothing.

At first.

I looked over the headings, cash at the beginning of period, activity, net income, net cash increase, cash at end of period. The beginning cash was a little more than four thousand dollars. The ending cash was over a hundred thousand—but that was how much I'd paid to buy in.

I scrolled down the page and found an entry for the money I'd paid for my equity in the gym, listed under Adjustments to Cash Due to Financing. Back to the top. The monthly net income in January was less than the electric bill. Add to that the cost of the kids he kept hiring and firing, the gym was losing money.

Until I bought in, Floyd was unable to pay the electric. All the new memberships from the record I'd set on the treadmill were a thing of the past, and thinking back, it didn't seem like there were ever a whole lot of new faces around, day in and out, after the event.

The only question was, why the buy-sell agreement, if Floyd and Lisa would have ended up running the company together if I died, anyway?

What was there to gain? Aside from a five hundred-thousand-dollar insurance policy on my life?

There was one more thing to check. I searched desk drawers until I found an envelope with *Columbus Life* on it. Opened it and found a phone number.

"I'd like to check on a policy."

"Your name, sir?"

"Nick Fister."

"Your date of birth?"

"March seventeen, nineteen eighty-one."

"And the last four digits of your Social Security number, please."

"Nine four four two."

"I have your policies here, sir."

"My policies? Plural."

"Yes, there are two. Let's see. You're the insured on the first policy. This policy is in premium paying status. Your other policy, the one you own with Mister Floyd Siciliano as the insured, this policy has lapsed."

"What does that mean?"

"It's not in force. You stopped paying premiums almost two months ago."

I tried to collect my mind through a maelstrom of suspicion... and fear. "So that means if I die, the death benefit gets paid, but if my business partner dies, there's no policy?"

"That's correct. You have until the nineteenth to pay the premium, and submit a reinstatement form, or the policy will be permanently lapsed."

"Oh, I see... Can you email me the form?"

"Of course, sir. My pleasure."

••

Mile 133: 21 Hours, 30 Minutes

MADDY: I don't know if you've listened to many of our podcasts—
NICK: Sure, quite a few.
MADDY: Well, you know the last question of the speed round is always, what's your favorite beer?
NICK: That's a good question. I've spent a fair amount of time thinking about alcohol—
TOMMY: Speed round!
NICK: Right. Well then, anything black. Cheers.
--DistanceHippy Podcast Pre-Race Interview

Behind, off my left shoulder, a burst of gray outlines the eastern horizon; warning shots from a sun about to rise. We've been alternately speed walking and slow-jogging Mount Whitney. The air cools with each step and after a day of baked death, the pine and earth scent rejuvenates. It's alive, and makes me long for an afternoon on my back in a tent with Edgerton.

She checks her watch. "Five thirty. You were an 8am start. We're twenty-one and a half hours in."

"Two miles to go, Deputy."

"Please," she says, "Annah."

Feet on pavement. Breathing. We cover a mile.

"Sunrise in twenty minutes."

To the east the sun forms a yellow radiance; the horizon looks pregnant with day. The sun rises at our backs, however, so our vision remains filled with gray shapes without colors.

Edgerton runs steady with me, sacrificing for me, to be with me. I reach out as if to touch her shoulder but she seems not to notice and I don't finish; I just enjoy the moment of unfulfilled grasp. Running has never reduced me to this sort of sentimentality, but I've never pushed this far beyond the wasteland.

A supersonic hummingbird zips by.

"What?"

Edgerton's eyes flare and her jaw drops. She looks upward to the slope on our left, a network of strident shadows and escarpments. A rifle report cracks sharp and echoes through the darkness. Awareness flashes through me.

Nicholas Fister.

"Move!" She cries.

Edgerton drives her shoulder into my broken elbow, pushing me against a steep rock bank. My skin is cool and I relish the warmth of her arm as she wraps it around me, her breast against my chest and her legs suddenly tangled with mine, man, woman, sweat and metal.

Gunshots.

We're against a boulder as another hummingbird zips by, and another.

She extracts herself from our haphazard clutch and I hang onto her a moment too long. "Wait. It's not safe."

Edgerton relaxes a moment into my arms and I exhale long and let go of a thousand torments I cannot name. Exhausted in every capacity I am subject to a thousand emotions I don't have the strength to withstand. I am grief struck, haunted, humiliated and doused in junior high puppy love.

"Nick," she says. "We're getting shot at. Get it the fuck together."

••

I release her and she smiles big with Desert Storm adrenaline.

"You packing anything in those shorts?" I say, "Like a gun?"

Ahead Barelegged Nova and her pacer, who appears of the same proportion as the fellow who drove her van and refused me water, look around, back at us and ahead—as they continue uphill and put more distance between us.

"That has to be Nicholas Fister shooting," I say. "He was a sniper in the military before they cut him loose for mental issues."

"That's a thirty caliber deer rifle from the sound. If he had a heat scope you'd be dead. He probably figured to have daylight as you passed through here."

Deputy Annah Edgerton looks ahead, down the mountain slope, and then to the embankment we lean into. She scratches just above her knee where mechanical limb joins flesh, and I realize I have been so self-absorbed I haven't asked about her running condition over the last twenty miles. At the same instant I realize she's never uttered a complaint, and has been devout in her obsessive support of my race. She has been perfect.

"You're the best chief I've ever had. So how do we win this?"

"See the curve of the road? I didn't see the flash of the second or third shot. I think the shooter picked a bad location. If we stick close to the bank all the way around the bend, there's no way he gets a clear shot."

"Unless he comes downhill."

"Yeah, but from the slope he'd have to get right up to the edge of the embankment. Can he do that before we cross two hundred yards?"

••

"Let's go."

We're off again, me in the lead, stretching my legs with all I've got. A dozen steps forward, Edgerton reaches to me and tugs me closer to the rock wall. Ahead, Barelegged Nova's pacer looks backward at us, says something to her, and they increase their pace. Nova swings her arms hard. She's speed walking, legs mostly stiff.

"You can pass her whenever you want," Edgerton says.

I stop running, wiped out from the burst. Edgerton matches my walking pace. I'm surprised at her agility on the uneven roadside surface.

"There's nothing we can do about Nicholas for now? No way to call for back up or whatever?"

She looks downhill. "Lisa won't pass with my truck—and radio—before the finish. So no one finds out about the shooter unless they heard the shots, or until we cross the line."

"All right. I have my breath."

I lean forward and fall into a run. My speed increases. Muscle, bone, sinew—my teeth—everything in me protests. Edgerton now runs a half-step ahead, a little more exposed than I. She points to her right as if to keep me steered against the wall of boulders and less exposed.

It seems the sun rises all at once. The gray shapes to our right become jagged conifers and boulders.

The burst of energy lasts only a moment and again I fight a sense of collapse, a sense I am losing the force that has kept me on my feet. I've burned everything I consumed since hitting zero. The adrenaline burst at the gunfire burned my last energy like dumping gas on a candle: useless.

I wobble.

"Edgerton!" I fall against a knee-high boulder. Sit, lean forward. "I'm not going to beat her."

••

"Yes you are. Get up right now. In this moment you can either give up or keep moving. You're here. Your body is going to do what you tell it to. But you have to be the boss."

"The boss is done."

I drink from my bottle, hoping the calories will flush straight to my legs, my back. I'm hazy in my mind, black at the edges of my vision.

I look up at Edgerton. She looks ahead to Nova, then to me. She twists and looks where we came from, then to the sky. "You know why your sister isn't here?"

"I know."

"She confessed to killing Floyd Siciliano."

"Don't—I don't need this. *I don't want this anymore.*"

"You know why she killed him? Because he raped your daughter. And you know why—"

"Christ! Won't you stop!"

"—she cares about that so much? Because your father raped her every time he put you in the potato cellar."

The water I drank comes up through my mouth and nose and I'm on all fours, coughing, sobbing.

"This is the last race of your life, Nick. This is your last chance to burn it all out, and as long as you're conscious, as long as you're alive, you've got to keep fighting. You have to keep moving or else everything you've lost is for nothing. You hear me? You keep moving now! Go to that dark ugly place and you stand there. If you quit without going there, you'll be dealing with this same ugly shit the rest of your life. Burn it out now! Get moving! You've got a mile to reach so deep you find all of it, and dredge it up and burn it. Put that pain straight—" she punches me in the shoulder of my broken arm, "—into the cooker and burn that shit up. Get up!" She strikes me again. "Now!"

..

My awareness comes and goes, my broken elbow presses against the ground, ankles in agony. I blink away the salt and water and my eyes twitch. Haze comes in and out, trying to find focus. I swallow bile and sweetness from the drink mix. Pull myself erect on my knees, drink the remainder of my bottle and pitch it. I tear open a Gu and squeeze it into my mouth.

"Move!" she says, pointing toward Nova.

I swing my left leg. My right. My left. An insight shines from above like a beam of light: I long ago ran out of my own pain. Somewhere along the line the pain became guilt because I'm causing the pain I'm converting.

To escape it, I became it.

I'm integral to the evil I loathe.

From the trees to our right, upslope, branches rustle and a figure crashes into my peripheral, leaping upon us.

Nicholas Fister.

Edgerton screams "GO!" as Nicholas lands between us, fatter than I remember, swinging his rifle stock like a pugil stick. Edgerton lashes out with her metal leg in a straight kick that collapses his knee sideways. As he staggers for balance she loops, swings like mounting a horse and boards his back as she smashes him into the ground. Edgerton jams her good knee into his back, twists his arm behind him until he is motionless save his quivering feet. "You move, I tear your arm out its socket. Got it?"

She has it accomplished before I can slow myself.

"Go!"

But I stop, walk back to her. This is the man who just shot at us. The man who broke my leg and drove me to retirement.

He wears a green ball cap and has blood residue in his nostrils where I punched his face. His hair is grown out, long

••

like mine. He wears a shirt with haphazard iron-on letters in the back that spell, *I'M THE REAL NICK FISTER.*

I want to drive my foot through his head.

Edgerton holds my glare, then her face changes. "Give me that belt. That Gu belt."

I remove it, take out the last Gu.

"Bring it here. Open, like that." She takes Nicholas's other arm and pulls it behind him, then leans to him.

Nicholas moans.

She holds both his wrists and wraps the Gu belt around them over and over until the belt is used, then clicks the ends together.

"Would you GO!"

I'm still shaking with myriad torments. I think of the coldness of the potato cellar—and how Mary will spend the rest of her life in a prison cell just as cold and terrifying. I think of how Mary suddenly hated me when she was eleven and I was ten, right after our mother left, and how I always thought she blamed me.

I think of Mary going from one bad man to another, as if she believed it was only the rotten men who would be interested. I think of Floyd Siciliano calling her a freak because, as she struggled to forge a sexual identity, she sought something that wouldn't leave her feeling filthy, then probably finally embraced some of it just to be done with the guilt.

And I think of what she must have felt learning Floyd Siciliano inflicted the same evil on Tuesday as our father did on her.

I see Tuesday standing at the mailbox with tears in her eyes, looking at me to do something to save her from the evil world I brought her into, and I abandon her.

∙ ∙

To run.

The muscles in my stomach convulse but I overpower them.

"GO!" Edgerton yells. "Now! Time is running out. I got this."

I run.

My legs and arms beat a new rhythm. I hate. I want dead men to rise from their graves so I can butcher them. I want to create justice where there is none and never will be; I want to inflict evil upon evil so it can feel the pain of being a victim.

I remember Mary the night my father took his dying ride to the hospital. When they left he was in the back seat, his wheezing head on Mary's lap. How difficult would it have been for her to clench his face to her breast, one last time?

When she read Tuesday's letter on the airplane she knew instantly neither I nor Lisa would stop Floyd from his next thousand exploits. So she cut off his cock, placed it on the television, and counted three hundred stabs to his groin.

My feet collide with the ground as if they want to beat it into submission. The shock makes me drive them faster. I twist out of the ace bandage, stretch open my left arm and it is not agony that greets me, but energy.

I run.

Nova looks back and then shuffles faster, but trips. She's fifty feet ahead, and coming around a bend I see the finish a hundred feet beyond her. Onlookers cheer and movement begins when they see me, high drama, a battle for the lead. I stride, stretch, push. My lungs are hot and all that holds my cells together is a desire to destroy something, the pain, the evil that causes the pain, either it or I must die, and I am willing. My cells burn with it.

I can't stand this life any more.

••

Nova stumbles and her pacer lurches to catch her but misses. She's on her knees. I near and she topples to her side, curls as I reach her.

A woman on the side of the road jumps and claps and cheers and smiles.

I feel as if I have never seen a smile before, and I wonder if behind the smiling faces, instead of perversion and infidelity, their lives are filled with grace and beauty. I wonder if they love one another. I wonder if I've spent my entire life in a room with no windows, so I chose the images I wanted on the walls and willed myself to believe they were outside.

Have I chosen illusions?

Needed hurt and found it?

Is the world evil? Or my eyes?

The crowd shouts and cheers and chants. Light slices through leaves casting long bolts of bright yellow, ripping open the shadows. The air is cold and mountain pure and somehow I've passed through the night—all of the night. The forever of night that has been my life, my career, my obsession.

God I want the light. The good.

The rage in me flashes away like a giant flame that disappears when the gas is burned off, just a frisson of transparent heat and a tingly feeling in my fingertips.

Looking at Nova on the ground, this girl who has fought dirty and ran hard, I break for her. For our blindness, for all of our races and the demons that compel us.

Reality whooshes in around me and I'm aware of the sounds, the cheers, Nova's pacer shouting at her as Annah Edgerton shouted at me. The finish line is twenty yards ahead. A hundred people line the mountain road. Pines, chairs, vehicles and reporters and cameras.

••

I say, "Get up Nova. You can do this!" My stomach is tight and my broken leg where it healed aches like bone in a vice.

Water rims my eyes.

Nova lays open-eyed but unmoving, still like a beachbound fish waiting for death. I lean and reach to help her and Nova's crew chief bends too and together we lift her, but she won't help herself. We lower her back the few inches we moved her.

My ankle throbs and my elbow flashes anew with white pain—has been flashing all along, but I've been elsewhere. Nova breathes in deep and sighs long. She closes her eyes as if to sleep right there on the road.

Nova's chief grabs my shoulder.

I meet his eyes.

He nods toward the finish. "Go. You beat her."

I drive my feet with everything. Lean into the hill and swing my arms at the shoulder—even the broken one—to help momentum. I'm intimate with this feeling in my legs; they whisper they're all in. They've given everything but are willing to continue on nothing.

The crowd chants Fis-ter, Fis-ter. Every muscle in me is violently ready to quit but none does, fueled by brightness ahead, gliding toward the hope that something down the road is better.

I cross the finish ribbon, look up at the clock. 21:51:14. A record, for today.

People slap me and crowd close. Strangers touch me as if to gain something from me and though I am enlightened it is with gratitude and awareness of the staggering depth of my inadequacy.

I must become someone else. Who I am isn't working.

••

A man with long hair steers me toward a canvas strung tree to tree, a backdrop for post-race interviews. He points to a seat and his mouth is a mash of words I can't comprehend. More than anything I want to make sure Edgerton is okay. Down the hill I see her marching a hobble wobbled Nicholas Fister toward us. I look around for a deputy and leave the yammering longhair by his tarp camera backdrop.

"Deputy," I say, moving toward him, waving my arm. "Deputy."

He's smiling, puzzled, suddenly alert.

I point down the hill. "Deputy Edgerton has a man right there. She needs help. He shot at us a few minutes ago."

The Deputy blinks, spins to his vehicle and in a moment the lights are flashing, the engine's roaring and he's ready to assist.

Again the longhair is at my side. "We want to congratulate you and take a few—"

"Nova," I say, and leave him, crossing under the ribbon that has been re-stretched for the first-place female finisher. Nova's chief remains at her side, cajoling her to move. I stumble downhill like I'm alternately floating or falling downstairs.

"Get up, Nova, you got this. Fifty feet. Get up!" Her chief says.

"Nova, you're about to set the women's record," I say. "Get up. There's no one behind you for miles. You have this by three hours."

I sit beside Nova and touch her hair, the side of her cheek. "Nova, you got to find whatever you have left. You're going to be the best there is. You look deep inside, Nova. I know you got some left. Now get up."

••

She locks eyes with me and with a groaning snarl wrestles the air and the ground until she is on all fours.

"You got it Nova. C'mon! Let's get this done!"

She plants her feet wide and, hands on the ground, walks herself upright. She wobbles. Her thigh trembles. Nova staggers. Her chief steadies her but backs away as she gains balance.

Nova takes a long stride that looks like she's been saving up all night for it. Her chief stays near, calling her champ, loving her, prodding her, then waits as Nova approaches the ribbon alone. She stops just shy, and looks back at me as if through a hundred miles of delirium.

Nova turns and crosses the line.

Again the longhair is beside me, tugging my broken arm toward the white interview backdrop, the chairs.

"Interview her," I say. "Talk to that one. Talk to Nova. She's the next thing. I'm retired."

I walk a few steps and turn. Done with the clocks and belt buckles. Records and medals.

Edgerton finishes speaking to the deputy who has taken custody of Nicholas Fister. She looks toward me with an enigmatic curl to the edges of her lips.

For the first time since the finish I see Lisa. She looks like flat paint, background. I spend no time wondering when she arrived.

I look back down the road to Edgerton.

Where I want to be.

THE END

..

Notes from the Author

Running a hundred miles is difficult. My longest run is 73 miles. I was trying for 100, and reached a point where, unlike Nick Fister, I gave in to injury. I'm not what you would call a talented ultra-runner. To those of you with the discipline and grit to complete the hundred miler, you have my admiration. To those of you who have completed Badwater 135, you have my utmost respect.

I'm sure there are distance runners who will take exception to some of Nick Fister's beliefs and strategies—but this novel is not intended as a manual for people who aspire to ultra-running greatness. It's a fiction about a person dealing with evil, falling in love with his own greatness, facing catastrophic consequences, and reorienting himself toward hope, and light.

I made Nova Bjorkman a bitch because the story wouldn't permit her to be sweet and likable. I've run a dozen ultras and have yet to meet a single runner—male or female—who was anything but awesome. Ultra-runners are the most generous, coolest people on the planet, and the volunteers who support the races are even cooler, and more generous.

If you enjoyed **Strong at the Broken Places,** please consider reviewing it where you purchased it.

Looking for another great gritty-athletic read? Allow me to suggest my novel **Solomon Bull**...

*W*ant *To Overcome Villains, Vandalize Sacred Cows, Have Sex with Dangerous People? Here's How to Experience the Vicarious Full-Throttle Brain Rush Now!*

You'll laugh too loud, stay awake too late, muse about new philosophies and read your underlined passages to strangers to make the world a better place.

Blue Ink Review calls Solomon Bull "a virile tale about a tough-as-nails Blackfoot Indian, a roaming badass."

Seattle Book Review, Manhattan Book Review, Indie Reader, and others all agree: Solomon Bull is an unflinching, adrenaline-soaked read.

••

Acknowledgements

I want to humbly note that Scott Jurek mentions in his fantastic memoir *Eat and Run* that he ran with an ankle sprain and went through a thought process that concluded with the realization the swelling would help him complete the race. Jurek also mentions the belief that the mind works for you or against you. I borrowed those concepts.

Also, homage is due to Christopher McDougal's *Born to Run*. He mentions the head works like a counterbalance in a tall building, and discussed a great deal about running form. His insights were instrumental in forming Nick's philosophy.

Kevin Amory is one of the best friends a person could have.

Last, you can learn more about Badwater 135, results, webcasts, training advice, books and resources—*everything Badwater*—at www.badwater.com.

Dedication Comments

This book is dedicated to Loren Fairman, who has done more over the years to encourage my writing than anyone except my wife. Loren first commented on a story snippet I posted on a writer's group, then beta read—super in depth—almost everything I wrote. He made suggestions, praised, encouraged. Only a very few people have mattered, in terms of whether my writing would exist in its present form without them. Loren is one I couldn't have done it without.

The Author

Clayton Lindemuth writes literary and rebel noir. Clayton is the author of *Tread, Cold Quiet Country, Solomon Bull, Sometimes Bone, Nothing Save the Bones Inside Her, My Brother's Destroyer*, and *Strong at the Broken Places*. He lives in Missouri with his wife Julie and his puppydog Faith, also known as "Princess Wigglebums" and "Stinky Princess."

Made in the USA
Coppell, TX
22 March 2020